THE FIRST FELONY

A DICKIE FLOYD DETECTIVE NOVEL

DANNY R. SMITH

ISBN-13: 978-1-7349794-9-7

Cover by Jon Schuler

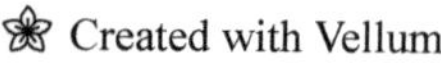 Created with Vellum

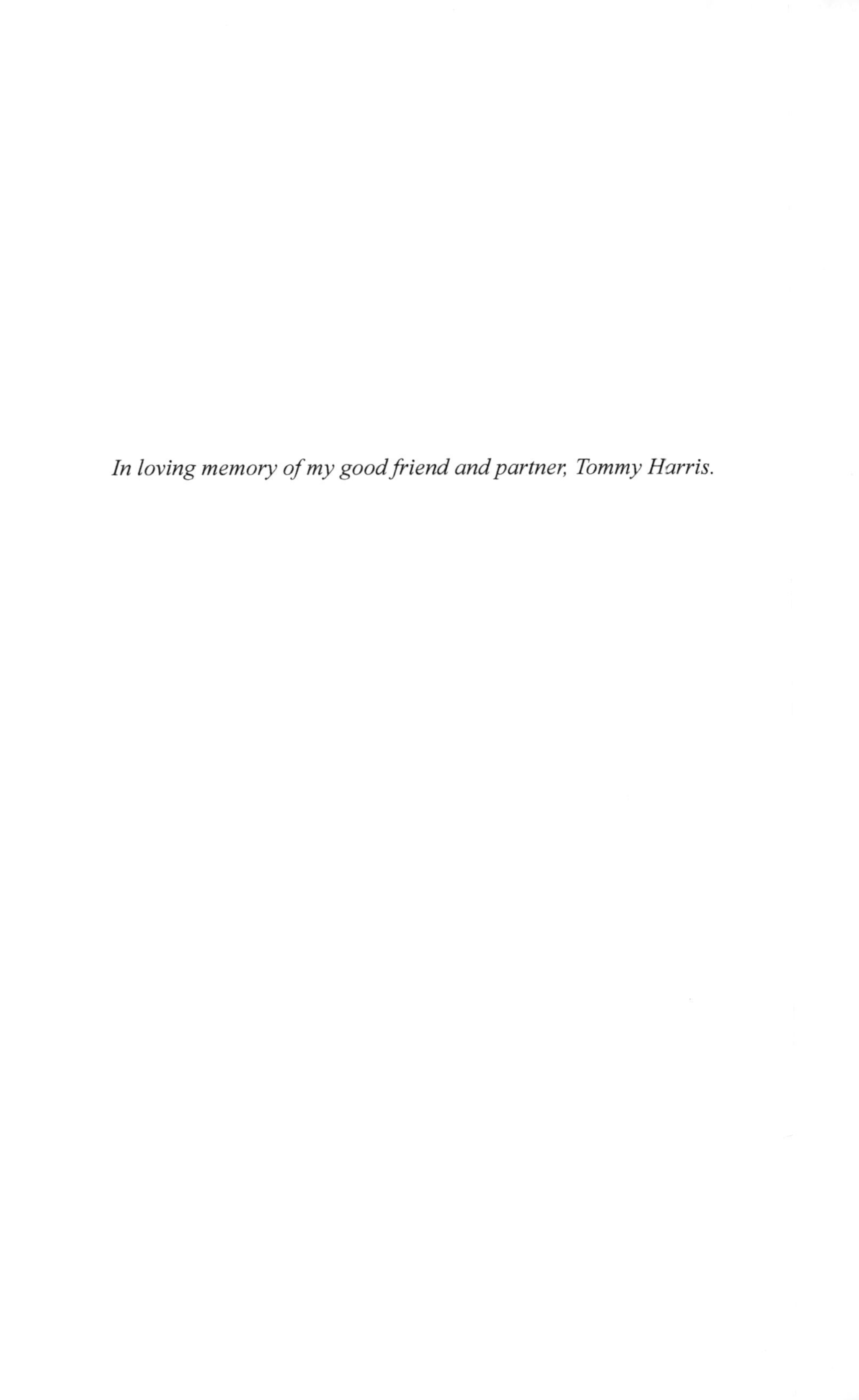

In loving memory of my good friend and partner, Tommy Harris.

We're gonna break out the hats and hooters
When Josie comes home
We're gonna rev up the motor scooters
When Josie comes home to stay
We're gonna park in the street
Sleep on the beach and make it
Throw down the jam
'til the girls say when
Lay down the law and break it
When Josie comes home
When Josie comes home
So good
She's the pride of the neighborhood
She's the raw flame
The live wire
She prays like a Roman
With her eyes on fire

Josie, by Steely Dan

1

DICKIE GNAWED AT THE END OF A PEN AS HE SAT LOW BEHIND THE WHEEL of Josie's Dodge Charger, an unmarked gray sedan equipped with the police package that boasted nearly four-hundred horses under the hood and as many foot-pounds of torque through its eight-speed transmission. It was ready to haul ass when the time came, and that time couldn't come soon enough for him. Haul ass north, hopefully, not south. If he were to head north, it would be because he was reunited with his partner and on his way back to L.A. where they should have remained. L.A. was where they belonged, not down here on or across the border. If he were to venture south, it would be for one reason only: he'd be going in to get her out—crossing the border to rescue Josie.

He never should have agreed to this. Josie shouldn't have gone to Mexico.

At the very least, she shouldn't have gone without backup. If you had an agenda that went against department policy, state law, and international conventions, the least you could do was take some precautions. Tijuana was a dangerous place for any American, let alone an unaccompanied woman.

He waited, praying a rescue mission wouldn't be necessary, his fingertips caressing the polymer frame of the Glock 19 he held in his lap. His finger rested on the edge of its trigger guard where it would naturally drop into a ready-fire position instantly if needed, the way he had been trained in combat shooting. Many years had passed since his academy days, but he still remembered the firearms instructor's words with fondness: "Keep your booger-picker off the bang-switch until it's time to party." There were things you never forgot because of how they were taught. The same instructor—a former Marine who had reminded Dickie of R. Lee Ermey in *Full Metal Jacket*—had said the car was your coffin, meaning you didn't want to be caught sitting in it with your head down while writing a ticket or after arriving at a call for service. He had said, "Un-ass the goddam car and be ready to party."

Dickie was ready to un-ass Josie's car if necessary, but he certainly didn't want to party—he wanted Josie to stroll back across the border with a smile on her face so they could go home. *Home.* He pictured Emily and Angelo embracing the final moments of a summer day, the boy's wavy blond hair damp against his mother's blouse as she breathed in the sweet, fresh fragrance of baby shampoo and read stories about dinosaurs or tractors or a little toy house and a young mouse and a cow jumping over the moon.

Dickie flicked his thumb back and forth across the magazine release of his pistol, his thoughts shifting back to the present. Two extra magazines secured in a pouch on his hip pressed against his side, a reminder that there were thirty more rounds available should he burn through the first sixteen—fifteen in the magazine and one in the tube. Because this wasn't Hollywood where you jacked a round into the chamber after the shit already hit the fan—and an emphasis that there were only thirty more should he have to "party." Had they come down in his Crown Vic, Dickie would have several hundred more rounds of 9mm at his disposal, stored in the trunk of his car along with a shotgun and several boxes of shells for it, a combination of double-ought buck and rifled slugs. Everything he needed and currently desired was a hundred and fifty miles away in the trunk of a sedan that sat ominously basking in the glow of yellow light in the Homicide Bureau parking lot. Josie's Glock sat tucked beneath the passenger seat, he realized, a model 48 with two extra magazines secured along with her badge, a six-point gold star with the California bear in the middle, the word Sergeant on the top rocker, Los Angeles County at the bottom.

The Glock 19 felt good in his hand, a fit like none other. When he first came on the job, they carried revolvers. Eventually, the department issued the Beretta 9mm pistols, a gun Dickie hated. It was big, bulky, an Italian-made boat anchor with rifling. A Fiero with bullets. Most cops liked them, and Dickie had to admit they were good guns, reliable and battle-tested. But they were not for Dickie. Once he began carrying the Italian job, his qualification scores plummeted from Distinguished Expert to Lucky to Qualify. To exemplify the point, Dickie had gotten into a shooting shortly after being forced to carry the Italian job, and he missed two shots he blasted at a fleeing felon. The bad guy had yanked a gun from his waistband as he ran into an alley in his (successful) attempt to flee from the cops, and Dickie had blamed the gun (not the loose screw behind the hammer) for his poor performance. Fortunately, Dickie was promoted to detective shortly after, and he was able to stuff the Beretta in the back of his locker and never carry it again. The gun policy was more relaxed in the detective bureau, and his carry options were greater. He began packing a Heckler & Koch P7, a 9mm autoloader he had picked up in a divorce sale from a colleague. He was far more accurate with it than he had been with the Beretta. He didn't shoot it as well as he shot his Smith & Wesson Model 14 revolver, a blue-steel classic with a six-inch barrel, but he shot it far better than the Fiero. And although he was fond of his H&K with its squeeze-cock safety configuration and sturdy German design, no weapon had ever felt better in his hand than the Glock. He owned the 17, the 19, and now the 48, too—his favorite for off-duty carry—each configured with Trijicon night sights, two subtle green glowing dots on the rear sight and a contrasting orange dot on the front. The sight design was brilliant, with no switches to activate nor batteries to maintain. They glowed in the dark, whether on your nightstand or in a drawer where you couldn't see them anyway, or against your lap in the dark of night as you sat in a San Ysidro parking lot watching the foot traffic of border crossers loading and offloading the trolley, buses, and taxis.

The McDonald's trolley station, as it was commonly called—officially the San Ysidro station—sat a couple of hundred yards north of Mexico and saw the bulk of border traffic, some hundred thousand crossings daily.

Its tracks ran north and south from a plaza where shops lined the platform, the business fronts just feet from the railways, and where metal benches were plentiful for the weary traveler. The McDonald's was the main attraction, it seemed to Dickie as he sat and watched, a 24-hour operation where those venturing north or south could grab a bite to eat and use the bathroom before continuing their journeys.

The air down here, thick and pungent, was a medley of sweat and stale beer, cigarette smoke and diesel fuel. It reminded Dickie of the hot summer nights in South Los Angeles when everyone was out, and you could feel the tension in the air, and you knew it was only a matter of time before violence struck. He had that feeling now too, and it left him uneasy. He was no longer that young cop who craved the action and the adrenaline it produced. Now he was married, and a father and his partner was a woman for whom—although she was perfectly capable of handling her own business—Dickie felt responsible.

Dickie couldn't see the San Ysidro crossing from where he sat, but he could envision it beyond the path that Josie had taken when she walked away after tucking her badge, gun, and cell phone beneath the seat. She had held his gaze for a long moment before assuring him once more that she would be fine, that she had been to TJ many times in her youth, and that she was comfortable being there. That was the point, she assured him —in any undercover operation, you had to be confident in your role in order to not be made as a cop. Of course, Dickie already knew that, but it didn't make it easier for him to accept that he had allowed her to go alone. Whether it offended her or not, he had reminded her that women were more vulnerable than men, that they drew more attention, and that they were, on average, at a greater disadvantage in hand-to-hand combat than their male counterparts. She had said, "Dude, you know I can kick ass." Then the car door slammed, and Dickie watched with great trepidation as she mixed with the masses that were headed toward "Ped East," a walkway that would lead her through a turnstile and into customs, then onto a foreign land where she would have no police powers, no weapons, and no backup.

Dickie imagined Josie in her role. She would likely pair with a stranger as they funneled into customs, an elderly man or woman. She'd speak to them in their native tongue, be friendly and conversational, and get through the whole process with a smile on her face and the appearance of being just another traveler. Then hail a cab on the other side and hopefully have an uneventful five-minute ride into downtown Tijuana.

A man stopped in front of the car and stared at Dickie, who held his gaze—returned it, in fact, with more intensity than the man might have anticipated. Most passersby minded their business. There were a few who lingered and mingled with watchful eyes and bad intentions, appraising the gringo in his flashy car, alone in the dark. They would be surprised to learn that Dickie's intentions were more sinister than their own, should they mistake him for a victim.

The man moved on, occasionally glancing back, only to find Dickie's piercing eyes tracking his every move. Once he was out of sight, Dickie returned to his thoughts about Josie and her travels south. Then, as he always had—and as most cops would—he began preparing for worst-case scenarios and considering his options. There was only one option if things went bad, which had been the greatest dilemma of this affair since they were on their own. If anything went wrong south of the border, Josie's only hope for survival would be Dickie's ability to get in and out of Mexico alive and free. That was no minor task if this detail turned into a mission. He pictured the freeway system that took you straight into the port of entry and decided he'd better bring it up on his map so that he could easily navigate his way there if needed. That would be the easy part, getting to the border. Then he'd have to get across in a cop car, undetected and undeterred. Would the Mexican cops recognize him for what he was, or would he slide through unchallenged? That was the next easiest part, in his estimation. The improbable feat would be finding Josie and getting her out of whatever situation she might find herself in without their bodies or Josie's county car being ventilated by automatic gunfire. And then came the impossible part: crossing back into the United States. The cops on the U.S. side were far more discerning with those coming north than their counterparts were of others going south. Dickie and Josie, in their police package Charger—if it came to it—would draw more attention from the U.S. Border Patrol than a panel van with its rear bumper dragging on the ground.

Dickie glanced at his phone as he pulled up a Google map. He memorized the route but wondered how long it would take him to get to downtown Tijuana, given the traffic and the process of going through customs. He wondered if he would be better off abandoning the car and going afoot as Josie had. But he dismissed the idea of it since moving fast would be of the essence if anything went wrong. Of course, if it came to going in after Josie, Dickie would do so armed and with no authority to carry a gun into Mexico, so he would be gambling with his life. Get caught with a gun in Mexico, and you'd do ten years in a Mexican prison—if you could live that long in the harsh environment and conditions you'd endure.

He should have talked her out of it. He should have insisted. The risk factor was far too great, and there was no reason they should have been taking these chances. Not for *him*, this so-called friend and mentor of hers.

But it was too late for regrets. The first felony had been committed, and Dickie was in for a penny, in for a pound, if it came to it.

2

———————

JOSIE FELT HER PARTNER'S WATCHFUL EYES ON HER AS SHE WALKED AWAY from the car and joined others funneling toward the border crossing known as Ped East. She felt the glances and stares from others as well, mostly those of men, ranging from appreciative to predatory. In almost any other scenario, Josie would return the gazes of the latter with an unmistakable message that she was not the victim type, but for now, she needed to blend with the masses, not stand out and cause some to wonder who and what she was.

Predators looked for easy prey, and Josie knew the importance of projecting strength in their presence. She had made it her mission to speak on the matter as often as possible. Josie had spoken at schools, churches, and community events where she emphasized situational awareness, telling the students to pay attention to their surroundings, put their phones away, make eye contact with people, and walk confidently and purposefully.

Depending on the audience, she would sometimes share a story from her rookie days on the job when she had been recruited to assist the vice detail in prostitution sting operations. She had been warned not to stare down those potential customers who would arrive alongside her in vehicles to engage her in conversation and negotiation; rather, she was to

7

quickly scan the vehicle's interior for immediate threats, such as other persons or weapons, but then to look away and watch her surroundings while speaking to the potential customer. Prostitutes are always on the lookout for their pimps, another john, and the cops. Those who trolled would expect that from a working girl, so if you stared him down instead, he'd make you for a cop every time. And then you wouldn't get the solicitation and the bust.

Shortly into her first sting operation, Josie had been approached by a lone white male driving an unremarkable four-door sedan, a typical rental car or businessman's company ride. She had sauntered over to the car in her short skirt and heels, scanned the car for threats, then leaned in and asked if he saw anything he liked, giving him a glance at the goods while forcing herself to scan the area as a prostitute might. The man said, "Do you have a little sister, someone 'bout half your age?" Josie let loose a string of profanities, and as the guy peeled away, she removed a shoe and hurled it at him through the open passenger window.

The vice sergeant picked her up in his undercover car and got her off the street and away from the operation. At the command post, he chastised her about losing her temper, told her to cool off for a while, and then told her they'd put her back out on the street in a half hour or so and give her another chance. Sitting before him barefoot, she held up her one pump and told him she didn't have a spare shoe. The sergeant chuckled and told her they'd take care of it. A few minutes later, the creep in the sedan walked into the command post with a badge around his neck and holding in his hand the projectile she had launched through his window. He smiled at her and said, "Are you my Cinderella, by chance?"

Josie had blown her cover that night, but fortunately, it had only been a test to see if she would and a learning experience from which to draw for the rest of her career. Now, as she prepared to cross into TJ without a weapon or any backup, it was imperative that she not react as her cop instincts would dictate but to role play instead. Tonight, she was just an average American citizen heading into Mexico like the thousands who did so daily. There was nothing to see here—no reason for gangsters, fugitives, or cartel members to question or fear her presence.

She meandered with the others along a winding concrete walkway, working up a sweat in the night's heat. It was good exercise, but Josie preferred to walk or jog in parks or at the beach or through neighborhoods with manicured lawns, not to be confined with others by twelve-foot concrete and reinforced-steel walls. There were benches along the route. Some of the elderly travelers and those who were carrying extra weight tended to stop and rest at them. Others—the youthful and fit, like Josie— walked briskly with their destinations in mind.

Josie wondered what others were packing and carrying across the border. Obviously, some of the plastic bags were filled with groceries or other merchandise, but there were people with suitcases on rollers like the type you see at the airports. Were they filled with more groceries and supplies you couldn't get in Mexico? Or were those people going on vacation or returning from one, the cases packed with clothing and toiletries? Josie couldn't help but picture the containers full of contraband—packages of narcotics and firearms. But the narcotics wouldn't flow in that direction, so maybe they were empty now but had been full when those who carried them had crossed into the U.S.

Finally, she reached the port of entry, a concrete wall surrounding a pair of large turnstiles that rotated horizontally and ushered you into customs, a one-way funnel to the south. Immediately inside were directions that instructed the *Mexicanos* to go to the left and "foreigners" to the right. She assumed the former would be less scrutinized, though surely they would be required to have proper Mexican national identification and documentation to enter through that channel. She'd remember to tell her partner about that so he could go off about identification being required everywhere other than the voting polls.

Her heart rate kicked up a notch as she approached the man behind a counter separated from the public by a plexiglass barrier, the man wearing a white uniform shirt with the Mexican flag on its sleeve, the shirt wrinkled and sloppy on his wiry frame. She greeted him in Spanish and flashed a smile.

He returned the greeting in a mix of Spanish and English, obviously recognizing her as a visiting American, not a Mexican national. "*Buenas noches, Señorita*. What brings you to Mexico, my frien'?"

"I'm here to see a friend, my friend." She flashed another smile and offered no further explanation for her visit while sliding her passport ID card through a slot in the barrier.

The name on the card: Maria Luna. Josie had revived the identity she had used as a young adult to get into clubs, one for which she had obtained a birth certificate and driver's license, unaware at the time that it was a felony to do so. A gray area, probably. Dickie had said, "Are you kidding me, Josie? That's a felony!" She shouldn't have told him, but as she stated then, this was the best thing for her to go undetected across the border. After all, a computer log was generated and maintained of the crossings. Who knew if any warnings might be placed on law enforcement officers the way the identities of fugitives were flagged. It wouldn't surprise her if that were the case because she wasn't the first cop to go into another country without authorization to pursue a killer, and Mexico was never fond of any such excursion.

The customs cop examined Josie's ID card but not nearly as thoroughly as he appraised her body when he stood on his toes and leaned forward, scanning her from top to bottom. He said, "You have no things." It wasn't a question.

She shook her head as she lifted her handbag as a declaration of her belongings. "I'm just here for the evening, officer."

His eyes were dead as he studied her for a long uncomfortable moment. Then he nodded, almost knowingly, as he motioned for her to move around to the side where a pair of other officials waited, a man and a woman who also seemed to be watching her closely. A secondary inspection point.

Josie moved along without comment, wondering what it was that this man seemed to know. It was as if he had expected her—as if they, the three of them, had expected her. Or was it that they always expected visitors *like* her, those who came late at night and traveled back a few hours later. But for what purposes? Josie imagined there were many, most of which would likely fall into some category or other of illegal activity. Smuggling, primarily. Humans, drugs, weapons... An American-born Hispanic woman who was intelligent and well-spoken in both languages would have a better chance at crossing back into the U.S. without a thorough inspection. As such, Josie fit a particular profile that might garner extra attention.

The man at the next stage silently demanded her purse with an extended hand. The woman maneuvered to Josie's side and told her to raise her arms as she placed her gloved hands upon her, beginning at Josie's waist and working her way down to her ankles, then returning to the waist and feeling her through her clothing upward on her sides, across her back, below and over her breasts. This wasn't done in a private room, and there were no explanations or apologies offered. The woman finished by fishing around Josie's collar and beneath the flow of her hair while her male counterpart finished searching her purse. He shrugged, and the woman said, "Okay," stepping aside and indicating with a nod of her head that Josie was free to proceed into Mexico. The whole process was another irony she'd share with Dickie just to get him going, the thorough screening process of those going into a country whose population demanded that there be no border at all.

Josie noticed a couple loading their suitcases and multiple bags of groceries onto a conveyor belt on the other side of the room—the side where *Mexicanos* were free to pass without much scrutiny. There were two more guards or cops or whatever they were waiting on the other side of a large X-ray machine, but they were chatting and looking at one of their phones, not the screen that revealed the inner contents of those items passing through the device.

At the exit, a pair of military men dressed in desert camouflage stood guard, armed with sidearms and automatic rifles slung over their chests and wearing body armor outside their uniforms. They, too, were mostly uninterested in the *Mexicanos* passing by, but they carefully studied Josie, and her fear of being targeted persisted. It was as if they knew she was coming, but how could they?

In her youth, Josie had come to TJ to party many times, but they had always driven across the border and returned in the same fashion. Walking in seemed to be a more closely scrutinized process, and Josie couldn't understand why that would be. Or was it her? That was the concern. But then she felt she must be overreacting, feeling paranoid. Probably because there was so much at risk in what they were doing, as she and her partner had considered and reconsidered. Dickie was against it, but Josie had held her ground. She told him how, as a kid, she would pile into a van with eight other teens and head down to hang out at the beach or *Señor Frogs*, where you could eat tacos and drink tequila and beer until you puked, which someone inevitably would. Dickie had said, "You're lucky you weren't jailed and raped." He had never been to Mexico and had no desire to go, he'd said.

"How are you going to get back?" he had asked in the early stages of their planning this trip.

"Same way I'm crossing over," she'd said, "walking."

He didn't like it. Said nobody should be walking around by herself at night in Tijuana, especially unarmed. She had countered, "I won't be alone for long."

That hadn't seemed to put Dickie at ease, but it ended the debate.

The night air felt thicker on that side of the border as Josie left customs with a feeling of unease and began her descent into Mexico down a long, winding concrete walkway lined with fencing and festooned with graffiti. There seemed to be a void between there and the city a short distance away, its bright lights and high-rise buildings a beacon in the dark of night. She passed several beggars who sat on the walkway expectantly, their sorrowful eyes following her. Soon she passed through another turnstile, and then it was just a short walk to the street where smoke rose from the grills of vendors, and taxi cabs sat waiting, their drivers milling about together as they eagerly watched each person entering their country. A sign welcoming all to Mexico advertised "Border Taxi Cabs" as safe, clean, and affordable, offering service to downtown, *Revolución*, *Xolos* Stadium, and "other city attractions."

Travelers with luggage were approached by the waiting drivers, who relieved them of their suitcases and bags and guided them to their coaches, working hard for their tips. One of them came to Josie and asked if she needed a ride. Yes, she told him, and he gestured toward the street and began moving beside her.

"*Donde, Señorita?*... Where to?"

She smiled at him briefly, just enough to show politeness, and answered him in Spanish and then in English—just as he had spoken to her—telling the man she was only going downtown. It was her way of letting him know he could speak to her in whichever language he preferred.

Surprisingly, he preferred English, though his accent was thick like many of the immigrants in Los Angeles. She figured he'd been there—

been there and likely sent back. Maybe many times. He said, "Any place in particular? Downtown is far and wide, my friend."

"*El Caballo Loco*," she said. "The Crazy Horse."

He stopped at her side and studied her a moment, then started again toward his car. "Very well," he said, with a hint of disappointment. "Is no problem."

3

___

The drive to downtown was short, the road leading into the city mostly free of traffic at the late hour. The northbound lanes of traffic, on the other hand, looked like the Harbor Freeway at six o'clock with a Dodgers game starting at seven. Or the Hollywood, San Bernardino, Pomona, Long Beach, and Golden State Freeways—at any time. As far as you could see there were cars sitting still, some idling with lights on, others not, each waiting their turn to cross into the U.S. It made Josie wonder how difficult it would be crossing back over tonight. She didn't remember ever waiting long to come back when she was young, but then again, she would be half-bombed and partying with friends in the back of a van, unconcerned with time or anything else for that matter.

They crossed the Tijuana River, and shortly after, they were among the bright lights and festivities on the streets of downtown. It seemed different to Josie after all these years, smaller and rundown. But she had been a kid the last time she came here, lacking the life experience she brought with her now. She thought about what Dickie had said, that she had been lucky she ever made it back alive, and she knew he was right. She had known it for a long time now. Josie compared Dickie's words to those of the friend she was going to meet. He had told her that Tijuana was a city that needed its tourists, and that as long as you were there to enjoy the city, they would leave you be. He had said, "You've heard the adage, 'You can shear a sheep a thousand times,'" and she had finished the saying for him, "'But you can only skin it once.'" She had also heard that pigs get fat but hogs get butchered.

"Exactly," he had said. "The murders you hear about down here are drug-related—almost all of them. The north zone, *Zona Norte*, is a place where everything goes, which makes it the main attraction for *Americanos*. You'll see cops everywhere, but they aren't there to hassle the tourists."

He had gone as far as to say that the cops in Tijuana were "sensitive" to the needs of its visitors, and they worked to assure their safety.

Dickie, on the other hand, had said the cops in TJ were crooks, that you couldn't trust any of them, and that you should avoid them at all costs.

She'd have to see. Maybe somewhere in the middle of the two conflicting views was where reality lived.

Most of the businesses were lively, though there were a lot of places closed this time of night, places strategically located near the border to serve their American clientele. Medical offices advertising plastic surgery. Dental offices. *Farmacias* stocked with Viagra, anabolic steroids, B-12 shots, and an assortment of narcotics for those who came for their augmentations. It was said there was nothing you couldn't get in Tijuana for the asking, and the *Americano* concept of needing a prescription to obtain pharmaceuticals didn't apply here.

The street was abuzz with activity, people loitering on the sidewalks, some moving along swiftly, all the activity accentuated by the bright lights of various clubs. A row of palm trees that lined the main drag glowed from strings of lights that were wrapped around them, each a different color. Like Hollywood, it was festive and energetic—and like Hollywood, Josie knew there was an underbelly that was dark and tragic.

The cab stopped on the street just before reaching the *Cabailo Loco*, a so-called gentlemen's club that featured a four-story hotel above it. In other words, a whorehouse. Josie hadn't been inside this one, or any others, for that matter—at least not in Mexico, anyway—and she was apprehensive about her impending debut. As a cop, she'd participated in several massage parlor takedowns, in addition to the times she had posed as a hooker herself in sting operations. She had a good idea of the type of people who would be inside—patrons and the working girls alike. But it was a completely different thing to be here in Mexico and to go into a place like this under the guise of being a tourist than to be on the clock with a crew of other cops. This felt dirty.

She leaned forward and handed her driver a ten-dollar bill, and slid out of the back seat while quickly doing the math: the current exchange rate was 1 to 18.71, which meant she just gave him 187 pesos. Was that a bad omen? The number 187 had a profound meaning in the lives of cops and killers, it being the California penal code section for murder. Josie couldn't help but contemplate the oddity of that number coming up before she ever stepped foot in downtown TJ, the way she would also cringe at the numbers 13 and 666 when they were presented in her universe. These things just felt like bad karma to her. Either way, she paid the gentleman and left his cab to stand alone in downtown Tijuana. She took a deep breath as her chariot pulled away.

Josie scanned her surroundings, looking for her contact person. He was to meet her outside the club because, as he had said, the gatekeepers of the *Caballo Loco* wouldn't let her in by herself. Women were welcome when they accompanied a man, as it wasn't uncommon for couples to patronize such establishments for the purpose of experiencing a ménage à trois discreetly. *What happens in TJ...* But a woman by herself could be a free-lance sex worker, and that was not allowed in these clubs—it was one of the few things in Tijuana that were forbidden.

Across the street, young adults laughed and uttered drunken words while a hype man blew his whistle and worked to draw more customers into the pub, offering free shots to those who entered and boasting two-for-one drink specials inside. Josie saw herself among the young crowd twenty years earlier, and she now considered that she had been a naïve girl who had risked much for an evening or weekend of kicks. And it hadn't only been trips across the border where she had been lucky to survive her wilder days—there had been the raves, the beach parties, the drunken road trips with reckless boys. But for the grace of God...

The two-for-one drink specials and free shots were nothing new. Josie remembered barhopping with her teenage friends and being drawn to just this type of entertainment, and she reflected on her last foray south of the border as a teen. One of her girlfriends was robbed and assaulted in the restroom of a similar establishment. Two Tijuana cops had followed the friend into the ladies' room and latched the door behind them. They demanded her jewelry and then ordered her to disrobe. She later swore to the others that they hadn't raped her but that the cops had kept her panties as a memento. Given the level of hysteria her friend had displayed immediately after the incident and for the entire drive home, Josie always wondered if she had decided to keep some things to herself about what happened that night in the bathroom.

Now that Josie was here again among the naïve revelers and shifty hustlers and thinking about her girlfriend's experience in the bathroom, she had to consider that Dickie's estimation of the dangers here was not overstated. Suddenly she felt very alone and vulnerable. As she kept her eyes on the doormen outside the *Caballo Loco*—the two men keeping their eyes on her—someone grabbed her from behind. She spun toward him and threw her arm in a large circular overhead pattern that freed it from the grabber and left her face to face with him, squared off and ready to fight.

The man retreated, his arm raised to protect his head and face as if he knew what might come next. And he did know, Josie realized as she focused on the eyes of the man. Because he did know her. He knew her well enough that he should have known better than to grab her from behind.

"Josie," he started.

"Jesus," she said. "You're lucky I'm not armed. What the hell—"

"I'm sorry. That was dumb..." His eyes were now scanning their surroundings, and Josie could see he was anxious. The man said, "Let's walk," and turned back in the direction from which he must have come.

Josie followed while noting her surroundings. Most people were oblivious to the two of them and hadn't likely noticed the minor clash they had had. This, of course, excluded the two men who stood outside the entrance of the *Caballo Loco*, each of them dressed in slacks and polos that revealed muscular frames. As doormen, they would have taken note of a minor ruckus and likely watched the participants until they were no longer in sight. She could feel the gazes of the two men following them.

Josie's contact walked at a fast pace, his long legs covering the ground effortlessly, and Josie hurried to stay up with him. He didn't look back, nor did he slow down until he came to the corner of the block where a crowd was gathered around a taco stand. A cloud of smoke rose from a grill of sizzling meat and hung on the corner like morning fog. He continued twenty yards past and stopped, turned to face her, but looked past her in the direction they had come. Apparently satisfied, he met her gaze and said, "It's good to see you, Josie."

Josie took a deep breath and controlled the tempo of her exhale to come down from the adrenaline rush that had hit her. After a moment, she looked the man up and down and said, "My God, Jerry, what has happened to you?"

4

───────

JERRY TOWNSEND HAD BEEN HER RABBI IN THE DEPARTMENT UNTIL HE vanished under a cloud of suspicion when his wife of seventeen years was murdered. Rumors circulated that Jerry was considered a suspect in the slaying, but the investigation had grown cold, and any speculation as to who may have killed her remained as such—speculation. Josie seldom even thought about Jerry anymore, as it had been a decade since he vanished, and everyone else seemed to have forgotten about him too. The case had been the talk of the bureau with many theories as to what might have happened and where Jerry may have gone, but even those murmurings had faded away with her memory of him.

Until his recent phone call asking for her help.

She might have owed the Jerry Townsend who had been her mentor, but she felt no obligation to the man who vanished rather than standing his ground and declaring his innocence in the matter of his wife's death. Josie had told him as much during the first conversation they had in a decade, just a few weeks earlier, and then she listened to his side of things as any good investigator would. What he told her seemed to be the ramblings of a delusional man, conspiracy theories that rivaled a Clancy novel, and unfathomable allegations of corruption, betrayal, and murder that reached the upper echelon of their own department. She didn't tell him her thoughts—she hadn't had to. He finished by asking her to do her own investigation, to pull the case and review what was there, and to see for herself if any of it made sense to her. He had said, "You're one hell of an investigator, Josie, and I need your help. I beg you to help me."

Beyond the taco stand, where the sweet aroma of grilled meat wafted past and nearly covered the stench of beer and urine that rose from the sticky sidewalk on which they stood, Josie said, "You look like shit."

He looked toward the ground, and Josie saw a weakness in him she had never seen, could never have imagined.

Jerry Townsend had been a legend in the sheriff's department. His career included a long stint in patrol, an assignment to the elite sheriff's SWAT team, and many years as a gang cop and supervisor. While still a patrol deputy—before he began his career at the Special Enforcement Bureau, which comprises the SWAT team and other specialized units—he had been wounded during a shootout that left his partner dead. They had responded to a domestic violence call and heard screaming inside the residence when they arrived. Jerry had driven that night. Before he could put the car in park, his partner had bolted toward the sounds of violence, shouldered through the door, and was met with a barrage of gunfire from inside. Jerry had only been a few paces behind him, and he saw his partner go down before his eyes. He ran inside, returning fire while he grabbed his partner and dragged him out of the kill zone. He was shot twice in the process. After his partner died in his arms, Jerry reentered the home and killed the assailant. This was before the time of handheld radios, so he had no way to call for help unless he risked retreating to his car, which would have exposed him more than re-engaging the suspect head-on. Already seriously injured, Jerry had reloaded his weapon and charged inside, killing the man who had killed both Jerry's partner and—they soon discovered—the woman who had called the cops, the mother of the suspect's children.

Josie knew the story from her first days in the department, as the legendary shootout had been the subject of a training film that was shown to all academy cadets. These reenactments were referred to by cops as Motorola Fuckup Films since they were produced by Motorola, a company that also manufactured law enforcement radio equipment, and because the incidents that warranted a training film always had a theme of how an incident might have been better handled. Several years later in Josie's career, she met the legend everyone knew as a cop's cop, Jerry Townsend.

By then, he was supervising a gang unit in East Los Angeles where Josie worked patrol. She and her partner had assisted Jerry's team in serving search warrants at multiple locations, looking for a killer and evidence of his crimes. They were coming up empty-handed and about to conclude the operation when Josie met the eyes of a bystander and knew instinctively that he had something to say. She discreetly provided him with her card and hoped he would call. Later that same shift, Josie and her partner were able to lead Jerry's team to the suspect's hideout based on an "anonymous" phone call she received. From that day forward, Jerry had taken an interest in Josie and her career, and it was no surprise that she was selected to work in his gang unit not long after.

She worked in gangs with Jerry for two years, and they became close friends. He left after being promoted to lieutenant, and soon after, he was promoted to captain. Although they never worked together again, they stayed in touch, often meeting for lunch or a beer after work. Jerry Townsend was a man Josie always respected, admired, and even considered to be a father figure. He was her department rabbi, a term used by some to describe a personal patron or adviser.

Now he was in Mexico, a shadow of the legend she had known. He had lost a lot of weight, grown a gray beard to match his hair that was now tied in a ponytail, and his eyes were sunken and dark. She wasn't sure if he was tired or strung out, though his pupils didn't show signs of his being under the influence of any drugs. The fact she looked for signs of it said enough about the condition in which she found her longtime friend and mentor.

He finally met her gaze. "It's not as bad as it seems."

Was he saying he wasn't in as bad a shape as he appeared? Or did he mean that the situation that drove him from the department he loved and the country he once served honorably wasn't as bad as many had speculated it to be?

"What's not, Jerry?"

"Nothing is ever as bad as it seems, kiddo."

Her mouth turned up in a partial smile, and she held his gaze that suddenly seemed warm and sincere, an old friend trying to get back from a bad trip.

He said, "You read the file."

She nodded, even though he hadn't asked but rather stated something he must have instinctively known. He probably knew she wouldn't be standing on a corner in Tijuana with him had she not read the file and learned some things about the case that bothered her, things that would stop an experienced investigator in her tracks and cause her to question everything she thought she knew about it before.

"And you read my letter."

Josie nodded again. The letter had arrived not long after the first phone call, and by then, Josie had already pulled the murder file from the library, taken it home, and read through all the reports and documentation once. Parts of it she revisited after reading Jerry's letter, which essentially told a tale that seemed so outlandish she knew that if others read it, they would write Jerry off as having lost his mind. Maybe he had, she considered more than once. But something else told her that no, she knew this man, he wasn't crazy, nor was he a murderer.

He nodded in return. "And?"

"We have a lot to discuss, Jerry, and I'm not sure this is the time or place." She quickly scanned their surroundings again to emphasize her point.

"Right, yes, I completely agree. Well, we can talk more as we go, but for now, I think it would be best if we go speak to my informant. Are you ready?"

Josie took a breath. "Ready as I could be."

He smiled. "Good. Let's go."

Jerry led the way back to the *Caballo Loco* and beelined straight toward one of the two doormen, the one who glanced their way as they approached. The other had his back to them and appeared to be speaking to a young lady dressed in a black mini with pumps and fishnets and a camisole for her top. Jerry had pulled his hand from his pocket as he and the doorman came face to face, and they shook hands. The man stepped aside, allowing them to enter the club, while plunging the hand that was shaken into his pocket. Josie had no doubt that a business transaction had just occurred, likely the way most business in Mexico was conducted.

Music spilled out as the door was opened. Inside, multicolored strobe lights streaked across a platform where half a dozen girls in various stages of disrobe danced in high-heeled shoes or go-go boots or barefooted, their bodies glistening in the lights. They stepped inside and paused momentarily as Josie took in the sights. There were several stages in addition to what she assumed to be the main one, all of which had seating and bar tops surrounding them for the clientele to enjoy close-ups of the talent. Most of these seats were occupied by attentive men of various age groups and ethnicities, though most were white. *Americanos*, she assumed. Most of the girls appeared to be young, and Josie was surprised to see that many of them were relatively attractive—as far as strippers and hookers went.

There must have been close to fifty of these girls, Josie realized, as her gaze panned the various stages, rooms, and plush booths where lap dances were taking place and business transactions were discussed. There were balconies that had more of the same—mesmerized men and mostly naked ladies. Jerry placed a gentle hand on the back of her arm to encourage her forward, leaned in, and with his voice raised over the thumping music that kept the girls grooving, said, "Follow me."

She dropped in behind him as he shouldered through the crush of spectacles and spectators, a medley of woodsy colognes and sweet perfumes nearly masking the harsh stench of body odor that hung in the thick, pungent air. At the back were several doors that Josie assumed to be offices or VIP rooms, but Jerry veered away from them and led her up a spiraling metal staircase to the second-floor balcony. Another set of doors lined the same wall on the upper level, VIP rooms set above VIP rooms, she figured.

Jerry walked directly to the door farthest from the staircase and tapped twice before opening it without waiting for a response. He walked in first, glanced around, and motioned Josie in behind him. The room was the size of a modern American living room, painted red and gold, and furnished with a bulky sofa and two matching armchairs that surrounded a small stage with a brass pole that rose to the ceiling. Three of the walls were covered by mirrors, making the room seem larger than it was.

The room was unoccupied. Jerry closed the door behind them, reducing the sounds of the night club to the distant melodies and thumping bass tones you might hear at a stoplight in L.A. if your car windows were up, the air conditioner on, and the source of the sounds was a couple of car lengths away. Josie knew instinctively that the room had been reserved so that they would have a place to talk. But where was the informant?

Jerry retrieved two bottles of water from a small refrigerator built into a bar and suggested with a wave of his hand for Josie to sit on the sofa. He handed her a water and opened the other for himself. After taking a long swig, he sat across from her in one of the two chairs, crossed one leg over the other, and took a big breath. He met her gaze and said, "Thank you for coming."

She wouldn't tell him he was welcome because she hadn't decided if he was. It felt safe in the room, but Josie had been uncomfortable walking through the club, and there was still the matter of getting out of there safely and back across the border. She pictured Dickie waiting in her car, knowing his anxiety would grow with each passing moment. She saw him in her mind, the serious man tugging at his mustache with one hand, stroking his Glock with the other, while conjuring all the bad thoughts he could in anticipation of the worst-case scenarios that might happen. Josie estimated that only an hour or so had passed since she left him sitting near the McDonald's, but it would seem much longer than that to him. Sadly, she knew it would be several more hours before she was back in his company, given the congestion on the roads heading north—and that was if all else went smoothly. She suddenly anticipated that moment when they were reunited, the way she looked forward to getting back on the ground every time she had been up in a helicopter.

Jerry broke the silence, apparently realizing that no acknowledgment of his thanks was coming. "So my informant will be here shortly, I hope. Time seems to matter less on this side of the border, but I made it clear to her that you would be in a hurry to get back."

"Jerry, why here? Couldn't we have met at a restaurant or some hotel that's not a brothel?"

He shook his head. "She works here—"

"Great. Your informant's a whore."

"—and she won't take the chance of being seen anywhere other than here with me or you or some other gringo."

"You're a client," Josie guessed.

He nodded sheepishly. "You could say that."

She shook her head and looked away.

"Josie, I've lived in a different world since Laura was killed. Nothing is the same as it once was. I live under this umbrella of suspicion, so I've run away from my life in America. I know some will never believe that I had nothing to do with her death—no matter what happens with your investigation—"

"Hang on, Jerry, I haven't agreed—"

"—I mean to say *if* you choose to look into this," he interjected, his hand raised to stop her. "But my point is, my life… well, I'm lucky to be alive."

She saw moisture in his eyes as he looked away, and it told her the meaning of what he had said. He wouldn't be the first nor the last cop she had known to seriously contemplate suicide, and if he ever went through with it, he wouldn't be her first friend to do so.

"Jerry."

A moment passed before he met her gaze again.

"I'm here to help you now. All you had to do was make that call, and see, here I am, south of the border, in a whorehouse to see what I can do." She flashed a smile to accentuate the levity of her statement.

He nodded and looked down again. "Thank you. I appreciate it."

The door opened, and in walked a naked angel.

She was young, almost childlike at a glance, wearing only skimpy white panties and matching tassels hanging from her modestly proportioned breasts. A set of wings was affixed to her back, and a halo was somehow suspended above her head. She wore her shiny black hair tight against her scalp, pulled back from her pretty young face, accentuating her caramel skin and almond-shaped, lifeless eyes.

The angel wasn't alone.

5

Two men followed and flanked her in the doorway, each of them dressed in slacks and sports coats that undoubtedly concealed weapons. One had no facial hair and a youthful face that made Josie wonder if he even shaved. The other had a scraggly beard. Baby Face and Fur Face—a dynamic duo. They were muscle, security, asset protection agents. The asset being Angel and her tight little money maker.

In her two-plus decades of law enforcement, Josie had seen countless young women and even girls who resorted to selling themselves to support their habits or just to survive. Some hadn't made the choices for themselves—child trafficking was all the rage in the twenty-first century. They were the ones who were tormented, beaten, and drugged until their souls were dead and submission was achieved. The others—those who hadn't been forced into The Life—came to the same place as the others but through their own bad choices or destitution. The commonality was the dead eyes, which came from their addictions. Because numbing the mind allows one to ignore the darkness of their soul once they've completely devalued their body.

The angel was no saint.

Jerry watched but didn't speak. Josie wondered if Angel was his informant. But if so, why the guards? There seemed to be a standoff of sorts, and Josie felt the tension in the room.

In Spanish, Baby Face said, "She will be your companion tonight."

Jerry shrugged as if he didn't understand them. Josie knew that he spoke some Spanish himself, and she figured he might have been playing the dumb *Americano* role. Baby Face met her eyes expectantly. Josie turned to Jerry. "They said she is our companion."

Jerry nodded as if to say okay. "Where is Mina?"

She turned her attention to Baby Face and said in Spanish, "He is asking about Mina?" – saying it in the form of a secondary question, as if she had never heard the name herself.

He shook his head while Fur Face gently guided Angel toward them. "Not available," he said, speaking in English with a heavy accent. "Is okay, or no? You no like?" referring to the beautiful child whore.

Josie met Angel's gaze and saw something that hadn't been there when they first came in—there hadn't been anything at all in the young woman's eyes then. But now she looked like a puppy in a pound: desperate, hopeful, and aware of her vulnerability. Josie didn't wait for Jerry to respond. "She will do fine," Josie said. Then she repeated herself in Spanish.

Baby Face nodded and turned on his heel. Fur Face—the dangerous one, Josie concluded—held her gaze momentarily before cutting his beady eyes to Jerry. His face twisted into a scowl, his eyes squinting, his nose wrinkled, and the corners of his mouth turned down. But he remained silent as he turned to follow his partner out. They closed the door behind them, and Angel remained where she stood in her wings and halo and tiny patches of cloth exemplifying her modesty.

Josie let out a breath that punctuated the relative silence in the room, and only the muffled sounds of music beyond the closed door could otherwise be heard. Jerry met her gaze and gave a faint shake of his head to reveal his concern about the situation, which she shared. Without knowing anything about these places and how they worked, she had to wonder why someone other than who they had expected had been provided to them. Josie assumed that Jerry had arranged for his informant, Mina, to come, yet she was deemed to be unavailable and substituted by the angel. So who was this angel, and what happened to the woman (or girl) Jerry had hoped to speak with tonight? Clearly, this wasn't business as usual, or the two goons wouldn't have accompanied her to the room—as far as Josie knew. Had they expected Jerry's disapproval? Josie hadn't seen Mina yet, but she couldn't imagine that Angel was any downgrade from her. Yet the goon squad showed up to accentuate the decision that had been made to substitute one for the other for reasons that were unclear to Josie. Did Jerry have any idea what those reasons might be? His subtle message to her had been not to say anything. He either didn't trust the angel, or he was worried about something else. And none of it was making Josie feel comfortable with having come into Mexico tonight, alone, unarmed, and, quite frankly, illegally.

Dickie crossed her mind again, and she wished she were on her way back to meet him. She longed for the moment when she reached U.S. soil; as it stood now, Josie couldn't be certain she'd make it back alive. It had been a mistake to come here, though she would never admit this to her partner if she made it out alive. This was a whole other arena and a different game than the one she was accustomed to playing.

Josie motioned the girl over and patted the seat on the sofa adjacent to where she sat. The young woman came slowly, watching them both with apprehension in her sleepy eyes. She sat at the edge, leaned forward, and moved her shoulder in order to tuck the wing behind the sofa's padded arm. Josie said, "Do you speak English?"

Angel shook her head.

Jerry said, "Let's not count on it."

Josie looked at him. "What's going on here, Jerry?"

"I don't know," he said, his gaze held on the angel. Josie knew he wasn't gawking at her nearly-naked beauty; rather, he was assessing the situation—assessing her. Though Jerry was just a man, after all, and Josie wouldn't blame him for gawking at a young lady as beautiful as the angel.

She said, "What are we going to do? This is a test, isn't it?"

He nodded.

Josie shook her head, leaned back in her seat, and looked at the ceiling. More mirrors. Lights and mirrors, the whole goddam place a funhouse façade. If she were armed, she'd take Jerry and this girl who was dressed as an angel and head for the border. But she wasn't armed, and she had no authority here. She was at the mercy of the Mexicans now—their government, those goons that brought Angel to their room, and probably the cartels—so she had no choice but to play this out, and every move would have to be carefully considered. She took a sip from the bottle Jerry had provided, and the cold water tasted exceptionally good.

The first contemplation, of course, was how to deal with Angel, the Trojan horse. Was she wearing a wire? Is that why she was sent there? The only places she might conceal one was in her wings or her halo, and the halo might be well suited for good reception. But Josie didn't think she wore a bug. It likely came down to one of two things: either something had happened to Mina, and the goons anticipated some pushback on the replacement, or Angel was sent in as a substitute to make sure that Jerry was a legitimate customer—that he and his companion were there for a threesome. The thought of it made Josie cringe. That would be the test she had asked Jerry about and had received an affirmative nod, indicating to Josie that he was on the same page. So how would they handle that? There was no way Josie would even pretend to engage in a sexual encounter with this young woman, and she wouldn't allow Jerry to either—certainly not in her presence.

There would be some risk to what she was about to propose, but so far, Jerry wasn't firing off any brilliant ideas himself. She looked at Angel and said, "Why did they bring you up to our room?"

Josie could see that she truly didn't understand what she had asked, so she repeated herself in Spanish.

Angel perked up. It was as if she finally had a part in the whole affair. She spoke in Spanish, addressing Josie directly. "They said the man paid for a threesome."

"What happened to Mina?"

She glanced away, came back to Josie's expectant gaze, and said, *"No sé."*

Josie looked at Jerry. He had no questions. He had apparently understood enough of the conversation, and he nodded for her to continue.

"How much do you charge for this?"

Angel looked from Josie to Jerry, considering. "One fifty. U.S.," she said in English. The important parts of the language were learned early in this business.

Josie looked at Jerry. "I'm going to take a big chance here because we have to get out of this predicament alive."

He nodded. "I'm sorry, Josie, I had no way—"

She cut him off. "Doesn't matter now, Jerry. We're just going to have to hope we can pull this off."

Jerry pushed out of his seat, went to the bar, pulled a beer from the fridge, and opened it. Turned and leaned against the bar, a spectator now.

Josie turned to Angel. "Take it off. Everything."

6

THE CRUISER SLOWED AND CAME TO A STOP IN FRONT OF HIM. THE DRIVER,
a black woman with short, cropped hair and big eyes, said something to
her partner, a white or Hispanic male. The passenger officer leaned
forward in his seat to see around her—to see Dickie, in fact. From the
angle where they had stopped, perpendicular to the front of the Charger,
they would have likely seen the red and blue lights hidden behind the grill
—at least, that's what you would expect from a trained observer—so
Dickie wondered if they had already figured out that he was a cop.

"America's Finest."

The declaration was printed across the door of the black and white
Ford Explorer just below the window where the woman sat staring.
Perhaps a little too prominently, this assertion. "To Protect and Serve"
adorned the bottom of the door, and a circular city emblem was in the
center. Along the top of the front fender, the words SAN DIEGO POLICE
identified their agency. Dickie hadn't known if San Ysidro was its own
city or a community in San Diego—he hadn't ever pondered it. But now,
with America's Finest bearing down on him, he had a good idea that it was
the latter.

He nodded as if to say *everything's fine*, he was one of them, so to speak—not to insinuate that he was one of America's Finest—but to give them the idea that he was a cop if they hadn't figured it out yet.

The car went into park, and the doors popped open. They hadn't figured anything out. Dickie put both hands out the driver's window and kept his eyes on the right hand of the woman cop, which was upon the grip of her holstered weapon. He said, "L.A. Sheriff's Homicide," and regretted that he had the moment the words left his mouth. He should have told them he worked Internal Affairs, Homeland Security, or anything other than where he actually worked. But he was so accustomed to identifying himself in such a manner that the words rolled off his tongue without any thought at all. Josie might have said, "Los Angeles County Sheriff's Department, Homicide Bureau, Sergeant Sanchez speaking," in her always formal tone, the way she answered phones at the office. Dickie wondered if she were on her way back to him yet and hoped that she was. But she was probably still down in TJ, eating street tacos and drinking Corona while he was bored to death and now preparing to bullshit America's Finest about why he was there and what he was doing.

The black officer continued toward him cautiously. Her partner went around to the passenger side of the Charger and shone his flashlight toward Dickie, who was thinking that for America's Finest, their tactics weren't the best. If he had been a fugitive trying to make it to the border, he would have dropped the Charger into gear and floored it, smashing into the cruiser while the woman was getting out of her car. The partner on the other side would likely have been knocked down while coming out of his door as well, and Dickie would be headed for the border by the time anyone was able to start slinging lead at him. But that was the thing about police work and survival—sometimes you only stayed alive by luck, and these two were lucky that Dickie was a good guy, not a bad one.

The woman cop's perfume wafted into his window as she neared him, a lilac fragrance spicing the summer breeze.

"You can put your hands down," she said, a pleasant tone that contrasted the scowl on her partner's face.

He was Hispanic, Dickie noted, now that the man was peering in through the open passenger window, his thick black mustache a beacon in the glow of his flashlight. Before Dickie followed her direction, he met the partner's gaze, Dickie's eyes a question the man understood. He nodded as if to agree with his partner that Dickie was free to lower his hands, and then he redirected the beam of his flashlight so that it wasn't directly in Dickie's face.

"Whatchya doing all the way down here, Detective?" she said, her lips parted in a slight smile.

Dickie smiled back, taking a moment to put his thoughts in order. He said, "Here on business, ma'am. How are you guys doing tonight? Staying busy?"

The partner was leaning in now, his eyes scanning the interior of Josie's car while the policewoman continued the conversation. "Always busy on the border, my friend. What type of business y'all handlin'?"

Dickie tipped his ball cap up a little as he slouched in his seat, showing how relaxed and comfortable he was in his jeans and tennis shoes. He didn't wear a fedora unless he was dressed in business attire, and for this little excursion, he'd thought to be comfortable, cool, and incognito. He would have been very content if not for the Glock beneath his leg. He hadn't wanted to make any furtive movements when they had pulled in front of him, so he had just tucked the gun that had been on his lap beneath his leg where it was concealed from view. Now he realized that it would be a great time to reveal the presence of that gun to them both before someone noticed some part of it protruding. He said, "We're on a case—by the way, my gun is under my leg here, just so you know. Had a dude kind of casing me a while back and been sitting here with it on my lap ever since—until you guys pulled up, that is."

"You're fine," she said. "So you were saying somethin' 'bout working on a case?"

"Oh, yeah… my partner and I came down to talk to an informant about an unsolved homicide. That's what I work, Unsolveds. Anyway, she's doing the talking, and I'm just hanging out here enjoying the show."

"She?"

"Yeah, my partner"—he started to provide her name but caught himself—"um, she's down there talking to the informant. She speaks Spanish, and I don't, so…"

The policewoman's big eyes narrowed, and Dickie wondered if she thought he was lying. He hadn't told her a lie yet but knew he was about to.

"She go across?"

He furrowed his brow as if the question surprised him. "Who, my partner? Oh no, the informant was coming here—well, down there," he said, thumbing the area generally south, "somewhere down by Customs, I believe."

"You didn't think you should go with her? It's sort of dangerous around here, you may have noticed."

Dickie nodded. "Well, my partner's sort of a badass." He grinned, and so did she. Her eyes softened a little more, and she seemed to like that Dickie had complete confidence in his female partner. He continued, "And the truth of it was, she didn't want me to go. Said having a *gringo* along would draw too much attention, that everyone would know we were the cops."

The woman cop looked across the horizon toward the south, contemplating. After a moment, she said, "Okay, then, Detective—what'd you say your name was?"

He hadn't, and at this point, he didn't think it was a good idea to provide it. What if Josie started an international incident? Wouldn't it be better to ride off into the sunset like the Lone Ranger, not bother waiting for the authorities to arrive and thank them for a job well done? It's what his buddy, Johnny B., used to say, and Dickie had become a believer of it himself.

So he said, "Floyd."

"Okay, Detective Floyd. You watch yourself down here, my friend."

With that, she turned on her heel and started back for her cruiser. Her partner followed her lead without any farewell. Their doors closed behind them, and America's Finest went on keeping this side of the border safe for women and children. Which it might not have been had Floyd actually been the one who was there rather than Dickie.

Dickie watched until they drove away and were out of his view. He then scanned his surroundings once more. A few people were eyeing him now that the cops had come and gone, likely wondering who he was and what was going on with the cops, but most were minding their own business. He watched the few who were coming north from the direction of the crossing, but Josie was nowhere in sight. He glanced at his watch, took a breath, and let it out slowly. The Glock was back in its rightful place in his hand, on his lap. His thoughts soon turned dark again, Dickie considering the worst and fretting over the status of his partner.

He started thinking about heading south.

7

———————

Jerry turned and faced the bar while Angel stood up from the sofa and removed her wings and her halo. Once the halo was gone, there was no reason to leave the panties and tassels in place. Josie told her again to take everything off, then she walked to the bathroom while Angel finished disrobing. Josie returned with one of two robes that were provided for guests, handed it to the young hooker, and invited her to have a seat again. She seemed smaller and appeared younger, a tiny dark angel wrapped in an oversized, fluffy white robe.

"You can join us now," she said to Jerry's back.

The three of them gathered in the small confines of the couch and sofa arrangement, with a small stage and brass pole as the centerpiece.

Jerry turned his head to Josie, sitting next to him. "What now?"

"We wait. What's the usual on these things, an hour? Half an hour?"

"Depends," he said sheepishly.

"Okay, we'll split the difference and hang out for forty-five minutes. Then we walk out of here and hope there's nothing to it."

He said, "She would leave first, in my experience."

Josie was disgusted to think about it. Jerry, her former mentor, now in his sixties, was accustomed to the workings of a Tijuana whorehouse. If she had known that before she came down to see him, she might not have bothered to come, even though she believed some of what he had told her about his wife's murder. Or at least she wanted to believe and was willing to explore it to the extent she could. But coming down to meet an informant had been a risk from the start, and everything had worsened since she arrived. There were the goons, who were probably cartel hitmen and would think nothing of killing them both. Then this girl, Angel… God only knew what she might say to her boss or those goons when this ended. Once Josie cleared this building, she didn't care what Angel reported, but the departure from here would be the risky part of the deal. And the elephant in the room was the missing informant. Where was Mina, and what might have happened to her? The goons had simply said Mina wasn't available. When Josie asked Angel, she said she didn't know. Was there more to her absence than a simple change in personnel? Josie suspected there was.

"Okay, fine," she told him. "Whatever the procedure is, that's what we do. But we get the hell out of here as quickly as we can without looking panicked." She held his gaze while waiting for his response, knowing she had been sharp in her tone. She didn't care; she was pissed. Anything that went wrong was on Jerry, and she just prayed it wouldn't be detrimental.

He nodded and said nothing.

Josie turned to Angel and said to her in Spanish, "You will be paid for your time, the one-fifty, but we don't want to do anything with you."

The look on her face was one of confusion as if she didn't understand the language.

Josie continued: "We had hoped to spend time with Mina, and nothing personal, but we aren't interested in having relations with you. But we don't want those men who brought you here to know that, okay?"

She nodded, seeming to get it now.

"They would be mad at you and suspicious of us."

Angel said, "*Eres chota?*"

Josie knew that *chota* was slang for cop, but why would the angel ask if she was a cop? Josie didn't like it, and it added to the anxiety she was having over this whole ordeal. But she remained in her role and simply said, "No, honey, we're not the police," and repeated it in Spanish. She said, "We're Americans just here looking to have some fun. But we had hoped to be with Mina. You don't have any idea what happened to her?"

Angel glanced at Jerry, then met Josie's gaze again. "I don't know. I haven't seen her in a couple of days. That's how it goes here—you see someone every day for a while, then you never see them again, and nobody ever mentions it. You don't want to ask questions, believe me."

Josie translated her words for Jerry. After a moment, he said, "Does she know her well?"

Josie asked his question, and Angel replied, saying she and Mina had been friends here at work. Saying it in the past tense. Josie told Jerry as much.

"Does she know where Mina lives?"

Before she asked, Josie thought about what Jerry might be thinking. He didn't know that the second they were out of this situation, she was heading for the border like hell on wheels, and she didn't plan on ever returning. Not even for Jerry—especially not for Jerry, the old pervert. In fact, her advice to him would be to get the hell out of Mexico himself, but she didn't think he would.

Josie asked Angel about where Mina lived, and the answer surprised her.

She told Jerry, "She says Mina lived upstairs in the hotel. I asked her if she lives here too, and she does. These girls are slaves here, Jerry… did you realize that? They're fucking sex slaves."

Jerry looked away and shook his head.

They sat in awkward silence for several minutes after that.

Finally, Josie said, "How long have we been here?"

He glanced at his watch. "About a half hour."

Josie pushed out of her seat, went to the refrigerator, and grabbed a bottle of water. She held it up and asked if anyone wanted anything, but neither did. She grabbed a second bottle, thinking she might need one for the journey back. She might have to run the distance, or worse yet, she might have to head east and try to go the way of the coyote, over the fence and through the mountains, or under something and across somewhere else. She didn't want to think about it. The dangers she'd find off the beaten path were likely worse than what she might encounter here in town. *The devil you know*, she thought. She wished she had a gun and thought about how she might get one, seeing herself doing business with a gangster in an alley and seeing it go bad, the gangster's friends thinking they'd take the rest of her money before raping and killing her there. She'd be better off trying to disarm Baby Face and shooting her way out of this place.

Josie returned to her seat. "In about ten minutes, we need to start getting ready. I'm going to give our little angel here some instructions about what to say if the goons start asking her questions when she walks out. We'll muss up our clothing and hair a bit, give her a couple of minutes, then get out of here ourselves." She turned to Angel and told her in Spanish, "Ten more minutes."

Angel nodded, then asked if she could use the restroom. "Of course," Josie told her.

Jerry waited until the bathroom door was closed. "We need to find Mina."

Josie shook her head. "We need to get the hell out of here before we can't. Jerry, something is off here, and I don't know what it is. Do you have access to any hardware?"

He shook his head. "No. They'd put you away for life if they caught you with a gun."

"Do you know where you could get one if you needed it?"

Jerry said, "This is *Zona Norte*. You can get anything you want here if you know who to ask and you're willing to pay. But again, you get caught with a gun in Mexico, you're fucked."

"Even a cop?"

"Especially a cop. I've got a friend who worked across the border, San Diego PD, spent half his years in their southern division. Did a stint back in the day working the BARF team, their Border Area Robbery Force. They did away with that unit and acronym years ago, but those guys worked undercover right here on the border," he said with a nod of his head as if the border were across the room. Josie wished it were. Jerry continued, "He told me their greatest fear was getting caught coming across into Mexico, even though they were on-duty cops doing their jobs. He said back then, you could accidentally end up on this side without even realizing it. The border crossings weren't as definitive then. If you got caught, he said, they might let you go back, but they'd keep your car and your gun and sometimes any cash you had. Cops robbing cops, if you can fucking believe it.

"Those signs telling you 'Last Exit' when you're coming down the highway? My buddy said sometimes they'd pass those chasing someone or whatever, and they'd have to call for their guys to come down and block traffic so they could turn around and drive back on the southbound lanes to avoid going into Mexico. Do you believe that? They couldn't even just swing around and come back through customs."

Josie shook her head.

He said, "They do that to the cops right across the border, imagine what they'd do to a couple of L.A. cops they catch all the way down here on Revolution?"

Josie said, "I didn't bring anything with me. No gun, no ID… nothing. But also, I don't plan on being caught."

"How did you get in without ID?"

"I've got ID, but it's fake. What I meant is I don't have any department ID with me. They have no way of making me for a cop."

Jerry smiled. "Shit, kid, they know."

Her brows furrowed, revealing her silent question.

He said, "Trust me, they know. They see it in your eyes."

"Well, I'll lie and deny."

"What's your cover story?"

"If we get jammed up?"

"If *you* do. I'm fairly well-known around here as an expatriate with a booze and broads problem. I'm not the only one."

"Do they know you were a cop?"

"Hell, no. Most people don't ask about a man's background when he minds his business, stays friendly, and tips the right people. On the rare occasion someone's inquired, I've told them I was in the security industry. Down here, that's an honorable profession, unlike law enforcement. Plus, if anyone cornered me, I could give them the name of an old partner who runs a security business in Vegas and could vouch for me."

She nodded.

Jerry said, "And why I'm here, I tell them I'm sort of on the run."

"Not entirely false."

He nodded in agreement. "It's another thing they respect here."

Angel came out of the bathroom, still in the robe. She stood behind the sofa and waited silently. Ready to leave the awkward gathering they'd had.

Josie said, "You're ready?"

She nodded.

"Okay, remember, we all had a really nice time here tonight."

8

DICKIE PASSED THE TIME GOING THROUGH THE FILE THAT JOSIE HAD brought with her and left in the car. He needed something to get his mind off Josie and her situation south of the border before he became irrational and decided prematurely that she needed to be rescued.

As he read the reports, some details of Laura Townsend's murder returned to him. Dickie hadn't been assigned to the case, but it was the talk of the bureau at the time, and he remembered hearing some of the details back then. How could it not have been the topic du jour? Jerry was one of those in the department whom everyone seemed to know and most liked. Then suddenly, his wife was murdered, and he'd become the topic of conversation in every locker room across the county, most of those discussions laden with speculation and unfounded accusations. Cops seldom waited for a jury's verdict before assessing one's innocence or guilt—especially when it was one of their own who stood accused.

What Dickie remembered of the case was that Jerry and his wife had been out for dinner and drinks, and when they returned to their home in La Crescenta late that evening, they allegedly surprised a burglar inside. The would-be thief shot and killed Laura, who had walked in ahead of Jerry, and then the killer fled through the back of the house. One of the questions that everyone seemed to ask at the time was why Jerry hadn't fired his weapon. The answer was that he didn't have it with him. That had caused a lot of suspicion because Jerry was known to always carry a gun, on and off duty, like most cops who worked and lived in L.A.

The other question that persisted was how and why his home had been targeted. La Crescenta was an upscale neighborhood where residents were attentive to suspicious persons and activities, and the crime rates were low because of it. Also, it was the sheriff's jurisdiction—Crescenta Valley station—a place that was slower paced than other parts of the county. Deputies there had time to patrol the streets and pay attention to the smaller, quality-of-life issues, which kept the riffraff out of their community and in the city not far away. Things like prostitution, gangs, graffiti, loitering, and drugs—the cops in that community had never let these things take hold, and it was a safer place to live because of it. So how and why did an armed burglar pick the upscale home of Jerry and Laura Townsend as his target? And a nighttime burglary, no less.

Like most cops, Dickie knew two things about burglars: they usually worked in the daytime when people were at work and school, and seldom were they armed. The average burglar is an addict, a petty thief who graduated to breaking and entering once their habits demanded it. There was a lot more risk in residential burglary than there was with being an opportunist thief, both in being caught and the length of time one would serve if convicted. There was no reason for burglars to carry a weapon, given the sentencing enhancements in California that went with being armed and the fact that most burglars didn't expect to encounter anyone inside their targeted homes. Burglars are sneaky, and they know how to make certain that a place is vacant before they enter. So those things also caused a lot of suspicion toward the case as it was reported: why would a burglar be armed? Why did he choose the Townsend home? Why was he committing his crimes at night? Why shoot the homeowner when fleeing was an option? Wouldn't the burglar have heard them arrive, the rumble of their car's motor, the shutting of car doors, voices, and heels clicking against the concrete…

"Something about it stinks," Dickie recalled hearing more than a few times.

Townsend had been the captain of Narcotics then, and there had been some speculation about a cartel hit. The Majors crew under his command had been very successful with their undercover operations and busts in the previous months, including one operation that netted nearly five million fentanyl pills, a hundred kilograms of fentanyl powder, two hundred grams of cocaine, four thousand pounds of methamphetamine, and four million in cash. In a press conference, Jerry had stood among the impressive display of seized narcotics, assets, and more than fifty firearms—about a dozen of which were military-grade weapons—and declared another victory in the department's ongoing war against the Mexican cartels.

It wouldn't have been the first or last time a Mexican cartel retaliated against law enforcement when they suffered a tremendous loss. South of the border, the killing of cops who tried to enforce laws against the cartels was common. In fact, they often went after the leaders, killing police chiefs, mayors, or anyone they deemed to be leading the efforts to weaken or destroy their drug empires. So the idea was that following the media attention of the drug busts, Townsend himself may have been targeted.

But it seemed a little sloppy to Dickie. Cartel hits were usually exacting, and he would have expected to see Jerry and his wife tortured and murdered in a way that sent a message to all American law enforcement. This killing didn't feel like a hit to Dickie. So what was the real motive? Had anything even been stolen?

What Dickie hadn't remembered about the case until he started thumbing through the murder book in the San Ysidro parking lot, reading a little and looking around every few moments to check his surroundings, was that the primary investigator had been Victor Robles.

Jesus, Robles again? Dickie shook his head in the darkness and thought about Robles and his former wife, Brenda Neely, now their lieutenant of Unsolveds. Robles had screwed up the case of a murdered councilman that Dickie and Josie had recently put to rest, but not until after an innocent man had spent seventeen years in prison. There were parts of that case that had obviously been botched, but there were also other parts where Dickie had wondered if Robles was somehow a dirty cop besides being a drunk. And now here they were, Dickie and Josie, looking into another case that had dark overtones and involved a questionable cop who was no longer available. Robles had killed himself not long after the Townsend murder. Was there something more to that?

Dickie made a mental note to check the timeline of those two events, the Townsend murder and Robles swallowing a bullet.

He looked at the firearms report and saw that no weapon had been recovered from the Townsend scene or elsewhere since that time. If the murder weapon had been used in any other crime, and the evidence related to that firearm had been recovered—items such as expended cases or spent projectiles—then the crime lab would have matched those items of evidence to the unsolved murder of Laura Townsend, and a report would be in the file. At least, in a perfect world, that is how it would work.

Dickie had to assume that Jerry's duty and personal weapons had been test-fired as a matter of procedure, but he didn't see any reports indicating so. Not a surprise, given it was Robles's case. That was something that would have to be verified if they were to look into this case in any official capacity. Even though Dickie knew instinctively that it wouldn't have been Jerry's guns that killed her if he were the one who committed the murder—any cop would be smarter than to use his own weapon. He would look into those things later if it came to that, if for no other reason than to eliminate the possibilities. In homicide investigation, a lot of the work you did was covering bases and eliminating suspects and theories through evidence and testimony. At this point, they were just scratching the surface —putting their asses on the line on a hunch and as a favor to an old friend of Josie's. A friend who some believed may have murdered his wife.

There was still no sign of Josie among the pedestrians heading north, and Dickie became more uneasy by the moment. His discomfort caused him to question this Townsend character of whom Josie was so fond. Dickie had never known him, though he knew of him and his reputation as a great cop, and he'd been around him here and there at department functions from time to time. But being a great cop didn't exclude the possibility that he had committed a murder—he wouldn't be the first who had.

The possibilities were many, but some of the thoughts Dickie had about what might have happened that night centered around the usual: love and money. Had Robles even explored those possibilities? An extramarital affair and an insurance payout? They say it's cheaper to keep her, but not if she's dead and you can collect on a life policy.

Josie had told Dickie about Townsend's theory on the case, some things he had told her in a series of written correspondence since contacting her by phone a few months earlier. These were wild, unsubstantiated accusations of corruption within the narcotics units and reaching the executive offices of the department. Townsend hadn't provided details, but his assertion was that he had been on to this corruption, and as such, he had been gathering evidence against the culprits. His plan, he had said, was to go to the feds with the information once he felt his case against them could be made. In one letter, he told Josie that he had never said this to anyone before, but that some of his files disappeared from his home that night.

Dickie stared off toward the south, hopeful but disappointed still. He thought about a burglar entering Jerry's home that night, armed, surprised by their arrival, and shooting the first through the door, Laura. Had the killer already found what he was searching for by then? Was he cradling it in his arms as he shot Jerry's wife and fled through the back? And what had he sought? Papers? Photographs? Something he could have stuffed into his pockets, or files filled with documentation that wouldn't so easily disappear under the circumstances?

And if Townsend's theory was correct, who was the killer? A deputy? An executive in the department? Because to follow this idea that it might involve dirty narco cops, you'd have to see it all the way through. You'd have to see a law enforcement officer cloaked in burglar attire setting out to commit murder. Or maybe only planning to steal something that might keep that person and others from going to prison and then being forced into a deadly encounter when the homeowner returned.

All of it seemed unlikely to Dickie—he just couldn't see the killer of Jerry's wife as a fellow cop trying to avoid being prosecuted for something far less severe than murder.

He flipped back to the first report and looked for information about the burglar's point of entry. A jimmied slider accessed through the backyard. No mention of dogs, a fenced yard, or locked gates. Those were things that should have been documented in the case file. A jimmied door meant nothing without context. Besides, Jerry could have configured the door that way before the cops came if the entire report of an intruder had been fabricated.

Why didn't the burglar kill them both?

Dickie could see a burglar being frightened and fleeing, but if he was so desperate that he would shoot his way out, why stop with the woman? After all, the man is usually the greater threat. In this case, that was a certainty. Would the burglar have known that? If so, would he have taken the chance of leaving him alive? Would Jerry not be a threat to identify the killer or aid in his capture?

He thumbed through the pages looking for a description of the killer. What he found didn't surprise him, a vague male suspect dressed in dark clothing, wearing a ski mask. In other words, a ghost. The burglar-turned-killer could have been anyone under the sun.

Dickie looked south again, now a little hot under the collar. How had he allowed Josie to go across the border to help this guy when there were so many unanswered questions about his wife's murder and Jerry's conduct in the days, weeks, months, and years that followed? And what was going on in TJ at that moment? Why hadn't Josie returned? Where was she, and was she safe? These things had Dickie sweating under his ball cap. He could feel the perspiration trickling from the back of his head, behind his ears, and down his neck.

He pulled his cap off, wiped a hand across his forehead and the back of his neck, then wiped it dry against his jeans. Dickie placed the various reports back into the file case and reached behind him, placing it on the rear seat. Then he fired the engine and revved the Charger before pulling it into gear, his heart pumping and his mind racing.

He started for the border with a knot in his gut and the Glock between his legs.

9

———————

ANGEL CARRIED HER HALO AND WINGS IN ONE HAND AS SHE WALKED OUT of the VIP room wearing a plain white robe and platforms that strapped around her glittery ankles, two hundred in cash clutched in her other hand. She'd never made an easier buck.

Josie knocked a few throw pillows off the sofas, ran the water in the shower for a few minutes, pulled the towels off the racks and, after dropping them on the shower floor to soak up some water, bunched them in a corner of the bathroom. She ran the faucet at the sink, splashed some water that smelled like rotten eggs onto her hair, and, with her nose wrinkled and her face puckered as if she'd just taken a bite of lemon, she mussed her hair to give it that fresh-out-of-the-shower look.

Jerry untucked his shirt and left an extra button open at the top, removed his ponytail, and followed Josie's lead with the faux shower head routine. He left it hanging in tangles, a mostly gray jumble of hair, telling Josie he would pull it into a pony while they walked through the club for effect.

He said, "I'll pay you back. I didn't expect to have to come up with two hundred bucks."

"No? What does Mina charge you?"

Jerry turned from her and went to the bar without comment. For a

48

moment, Josie regretted the jab she'd landed where it smarted. But as she watched him pulling a beer from the refrigerator, seeing the stoop in his posture, the clumsiness of his movements, her disgust for this man who had been so influential to her grew. She said at his back, "You're not the man I loved and respected."

He slowly turned from the bar, his eyes examining the entire room before meeting her gaze. She thought he looked defeated and demoralized. Regret welled up inside her as if she had just cursed her mother or disrespected a superior. She had meant for her words to be hurtful, and they had been at least that. And now she was sorry they had left her mouth, even if what she said had been the truth. She watched as he ambled over to the sofa, lowered himself onto it, and let out a huffy breath.

After a long moment, Jerry looked up at her. "We have to kill some time before we leave, so I'd like to tell you about Mina, about Mexico, about my wife's murder, and what I had hoped you would take away from this trip."

"I'm hoping to take my ass back to America alive at this point, Jerry. That's about it."

He nodded. "I know. I think we'll be okay." He gestured toward the overstuffed armchair that sat next to him. "Can we talk?"

Josie went to the chair opposite where he'd suggested she sit and lowered herself into it. She crossed her arms and her legs and set her gaze on the bar at the other side of the room. Her message should have been clear: *you don't tell me where to sit, and I'm so disgusted with you I don't want to look at you.* She didn't say anything—she just waited in silence, listening to the thumping music beyond the walls of their revolting den of sin.

Jerry began, "I shouldn't have dragged you into this. I should've just lived with what happened and died with those regrets because they were manageable. Now I've made an enemy of someone I've always respected greatly, considered the daughter I never had, and whose friendship I cherish."

She could see he was looking directly at her, but she willed herself not to give in or look him in his eyes. He didn't deserve forgiveness, and she wasn't prepared to give it.

"Where do I start?" he seemed to wonder aloud. Then, after a moment of apparent contemplation, he said, "I'll start with Mina."

Josie said, "Start with the night your wife was murdered."

That hung in the air for a moment. "Okay, I'll start there.

"No, actually, I have to back it up a year or so. Let's just begin with this: Not long before I was transferred to Narcotics, Laura and I were invited out for the evening with a very unlikely group: Commander Don Wilkins and his wife, Carolyn, County Supervisor Charlene Anderson and her husband, Tom, and an old radio car partner of mine, Benny Carmen. Benny went stag, having been between wives at the time."

"Benny Carmen. You're referring to Chief Benjamin Carmen, I suppose."

"Yeah, Benny. How he made chief, I have no idea. Last I heard—this was back when I left, and think that Benny has retired since then—but the new sheriff was considering him for the assistant sheriff position. Do you believe that? Well, you didn't know Benny. Anyone who knew Benny can't fucking believe it. Don't get me wrong, Benny was a good cop—a solid dude who knew crooks as well as anyone I ever worked around. But he was also a bit scandalous. Benny came from Chicago, and you got the feeling it could have gone either way with him, law enforcement or a life of crime. Maybe muscle for the mob. I'm not saying he was a criminal, but he was certainly on the edge at times. He was very cunning and definitely played by his own rules.

"I remember one time back in patrol, Benny and his trainee popped a rapist, caught the guy in the act with a knife to the throat of this young girl in a public restroom. They take the guy down without too much trouble, and within minutes all the troops are there, including the brass. Benny's pissed that this rapist didn't get his lumps, and now that he was wearing handcuffs and the world was there to see, it wasn't going to happen. The crook knew it too, and he started getting mouthy, having fun with it. Said he would rape the girl again when he got out of jail, then asked Benny if he had any daughters. You can imagine how that would set off any cop—"

Josie said, "I would've shot him."

"Right?" Jerry agreed, and their eyes met but for a moment. He went on. "Problem was, the dude was untouchable at that point with everyone there—or so you would've thought. Benny grabbed the rapist by his arms

—the guy's cuffed behind his back—and he tells his trainee, let's load him up and get him out of here. They're walking him to the radio car, the trainee leading the way, and Benny behind the suspect, holding him by both arms right in front of him. All of a sudden, Benny screams, 'He's got my nuts!' The trainee spins around and sees there's no separation between his partner and this rapist—like the dude backed up into Benny and grabbed him. So the trainee instinctively attacks the guy, cracks his head open with three or four consecutive blows from his flashlight."

"Nice."

"Yeah, and Benny never raised a finger to the guy. The dude got what most cops would say he had coming, and it looked as clean as it could be, this guy having grabbed Benny's nuts and squeezed 'em till Benny was about passed out. There were plenty of witnesses who saw the whole ordeal, heard Benny cry out in pain, and saw the horror of it in his eyes. But the thing is, it never happened—the dude hadn't done a thing. Benny, that devious bastard, had pulled the dude back against him, held him there, and started screaming to set the whole thing in motion."

Josie frowned questioningly.

"Yeah, I'm telling you… he copped to me later over beers that the dude had never touched him."

"Brilliant, really," she said.

"But devious. That's my point, and it matters. All this comes into play. Stay with me, Josie—I'm telling you. There are things you won't believe about some of the shit that went down in that fucking year, the worst year of my life."

Josie crossed her legs and took a swig from her bottle of water. This was interesting to her, though she knew to keep an open mind that Jerry could also be full of shit.

"This dinner date with Benny and the commander and a county supervisor turned into a drink fest, and the whole time, I'm thinking, why'd Benny invite me out with this crowd? Benny doesn't do anything without a purpose, and all I can think of is he wants to get me in this circle and pull me up by my strings, if you know what I mean. Like they were grooming him for high executive office, and he was thinking of bringing me along. That's how I saw it, anyway."

"You were a captain," she said, not a question but a statement.

He nodded. "Yeah, but a dead-end captain at that, unless some miracle were to happen. I didn't have enough years left, and I hadn't played nicely enough with some of the other administrators to be looking at any further promotion. In other words, I was president of the Nothing Coming club at that point in my career, and I wasn't about to play the game for anyone to change that.

"A few months later, I'm transferred into Narcotics. I'm thinking, where'd this come from? I'd never worked Dope, hadn't ever had the desire to. Wouldn't know a kilo of cocaine from a block of cheese. But whatever, I guess—know what I mean? It's not like the captain of Narcotics would have to know how to buy dope in order to command the unit, right? Like half your bosses at Homicide, they probably wouldn't know a crime scene from a putting green. And as a captain, you don't have to. You're an administrator, and that's it.

"By then, Benny's the chief of Detective Division, so he's in charge of Narco. I figured he was putting me in that spot to have an ally at the helm. Or maybe he was just being a good friend, I didn't know. Being the captain of Dope was definitely a coveted assignment, so I didn't want to question it too much, you know? I took the job and said thank you.

"A few months after I'm there and I've sort of got things figured out, I notice there are some bizarre things going on with some of these big dope busts."

"Like," Josie said, glancing toward the door and then at her watch. She felt they needed to give it a few more minutes before leaving, but she eagerly anticipated their departure.

Jerry looked across the room beyond her, past the walls that enclosed them, likely back to a place he saw as a turning point in his life. He remained there momentarily before cutting his eyes back to her.

"Well, quite bluntly, theft. Major fucking theft."

Josie didn't react; she just met his gaze and held it, waiting for him to continue. Now she would watch closely for any sign of deception.

"At first, I was sort of blind to all of it, being out of my element. And maybe I didn't want to see some things that might have made me stop and contemplate what it all meant. Things like how the chief—my old buddy, Benny—would be involved in some of these larger busts, coming out in the field and even doing some of the tasks, such as transporting large quantities of money and drugs back to headquarters."

She nodded nearly imperceptibly as she followed the dots, seeing where they were going before Jerry arrived there himself.

"And not just him, but also the commander, Wilkins, showing up at various drug raids and rolling up his sleeves.

"One night, after one of these spectacular takedowns where we seized millions in cash and hundreds of kilos of cocaine, those two showed up at the location together. Then Benny says he and the commander were transporting the cash, and in his trunk it went. An old buddy of mine from SWAT asked me that night, he said, 'What the fuck is up with that?' I didn't know, but I had a bad feeling, and this SWAT copper drove home the point with his question.

"They leave, and we're still at the location for a while, tying up loose ends. When we get back to the office where the inventory was supposed to take place, Benny and Commander Wilkins are nowhere to be seen. They arrive a little later with their trunk full of money, but how much lighter was that load? And where had they gone? Those were questions that I kept to myself, but they stayed with me long after.

"The next day, everyone comes in later than usual, having been up all night on the warrant. It's like three or four in the afternoon, and the plan was we were going to finish up any reports, prepare for a news conference, and then go celebrate the team's victory. That was something else, by the way. There were always big celebrations, but I had never considered who paid for it all. Nobody ever asked for a donation, yet the bar was always open, and the food was there for the taking wherever we gathered.

"Anyway, I walked through the squad room, and everyone was busy on their phones or had their faces buried in paperwork. Not a single greeting or acknowledgment from anyone, but I just wrote it off as they were busy—there'd be plenty of time for visiting and patting each other on the back soon enough, right? Then I go to my desk, open my drawer where I'd put my gun while in the office, and there's this fat envelope sitting there. I must've turned white. My stomach turned over, acid came up into my throat, and my blood began pumping through my ears. Because I knew exactly what I'd find inside that fucking envelope.

"I shut the drawer, looked out into the squad room, and not a single eye looked up."

"Jesus, Jerry. What'd you do?"

"Well," Jerry started, "I didn't know—"

There was a knock on the VIP room door, and it flung open almost immediately after. The two goons had returned.

10

THE SIGN WARNED IT WAS THE LAST EXIT, HIS FINAL CHANCE TO TURN OFF before entering a sovereign nation as a law enforcement officer, armed, unauthorized, and unsanctioned. He figured there were at least two felonies attached to those actions if he were to continue, adding to the one he and Josie had already committed when she crossed over.

At the last second, he swerved onto the exit and hit the brakes, veering onto the shoulder of the offramp. The Charger ground to a halt much quicker than his Crown Vic would have, defining the term "stop fast," and resembling what a race car driver must feel when the parachute opens behind his dragster. Dickie sat at the side of the exit and thought for a minute—pondered, really. Pondered and plotted and considered the pros and cons of going south. There were many cons and only one pro, and that was to find Josie and make certain she returned safely.

Josie had left her phone along with her badge and gun, and she had taken a burner phone with her. The idea being that she didn't want to leave a digital trail of her going south, especially with a county phone. She hadn't programmed Dickie's number into the burner as she had it memorized, and they didn't want any such identifier associated with the phone should it fall into the wrong hands. The problem with the burner was it didn't have location services, so Dickie wasn't able to trace her movement.

As he considered this, he pictured her coming across the border now or even in the next few minutes or hours while he worked to find her in Mexico. How would he even begin his search? He'd never been across the border himself, and he didn't have a clue how to find his way around Tijuana. For that matter, he didn't even know if he could make it past customs. If, for some reason, he was profiled for a search, it would be straight to the Mexican clink, where a *gringo* cop wouldn't fare well. And Josie would be standing in the parking lot at the San Ysidro station, looking around for her partner and her Charger. In fact, he considered, she might have been there already.

Dickie made his decision to return to the drop-off point and wait, trust that his partner had things under control, and try his best to be patient, an attribute that didn't come naturally to him outside of interrogation rooms. He shifted into gear and peeled away from the shoulder, throwing a rooster tail of dirt and gravel until the rear tires found purchase on the asphalt and burned rubber. The vehicle fishtailed and straightened as he came to the next turn, which would take him back to the San Ysidro station. A siren startled him, and he looked in his mirror to see wig-wagging headlights and red and blue strobes in the dark of night. It was America's Finest —again.

11

"THE BOSS WANTS TO SEE YOU BOTH BEFORE YOU LEAVE."

It was Baby Face giving the orders, Fur Face at his side again. Josie glanced from the goons at the doorway to see Jerry staring at them. His eyes betrayed nothing of his emotion, but his jaw was clenched, and his brow wrinkled. She knew inside he would be the same as she, unnerved and assessing the level of threat, which was no doubt high. Her question was, do they make their move, try to fight their way through the two goons, across the packed club, past the bouncers at the front door, through the city, and across the border? Or do they take their chances on this meeting with the boss, whoever that might be? The first option seemed impossible. The second one offered the glimmer of hope that they wouldn't be taken out to the desert and executed for being cops, though that is exactly what Josie feared would be the case. Even the angel had questioned if they were cops—surely the goons had their own suspicions.

She would follow Jerry's lead. Even though he was a shadow of the man he once was, he was a warrior at heart, a great cop, and a survivor. She trusted his instinct and would continue to do so here on his home turf unless something changed that for her.

Jerry rose from his seat, and she followed suit. She could see the wheels spinning, so she prepared for whatever might happen. They could go along quietly, or Jerry could tear into one of their throats at the door, at which time she would have to unleash equal violence upon the other. Josie was ready if it came to that. She was already thinking groin, eyes, throat. As an instructor at the academy had said, you fight like you're the third monkey on the ramp to Noah's boat, and it was starting to rain. You don't allow them to waste you in some dirty stinking alley.

As they closed the distance, Josie wished for Dickie to appear in the doorway behind them, a gun in his hand, vengeance in his heart. But she knew it wouldn't be. Dickie wouldn't panic and come across the border prematurely, not unless there was some compelling reason for him to do so, and as far as he would know, there was not.

No, it was up to Josie, her old mentor, and possibly fate.

At the door, Jerry paused within striking distance of Baby Face, the heftier of the two—a big Baby Huey. Fur Face stood a few feet from his partner, purposefully, Josie figured—a tactical separation. Jerry began fiddling with his hair, pulling it back into a ponytail, which put his elbows up high, a great starting position for an elbow strike to Baby Face's temple, the type of blow that would at least ring his bell, at best knock him out. Josie felt her adrenaline rush, the pre-fight pump she'd felt many times before. The anticipation was always worse than the conflict, at least so long as you didn't get your ass kicked. She had no intention of letting that happen, even with these two big creatures at the doorway. They might be an old man and a girl, but they were seasoned fighters with warrior spirits, and they'd leave it all in the ring if it came to it.

Jerry smiled at him. "The boss, uh?"

Baby Face nodded.

"Is there a problem? We had a nice time with the lady, and she was generously tipped," he said, still messing with his hair, tying a pony.

Jerry's comment made Josie wonder if they should tip these two idiots and buy themselves a ten-minute head start. Everyone could be bought in Mexico, right? She placed her hand on Jerry's lower back and said, "Honey, maybe we're supposed to tip these gentlemen, too."

Baby Face shook his head and smiled back. "Doesn't work that way." Then, in Spanish, looking Josie in the eyes: "The boss is very interested in meeting you. Come now, let's go."

Jerry followed Baby Face out with no resistance. Josie silently let out a long breath that filled her chest, feeling relief that the violence she had anticipated and mentally prepared for hadn't materialized—at least it hadn't yet. She was relieved but also not sure it wouldn't have been the better choice given their situation, which seemed dire to her. Now she'd have to wait and see.

The two goons sandwiched them, Baby Face leading the way, Fur Face following just outside Josie's reach if she were to pivot and throw a backhand punch. She wondered if he was that smart or if it were a coincidence. She figured he knew to measure distance just as anyone with any fighting experience would. Josie had learned it from her kickboxing coach, George, who owned a fighters' gym in East L.A. He was deadly with the focus mitts, and if you didn't guard your distance or if you failed to keep your hands up, you'd find George's mitt upside your head in the blink of an eye.

They descended the staircase and turned down a hallway that Josie hadn't noticed when they came in, a small, dark passage that led to the far corner of the building. Josie imagined there would be a back door, perhaps to an alley, and she wondered if they'd missed their opportunity to survive. The way she imagined the setup now—a boss with more goons in a back room, a door leading to an alley where a car waited to take them or their corpses away. She hated to admit they were now at the mercy of others, or, at the very least, they'd have to be able to talk themselves out of the situation.

The sounds of the club faded as they continued into the darkened hallway, the smell of cigars and cheap cologne permeating the narrow path. They reached the door, and Baby Face stopped, wrapped his knuckles against the wood lightly, and cocked his ear toward it as he waited.

Time seemed to stop in those next moments, and Josie felt her body tense again. She noted that the hallway continued for about ten feet beyond where they stood waiting at what she assumed to be an entry to the boss's office. At the end of the hallway, there was another door adorned with signs in Spanish that said No Exit and Emergency Exit Only on them. It occurred to her that this was their last chance to make a break. Either do something now or continue into the boss's office and take their chances. If they made their move now, it would be but a moment of extreme violence where they stood waiting and then a dash for their lives. Crash through that emergency exit at the end of the hall before the office door was opened. She willed Jerry to turn and look at her.

He did—the power of a stare and subliminal will revealing itself again. Jerry turned and caught her gaze, and she knew he was on the same page, that they needed to act now or do nothing and leave their fate in the hands of this boss, likely a man connected to one of the cartels. Probably a fat man in his forties with a receding hairline wearing a polyester suit and a silk shirt, unbuttoned. Gold chains and medallions nestled in a blanket of chest hair, a pencil mustache and beady eyes. Josie already hated him.

The follow man, Fur Face, maintained a distance just out of her reach. She would have to make a move before delivering any kind of blow. Ten years ago, she could have kicked him in the head before he could flinch, but those days were long behind her, gone with the six-pack abs and bulging quads. She could still deliver a leg kick, sure, but that required significant movement that would telegraph the attack. Perfect timing and placement would be required if there were any hope of striking the lateral femoral nerve to take him down. And if he were armed, which Josie had to assume him to be, she would have to quickly follow up a leg kick with something more disabling, like a throat punch, or she could drive her thumbs into his eyes. She assumed Jerry could handle Baby Face if his timing matched hers and if they each caught their opponent off guard. The first to strike usually had the advantage in a fight, especially if that action was efficient and unexpected. But timing was indeed the issue. She would follow Jerry's lead since this was his playground, and to react to his action would create a lag that could cost her any advantage she might otherwise have by striking her opponent first.

It became a moot point a moment later as the door opened and a third goon appeared, this one more muscular than the other two, built like a bodybuilder, not just a bouncer who ate and drank more than two horses. His hair was neat and slicked back, gold chains showing beneath his open collar. A pretty boy. He stepped aside, and Angel walked out. She met Josie's gaze and held it a moment, her soft eyes sending a message that she had not betrayed them. Or at least that was what Josie hoped it had meant.

After she passed, Pretty Boy stepped back and opened the door wider, motioning them with a jerk of his head to enter. Baby Face walked in.

Jerry followed, and Josie acquiesced as well. There was no chance now for them to make an escape through the use of force. They would have to talk their way out of whatever situation awaited them or hope for mercy. The latter was never a good strategy. Fur Face followed her, and Pretty Boy closed the door behind them and locked it.

The inside of the room was small and dark, with black and red furnishings and gaudy paintings of naked women against elegant vintage gold frames. They reminded Josie of the art that adorned a bar Dickie enjoyed in Sierra Madre, the pirate-themed bar with its hand-painted ladies in various stages of undress, said to have been the work of a man who painted the canvasses of bullfighting arenas in Mexico, and who had been commissioned for his work at the Sierra Madre bar in exchange for a lofty bar tab. She was taking in the scenery and avoiding the stare of a small man behind a desk, someone she had glimpsed when they first entered but otherwise chose to ignore. The boss, no doubt. He was very different than what she had expected, this boss with his pressed shirt and tie who appeared more like a banker than the proprietor of a whorehouse.

With a thick accent, he asked in English, "You like the artwork?"

Josie met his eyes and smiled. "Very much, *señor.*"

"Pick one, and take it with you when you go. I have many. The artist was a friend of the family, but he was killed by my great uncle when they found he painted a picture of his executioner's daughter." He shrugged and twisted his nose, showing disinterest and distaste, the latter of which struck Josie as ironic. "Maybe this one over here," he said, rising from his leather chair and gracefully moving across the room where a painting of a young woman with angel wings hung on the wall among others but was highlighted by a small lamp over it. He regarded the painting a long moment, then turned his gaze to Josie and smiled. "It would be a souvenir for your visit, no?"

Josie stepped closer to the work—closer to the boss, in fact—close enough to breathe in a strong scent of woodsy aftershave, something old-fashioned like Old Spice. She cocked her head as if admiring the art, a close resemblance to the young woman she called Angel, the young hooker with whom Josie was thought to have had relations. She said, "I like it very much, but I've walked across the border this evening and wouldn't wish to carry it back. Maybe on my next visit?"

Jerry stood silent, as did the three men who now encircled him—the four of them spectators of the art show.

The boss seemed to consider Josie's words, his hand stroking his chin as he nodded slightly. Then, suddenly—as if stricken by a moment of genius—a smile stretched across his narrow face. He said, "I tell you what, *señorita*. My men will drive you back to the border when we finish our business. They will put the painting in the cargo, and you take it with you as a gift from me. You will like it hung on a wall in your home—in *la Ciudad de los Ángeles*, no? Is where you are from, no?"

His smirk told her he wasn't guessing, that somehow he knew more about her than she could have imagined he would. But how could that be, and what did he know?

"Yes, Los Angeles is now my home," she said, holding his gaze with an air of confidence. "But I am from *Chihuahua, señor.*"

He regarded her again—questioningly or maybe surprised—then nodded thoughtfully and returned to the seat at his desk. Josie considered his expressions and wondered if he was satisfied with what she had told him or if he still had questions. She had a better idea a moment later when he cut his eyes to Jerry and held *his* gaze as he continued his conversation with her in Spanish. "But your friend," he said, "he is *Americano*, no? And my people tell me he noses around too much and that I shouldn't trust him." He shifted his gaze back to Josie. "What do you think? Can I trust him, or shall I disappear him?"

She glanced at Jerry and saw in his eyes that he understood much of what was said about him. Certainly, he at least got the gist of it. Josie met the boss's gaze with warm eyes and said, "He is my lover. I would be very sad if he disappeared."

The man held her gaze for a long moment, his eyes narrowing as he pondered her words. Finally, he said, "Very well, I shall not disappear him."

"Thank you."

He looked at the office goon, Pretty Boy, who had greeted them at the door, and said, "Carlos, take the *gringo* out back and shoot him in his head, *por favor.*"

12

―――――

Josie lunged at the man, started to yell "No!" but before the words came out, a deafening crack reverberated through the room.

The boss man sprang to his feet, his stare intense and alarming. His right hand remained flat on the desk where he had slammed it down, the other rose slowly until he was pointing a finger at her.

Josie broke from his gaze, looked for her partner. Her vision had narrowed from the stress of the moment, but now her focus softened. Jerry hadn't moved. His eyes were wide like those of a startled child.

The boss man then laughed.

As if a director had called for a new scene and the actor before her had been transformed from a villain to a gentleman, the boss now stood smiling at her, his eyes soft and warm. She could no longer see the darkness of his soul that his eyes had briefly betrayed during those preceding moments.

"Of course, I am kidding," he said, now holding his arms out in a welcoming gesture. "What do you think of me, I'm a murderer? I would kill a man—for what? What reason would I have to kill this *Americano* you call your lover?"

Josie stood frozen, unable to speak and unable to slow the processes that raced in her mind as she tried to make sense of everything happening.

"Please, sit," he said, gesturing to one of the chairs on the other side of his desk. Then he repeated the offer to Jerry.

Josie caught Jerry's eye again as they lowered themselves into chairs. She could see that he was as fearful as she. They were the mice, the boss a big cat swatting them with his paws and making a sport of the capture before killing and eating them. Anger welled inside her. She committed to herself—momentarily reflecting on a terrifying incident when she had spent several days tied to a makeshift bed in the cold confines of a mountain shack, her fate hanging in the balance—that she would never again be held captive. Either this Mexican *jefe* would allow them to walk out of there of their own accord, or she would fight to the death then and there.

He motioned toward the back wall and directed his words to Pretty Boy Carlos. "Take down the angel for our guest, Miss"—he turned his eyes to Josie again—"What name were you using here?"

"My name is Maria Luna," she said.

"Of course." He smiled at her in a manner that said he knew she was lying, then shifted his gaze back to his man. "For Miss Luna. I would like for her to have this one." He cut his eyes to Baby Face. "When we are finished here, you will escort her to the border and see that she gets across safely."

Josie saw that Jerry was picking up enough of the language to understand what was happening. She could see that he was fearful, perhaps desperate now. Jerry confirmed her suspicions a moment later, speaking for the first time since they had been whisked from the VIP room. He said, "Mr. Campo, we've been respectful of your club and the employees. We have no agenda here, we're just—"

The boss man raised his hand toward Jerry to stop him and then admonished him in English. "You've come here under false pretense, Mr. Townsend, as if this is *your* place of business rather than mine. You're an expatriate with a questionable situation in your own country, a suspect in the murder of your wife, I believe. No?"

"How would you know—"

Campo held his hand up again. "It is neither my problem nor my concern. You are welcome here as a customer, but you are not to conduct business here. You are not to harass my employees and interrogate them. Are we clear?" Before Jerry could answer, Campo added, "It would not be good business for me to disappear you. I'm certain that somebody some-where is waiting for your friend here to return to them and would know that the two of you came to my club tonight. I'm simply making clear to you that I know who you are—who you both are, actually. He cut his eyes to Josie. "Yes, Miss Sanchez?" he said and smiled. "Just to be clear, I will not be so kind the next time you conduct your business here and waste the very valuable time of my people."

They sat in silence for a long moment. Finally, Jerry said, "What has happened to Mina?"

Campo rocked in his chair and held Jerry's gaze. "She has sought employment elsewhere, I believe." He shrugged. "Things didn't work out for her here."

"May I ask a favor of you, sir?"

Campo frowned. "I owe you a favor now?"

"No sir," Jerry said, "you absolutely do not. But I'll owe you one, how's that?"

The *jefe* smiled widely. "You have balls, Mr. Townsend—I will give you that. What is this favor you would ask of me?"

"May I accompany her to the border?"

His gaze alternated between Josie and Jerry as he considered the request. "You are returning to the States?"

"Yes, I would like to accompany her across. I may return as I have made this my home, but I will be more forthright with you if we ever have future dealings." Jerry dropped his head momentarily, then looked up with pleading eyes. "I'll be honest with you, sir. I am only trying to clear my name of these allegations you've referenced. I don't intend to harm anyone, nor do I mean to disrupt your business or harass your employees. I will never make the mistake of conducting business here again. The only reason I came here is that I needed my friend to speak with the woman who had information about my wife's murder."

"This woman is Mina."

Jerry nodded. "Yessir, Mina."

"What is it Mina seems to know that might help you? How would she know anything about your wife's murder?"

Jerry settled back into his chair, considering. Josie could see that he was conflicted about how much to say. It was one thing for them to talk their way out of the situation and quite another to say too much and have it cause someone to lose their job or life. She wondered if Jerry had spoken with this man before—after all, he knew his name, and until just a moment ago, when Jerry addressed him by it, Josie hadn't had a clue. Campo had not introduced himself, nor were there any identifying placards on the door or desk to reference. So either Jerry knew him, or he knew of him before this meeting. She wasn't sure if that mattered or not. She wasn't sure if it was good or bad. All Josie cared about was getting out of there alive. For the first time since Angel had entered their VIP room, she started to believe they had a chance to walk away relatively unscathed. Or perhaps they would ride away with the goons if all went well.

The room remained silent while Jerry gathered his thoughts. The boss was patient; Josie would give him that. It was the way of Old Mexico, where the passage of time meant nothing—there was always tomorrow. Josie's uncle, who trained horses in her hometown of *Chihuahua*, would never rush the progress of a young horse. He was careful not to apply too much pressure and cause them to be apprehensive or fearful. He told her this was the way of the *vaquero*, who understood that today or tomorrow made no difference to the horse.

Jerry addressed Josie as he began. "I had wanted you to hear this from my source."

Campo said, "Mina."

He nodded and continued, now speaking directly to *El Jefe*. "Recently, a year or so ago, I met Mina in the bar, and we spent time together here in private rooms and upstairs. I paid for her services. We became friends." He looked Josie in the eyes so she could see he was sincere about what he was saying. Jerry looked back at Campo, and Josie was surprised that he nodded. She didn't know if he was encouraging Jerry to continue or agreeing with what Jerry had said.

"We began seeing each other away from here, but only as friends. I know it sounds crazy, but it is true. And over time, I told her about my life in America, my career, my wife, and how everything ended unexpectedly. As I told her that part of the story, I saw something in her eyes, some type of knowledge or familiarity with what had happened. And then she began to pull away as if she were repelled by what I told her. At least, that's what I imagined it was.

"Then I met a man who knew her. The truth is, I knew that he was a regular customer of hers as well, so I went out of my way to befriend him. This guy was always here, someone that everyone seemed to know."

"Dr. Fleming," Campo said.

Jerry nodded. "Yes, Dr. James Fleming." He looked at Josie. "Dr. Fleming is a very successful cosmetic surgeon in Los Angeles, and he has an office here where he works a few days a month, providing the same services but at a much lower rate to cash-paying customers. He also is known to do a lot of charity work here in Mexico. I think he performed surgery on Mina, even."

Campo nodded along, neither surprised nor in disagreement with anything Jerry had said.

"Fleming and I became friends, and not only because we are both Americans. It turned out that the doctor was an avid supporter of law enforcement. As a med student, he did his residency at LCMC—the L.A. County Medical Center—working mostly in the E.R., where he says he saw everything a doctor could ever see. Including a dead cop. An LAPD officer had been gunned down, and Fleming was on the team who tried to save him on the table. Chief Gates showed up not long after the officer expired, and he stood and wept while holding the dead officer's hand. Doc said he'd never been so moved by anything in his life, and it solidified in his mind and heart how beautiful these men and women were who sacrificed so much for society. Those were his words, nearly verbatim.

"The officer's name was Enrique Torres," Jerry continued. "Dr. Fleming will never forget it."

Campo waited, seemingly unmoved by the story.

"So we were able to speak quite candidly, and eventually, I told him about my wife's murder and some of the things I suspected may have been in play at the time."

"Which was what, exactly?" Campo questioned.

This was what Josie had waited to hear as well. Jerry had said very little about it on the phone or in his letters, just that he believed that his wife's murder was related to corruption in the department. He had said he preferred to tell her in person and to do so in the company of a woman whose story could corroborate parts of his own. That's why Josie was there, but she never imagined that she would be sitting in this man's office getting the details with armed men surrounding her and still an unspoken threat hanging in the air.

Jerry crossed one leg over the other, settling in.

Campo said, "I've been so rude. Would either of you care for a drink? Water or coffee, perhaps a beer or tequila? We have very fine tequila here" —he gestured with his hand as if showing them the direction of the distillery— "made just across town by a *compadre*."

Jerry shook his head. Josie asked for water. *El Jefe* glanced at his office man, and a bottle of Arrowhead appeared a moment later. It wasn't her preferred brand of drinking water, but in Mexico, she welcomed the familiar brand name and a sealed bottle. The bottle she had taken from the room would remain in her purse—she still wasn't sure what might happen next, and extra water might become a lifeline.

"I was transferred into a narcotics unit," Jerry continued, "and within a few months, I began to suspect that there was theft occurring during the raids of drug houses."

Campo stopped rocking, sat straight up in his chair, and shifted his chin in Jerry's direction slightly. Clearly, this was of great interest to him. "Yes, go on," he said.

"I'm actually sure of it, to be honest with you, Mr. Campo. There were things that happened that were impossible to ignore, and within a short time of my being assigned to the unit, they tried to get me dirty."

"Your *comrades*," Campo said.

Jerry nodded. "Yes, the cops in my unit."

"I see," he said, his thumb and index finger gripping his narrow chin.

"And it was equally clear that the corruption went upward, that my chief and the division commander were complicit. Worse yet, I feared that there were politicians involved as well. One of the county supervisors was close with the chief and the commander I mentioned, and on the night Laura was murdered, they—this chief, the commander, and the county supervisor—had taken us out for dinner and drinks."

"They set you up," Campo said. Josie wondered if he was guessing or knew it for a fact.

Jerry shook his head. "I think they kept me out so that someone could search my home. It wasn't the first time Laura and I had accompanied the group to dinner and drinks—a similar night out preceded my appointment to Narcotics. As far as the night she was killed, I think we surprised the intruder by returning early. Looking back, it seems that those we were out with that night did everything they could to keep us out later, but Laura didn't feel well, and she insisted that we go home."

"What would they have been searching for at your home?" he asked.

Jerry took a deep breath and glanced at Josie before turning back to Campo. "Two hundred thousand dollars, for starters. But I also think they believed I was building a case against them, maybe keeping notes or reports. Who knows, maybe they thought they'd find evidence of me having gone to the feds."

"But you didn't?"

"Go to the feds? No. Hell no."

Campo raised his brows in question.

"Look, I didn't know where to turn or who to trust, and they were right, I was trying to build a case. But until I knew for certain who was involved, I wasn't about to go anywhere. The only person I ever spoke to about it was Laura—" Jerry's eye dampened, and he took a moment to compose himself. "I honestly didn't know where to turn."

"And the money?"

Jerry held his gaze for a moment, considering. "They didn't get it."

13

"TWO HUNDRED THOUSAND?"

Jerry simply nodded in response.

They were riding in the back seat of an Escalade, concealed behind limo-tinted windows, a soft blue glow emitting from the instruments. Its leather seats were firm and cool and slicked by Armor All, hints of the protectant's orange essence blending with the aroma of a pine-scented air freshener. It was quiet inside, the vehicle nearly soundproof with only the sound of its air conditioner humming in the background. Baby Face was behind the wheel, Fur Face riding shotgun.

Josie wanted to ask where the money was now, but this wasn't the time to ask that question. Not in front of the goons. She wasn't even sure she wanted to ask later, in the company of her partner. Maybe she would ask him after they were dropped off near the border and while they walked to the San Ysidro station if this journey went as planned. The thought of them being driven out to the desert and executed still lingered.

Instead, she asked about the money. "So they put stolen cash in your desk."

"In envelopes, yes, after these successful raids." Fur Face's head moved slightly left, paying attention to their conversation. "There was no way to know who put them there. At first, I thought it was an internal affairs type deal, a sting operation or whatever, like putting a bait car out on the street and waiting for some dude to rip it. Fucking entrapment, you ask me. Anyway, I didn't know what was going on, so I took the envelopes home, put them in the safe, and told Laura not to touch them— not for any reason other than to hand them over to the authorities should something happen to me."

He turned and stared through his window into the dark, the city's lights growing smaller as the goon squad took them north. Josie could see that his eyes had dampened again, and she figured it was because Jerry was thinking about his wife and reflecting on all that had happened. Or perhaps he, too, wasn't sure they were being taken to the border to be released.

In almost a whisper, she said, "Unbelievable."

He looked at her and nodded. "I shouldn't have gotten you involved."

Josie wished that he hadn't, but she couldn't tell him that. The entire thing seemed surreal. Everything from Jerry's wife being murdered to his subsequent disappearance to this ordeal they hadn't yet survived in Mexico, and the idea that there were executives within the department who were involved in ripping off drug dealers and committing murder. Of course, she wished she wasn't involved in this—she wished it were just a bad dream. But if she believed what Jerry told her, she couldn't turn her back on a friend who had lost everything. And she did believe him.

"It's too late for that now, Jerry."

"I know."

"So we take a look at it. Try to put some pieces of the puzzle together."

He seemed to consider it for a moment. "The thing is, we have to be smart and discreet. Nobody can know you're looking into this, and nobody should ever know that we are in contact. I can't take a chance of losing anyone else."

Fur Face glanced back, and Josie couldn't help but wonder why. She was more comfortable now that they were, in fact, being taken to the border to be dropped off, as they seemed to continue north and they remained on main thoroughfares. But she was still prepared for the worst.

Dickie, who was likely having fits by now, would be ecstatic to see her. But then he would wonder why Jerry was with her, and he might not be too happy about it. She would have the entire ride back to L.A. to tell him about their evening, but she would need some time first to absorb it all herself. The entire night now seemed unreal to her, and it wouldn't be until she was safe in the U.S. that she could calmly reflect on all of it and connect the dots. As it stood now, there were parts that didn't make sense, missing pieces that left her without a clear picture in her mind. Like with Mina—what happened to her? Why would she disappear, and what did Campo really know about that? Who was Campo, anyway? His interest was piqued when the topic of drug rip-offs was mentioned, and then he paid closer attention to the mention of the money Jerry had been given. Was he part of the cartel? Probably. Josie knew that at the very least, a business like his would pay taxes to one of the Tijuana cartels—that was the price for doing dirty business in Mexico.

A cell phone rang, and Baby Face answered, saying, *"Bueno... sí... bien... adiós."* He disconnected and looked back at them but said nothing.

The muted lights of the city behind them were replaced by the bright lights of the border crossing not far ahead. A ribbon of glowing red marked the line of cars waiting to cross into the U.S., and the roadsides were again busy with pedestrians and vendors alike. Josie felt a mixture of excitement and apprehension, knowing they weren't safe until they cleared customs.

With the crossing in sight, Baby Face steered the SUV to the side of the road and stopped. He left the engine idling and shifted in his seat to look back at them.

"You'll walk across from here. Mr. Campo has an interest in the outcome of your investigation. He has asked that you inform him of any developments."

Josie frowned. They were going to report their investigation of an L.A. murder to a cartel member in Mexico? She didn't think so.

Jerry said, "I'll come to see him when I return, and I'll bring a gift to thank him for his kindness."

Fur Face handed Jerry a cell phone. Baby Face said, "It's a burner. If it rings, answer it."

He nodded. "Okay."

Fur Face opened his door and started for the back of the SUV. Baby Face continued. "A couple things before you go. Be careful of these filthy Jamaicans and Haitians that are crowded around the border here. They'll try to sell you things and con you into other things, and they'll beg you for money. Do not even speak to them. They're only here because they think the border will be opened by your president. They are not welcome here by our people."

The back hatch slowly opened, and warm air blew in and lifted Josie's hair. She pushed it back behind her ears and remained focused on the driver, who had more to say.

"If the border patrol asks your business, do not mention Mr. Campo or the *Caballo Loco* as a place you visited. You will have the painting Mr. Campo gave you as a gift, and you can tell them you came to buy some art."

Jerry said, "Okay."

But Josie wondered why they would receive this instruction. Could it be that the border patrol flagged Mr. Campo and his associates? It wouldn't surprise her, but she still found the warning to be odd.

"And that is it, *amigos.*"

Josie's door flung open, and Fur Face stood waiting outside, a framed angel held in his hand like a suitcase, the painting exceeding the height and width of a carry-on bag. Josie slid off her seat and onto the pavement that was still warm from the day's hot summer sun—she could feel the warmth through the soles of her flats. Jerry had slid over and followed her out, crowding Josie at the door as she received the painting from Fur Face and took in her surroundings. Jerry put his hand on the small of her back, letting her know he was directly behind her. She was glad at the moment that he was with her.

Fur Face stepped aside and tried to smile, but it appeared more like he had gas. They moved past him together and turned to face him expectantly.

"*Adiós,*" he said, flinging the SUV's door shut behind them. A moment later, he was back in the SUV, and it glided away from the curb like a ship in the night.

The two *Americanos* turned on their heels and started for the border crossing, an angel in their midst.

14

Dickie had returned to the parking lot at the San Ysidro station after the conversation with yet another one of America's Finest. Throwing gravel from the shoulder and squealing the tires of Josie's Charger had drawn the attention of a sergeant with graying hair, slouched shoulders, and a uniform shirt that was stretched tight across his torso, and not just because of the protective vest he wore beneath it. He was an old-school cop, a veteran nearing retirement with tired eyes that still noticed every detail. A younger cop might have written Dickie a ticket for exhibition of speed or reckless driving, but the old timer had sauntered to the window and asked quite matter-of-factly what seemed to be Dickie's major fucking malfunction. He had started to inform the sergeant of who he was—rather, what he was—but the cop had cut him off before he could start, saying, "Yeah, I know, you're a cop. The question is, where are you from, and why are you driving like an asshole in my city?"

There had been times in Dickie's career when conversations that started in that direction had taken a turn for the worse, but tonight something had kept him from overreacting. Perhaps it was the presence of this cop that commanded respect. Or maybe it was his tone and the no-bullshit approach he had taken—that was something that Dickie could admire and to which he could relate. Or it could have been that Dickie realized he was in the wrong and at the mercy of the man behind the shield.

Dickie had apologized for his driving and then put it out to the sergeant, instinctively knowing this old-school cop would handle the situation properly. He'd said, "I'm sorry, sarge, I'm just a little stressed out down here, out of my element and probably in over my head." Then he told him who he was and where he worked and admitted that he had been contacted by a couple of the sergeant's officers a short while before. Dickie admitted that he had lied to the officers about his name and that he had stretched the truth about what he and Josie were doing down on the border. After Dickie explained all of this, the sergeant suggested he get back to the crossing so he wouldn't miss Josie's return, and he said he'd follow him over, and they could continue their conversation there.

They were facing south, watching the stragglers coming north while leaning on the hood of the sergeant's black and white Ford Explorer, drinking coffee the sergeant had picked up at McDonald's. The warmth from the cruiser's engine reminded Dickie of hot summer nights in South Los Angeles, working patrol out of Firestone station. They'd stop for a cup or a quick bite to eat, and the hood of the radio car served as their table. Food containers and cups of coffee or soda adorned the shiny black surface among greasy handprints of gangsters and crooks who'd been told to grab the hood while they were searched for weapons and questioned about their illicit activities. Some were hooked up and hauled to the pokey while others were thrown back into the pond—the proverbial little fish of the night, a sacrifice to the arrest gods. Dickie regarded those days and nights as the best years of his life, and at times he wished he'd stayed on the streets like this old-time cop at his side. There was something to be said for closing your locker at the end of a shift and starting anew the next day. As a detective—especially as a homicide detective—you were never again above water or starting with a clean slate. It was a part of the job that wore most cops out.

The sergeant, whose name tag read Johnson and who had neither introduced himself nor provided a first name, began: "You heard about the lawyer and his wife who were killed down in Ensenada?"

Dickie shook his head, thinking it sounded like the opening line of a bad lawyer joke, but he knew instinctively that it was anything but that.

"Probably related to their work," he continued. "The lawyer represented one of the cartels down there, and he must've stepped on his dick. Then there was the security guard from La Jolla who was beaten to death at one of the TJ bars not too many months ago. Year or so ago, a fire captain from Orange County got whacked in the *Zona Norte*, down there fucking around doing who-knows-what. Then on a fairly regular basis, there'll be ten or twenty people mowed down by military weapons, gunmen bursting into nightclubs or cockfights or taking down a bus full of people after barricading a road. It's fucking savagery down there, and ain't no way in the world I'd go across or allow anyone I loved to go—not in this day and age."

Dickie grunted a thoughtful "huh" as his gaze remained to the south, anxious as the moments slipped by and silence prevailed, punctuated only by the background noise of the trains, the buses, and busy travelers hustling north.

A few moments passed, and the sergeant said, "Years ago, we had a border team stationed right down here at the crossing"—he nodded in the direction each of them was already watching—"had a trailer set up and their whole job was to deal with all the shit coming back from TJ. Kids that were too drunk to get home, others who had complaints about being robbed or groped or raped. Some came back with stab wounds or broken noses and missing teeth. But hey, TJ's a good time!" He chuckled at the absurdity of his statement. "And back then, we knew the border patrol, know what I mean? Like they were just feds working in and around our city, kinda like when the feebies or ATF come into your jurisdictions, right? You lend them a hand, and they sometimes work with you. Used to be you'd get a carload of illegals, you'd just radio for the border patrol to pick them up. No paperwork involved. They'd haul their asses back and kick them across the border. Back then, you needed someone brought over —you know, unofficially extradited—that could happen too. It wasn't ever used for anything minor, but some asshole kills a cop or a kid, and we know he's there… well, there was a day the asshole would somehow magically appear on our side of the border where a copper just happened to be waiting."

Dickie could see how it might have been working the border in those days. Watts was a wild ride when he worked the streets of South L.A., and he imagined he could have had just as much fun and adventure down here.

"But not anymore," Johnson said. "My point is, don't let your partner go over there again. It just ain't worth the risk, whatever it is you're hoping to accomplish."

More silence followed, then Dickie finally asked. "What are my options if she doesn't come back soon?"

The sergeant looked down at his coffee, considering the question for a long moment. Then he pushed off the fender of the car and turned to look Dickie in his eyes. "Let's hope it doesn't come to that. But between you and me, if this goddam stupid thing you're doing goes bad, I've got a few favors down south I can call in. Nothing anyone could ever know about."

Dickie nodded and pondered the possibilities. He figured this cop for a thirty-year veteran who had no doubt made numerous connections over the decades from both sides of the border and both sides of the law. Every good cop had informants, and he figured Johnson had his share of at least those who could get information down south.

Dickie said, "What about our guys here?" nodding toward the border crossing south of them. "Will they give us any love if we have to do something drastic?"

"Customs?"

Dickie nodded.

Johnson shook his head. "Not likely. Not these guys. The border cops of twenty years ago? Yeah. But if I had to get something done down here now, or if I had to get someone out of there, it would be a black bag op, if you know what I mean."

Dickie knew exactly what he meant. Off the record, secret squirrel shit. No reports, and nothing ever happened, no matter how it ended, as far as anyone else would know. He'd known of a few of those types of operations in his day and might have been involved in one or two as well. But that was the thing; you never admitted it nor mentioned it. He said, "I know what you mean, sarge... I know exactly what you mean."

And he realized he was in the company of one of America's Finest.

15

SHE COULD HAVE KISSED JERRY WHEN THEY CLEARED CUSTOMS AND WERE standing on U.S. soil, for all the joy she felt at that moment. But despite the relief of being safely back from an excursion that nearly turned into a nightmare, a measure of anger stirred inside her for what they had endured in the lawless land of Mexico. She couldn't imagine being lectured and taking orders and insults from a drug-dealing pimp in America. She would've had her foot on the dude's throat, and it would have been she who was calling the shots. If she ever caught Mr. Campo on her home turf, there'd be… well, she would…

Her train of thought was derailed when they were close enough that she saw Dickie standing in the lighted parking lot, a cop at his side. She froze in her tracks, and Jerry stopped next to her. Two old friends side by side on American soil, exhausted and bewildered from a mission to TJ gone awry. There was something about near-death experiences that made you feel more alive, or, as Winston Churchill famously said, there was nothing more exhilarating than being shot at and missed. Josie could argue after tonight that there was one thing even more terrifying than that, and that was having the idea that you might be pulled into an alley and shot or be driven out to the desert and murdered after who-knew-what-else. She'd experienced the immediacy of bullets flying past her, as well as the anticipation of death or worse, and she felt the former was less stressful than the latter. It was the difference between being told you had so long to live and dying in your sleep from an aneurysm.

Josie stood in silent contemplation, the portrait of a naked Mexican angel held along her one side, the phantom of a legendary lawman posted on the other, her partner across the lot chatting with the cops—a trifecta of paradoxes.

"That's your partner?"

They were looking in her direction, Dickie and this cop he was entertaining, and she had to assume he saw her. However, she had to consider that they were far enough away that he might *not* see her. Plus, it was nighttime. Dickie didn't see as well at night anymore. He'd complain about needing glasses now when he drove after dark, and that would lead to all the other complaints of aging before his time—the job did that to you, he'd say. What would surely throw him off, though—if he were looking at her and trying to decide if it were his partner coming back—is that she was in the company of a longhaired Deadhead who could also pass for a homeless addict. Dickie certainly wouldn't expect her to be accompanied by some derelict, nor would he imagine she'd be toting a giant, gaudily-framed portrait of a naked angel with her, like a depraved tourist.

But Dickie was sharp, and she had to consider that he might have seen her but hadn't acknowledged her or reacted to her presence for a reason— for instance, the cop at his side. Who knew why the uniformed cop was there or what Dickie may have told him about what he was doing at the border. But maybe Dickie was playing it cool until the cop was gone.

"Yes," she finally said, "that's Dickie. Don't know what the cop is doing there, though."

"I guess I've never seen him without a fedora. Looks different in his jeans and ball cap."

"It's his undercover disguise."

Jerry said, "Not much of a disguise… still looks like a cop."

She looked around, spotted a place to sit, and nodded as a way to direct Jerry. "There, those benches. Let's go have a seat like we're waiting for a train and see what he does. I think he sees us but, for some reason, isn't reacting to our being here."

They moved along the sidewalk. With few others about at the late hour, Josie guessed it must have been close to midnight, but she didn't care enough to fish the throwaway phone out of her pocket to check. She hadn't worn a watch this evening, just as she'd never worn a watch when working undercover. Crooks were as unconcerned about the time of night or day as they were about a dip in the stock market or the rate of capital gains taxes, and something as simple as a watch on your wrist could blow your cover. As Josie moved to the bench and took a seat, she mostly avoided eye contact, though she couldn't help but glance at Dickie and the cop a couple of times just to see if she saw any recognition. Jerry remained standing and took the opportunity to light a cigarette while scanning their surroundings.

Dickie pushed off the cop's car he'd been leaning against and offered her only his back as he stood facing the cop. Now she was certain he had seen her. She had been gone for several hours, and there was no way Dickie would stop watching the direction from where he expected her to come if he were still looking for her.

She said, "He knows we're here."

"Wants the cop to split, uh?"

Josie nodded. "Yeah, I think. Probably doesn't want to have anything else to explain. He sure wasn't expecting me to drag you back with me, you and the angel."

"It's quite the piece of art. It'll look lovely in your home."

"My mother would love it. Think I'll hang it in the dining room, give her something to talk about other than my failure to provide her with grandbabies."

Jerry chuckled.

But Josie was thinking about the other angel now and about Mina. She said, "What do you think happened to her?"

He seemed to consider her question for a moment before answering. "Mina?"

She nodded, her gaze still fixed on her partner's back across the lot.

"I don't know, Josie. I'm not sure I want to think. It's a different fucking world down there, and some of the possibilities are unsettling, to say the least."

She had the same thought. "We should have kidnapped the angel while we were there."

Jerry dropped his cigarette, snuffed it out with the toe of his shoe, and took a seat next to her. He drew in a deep breath and let it out slowly. Said, "We can't save them, Josie."

Josie turned her gaze to the south, seeing the young angel in the VIP room, a woman before her time. "She was so young. It's sad, really. You wonder if she had a choice or was forced into that life. You know, human trafficking and all."

Dickie and the cop shook hands, and the cop started for his car. Dickie made his way to the driver's door of Josie's Charger, never glancing toward them as he did. Now she was certain he knew they were there. Josie stood up, picked up her angel, and waited.

"There's no way to know," Jerry said. "Mina worked there in order to feed her family—her mother and three siblings. Her father was killed after being caught in the crossfire of rival gangs in the middle of town. Being the eldest child, she had to do something, and there was no way to make the kind of money she makes at the club by doing anything else. Not in Mexico, anyway. Not for an uneducated Mexican girl."

"Made," Josie corrected, a subtle reminder that Mina no longer worked for Mr. Campo, as far as they knew. Perhaps the past tense of the situation was even more dire than that.

Jerry had his eyes on the ground. After a moment, he looked up at her and said, "When I go back, I'm going to find Mina or find out what happened to her. And if I can, I'm going to help her out of that life. Because maybe I can at least save *her*."

The cop pulled away and drove off into the night. Dickie started the Charger, revved the engine, turned on the parking lamps, and let it idle.

Josie started for the car. "Come on, Jerry, let's get the hell out of here."

16

THEY REACHED THE CAR, AND JOSIE LEANED DOWN TO LOOK THROUGH THE open passenger window at Dickie behind the wheel. He didn't appear happy to see her, or maybe Jerry's presence had him off balance. "Shut it down, partner; we have to figure some things out. And pop the trunk, will ya?"

He looked around for a trunk release.

"Left side of the steering column."

Dickie found the button and pushed it, and the trunk lid slowly lifted, a glow of light escaping from inside.

Josie went to the trunk and hoisted the angel inside, face up, the naked woman staring into the sky before the lid slammed shut and she was alone in the dark. Dickie killed the engine and stepped out, came around to the back of the car just as Josie was closing the lid.

"What the hell was that?" he said, referencing the painting.

"Long story, partner." She motioned for him to follow her, and then she moved back to the side of the car where Jerry waited. "Jerry, this is my partner, Dickie Jones. Dickie, Jerry Townsend." The two shook hands but didn't exchange any pleasantries. Josie popped open the passenger door of her car and retrieved her gun, badge, and cell phone from beneath the front seat where she had stored it.

When she closed the door, Dickie met her gaze. "What's going on?"

She sighed and nodded to Jerry. "That's a good question. Jerry, would you care to field that one?"

Jerry glanced away and stroked his gray beard, then turned his attention to Dickie. "Thanks for coming down here and letting Josie come across. It went a little bit sideways because my informant has gone missing. But in a nutshell, I've gotten to know a woman named Mina who works at one of the clubs down there—"

"Whorehouse," Josie interjected, not looking up from her phone as she scrolled through messages and emails.

"—who knows something about my wife's murder."

"What does she know?" Dickie asked.

"That's the thing, I'm not sure."

Dickie frowned.

"I had gotten to know her well, and we shared a lot about our lives. I know it sounds crazy, but... Eventually, I told her about my life in L.A. and my wife being killed, and I even told her my theory about why it happened."

"Which is?"

"I believe they were in my house that night looking for some things that could take down a bunch of dirty cops. At the time, I was commanding a narcotics unit that I eventually figured out had been ripping off drug dealers. I think they thought I was going to rat them out."

"Were you?" Dickie asked.

He nodded. "As I told Josie, and now this *jefe* of one of the clubs down in TJ, they had been trying to bring me in by getting me dirty with the money, an envelope here, an envelope there... pretty much every time we had a successful operation and seized a lot of cash and drugs, there would be a payday."

"How much, Jerry?" Dickie wanted to know. "How much cash did they give you?"

"Nearly half a mil."

Josie jerked her head up from her phone. "Half a mil? You said two hundred thousand."

He shrugged. "I almost said fifty K, but I didn't think Campo would buy it—he'd know I was lowballing it. So I said two hundred. There was no way I was going to tell him I had half a million dollars of cartel money stashed away. Chances are, he's going to be asking for it."

"You still have it?" Dickie asked.

He nodded.

"Where?"

"I put it in a safe deposit before I headed south."

"All of it?"

Jerry nodded. "I've got my retirement, which is more than I could ever spend in Mexico. I don't need their dirty money."

Josie saw that Dickie was assessing the man, doing what he did—Dickie the human lie detector. He held the former captain's gaze for a long moment, and Jerry never looked away.

Dickie said, "So you've sat on this money for a decade. Didn't you think it should be turned over, that you should've come forward at some point with it?"

"Yes, I did. But the timing was never right, and then they were looking at me for the murder, and I just kind of flipped, man, to be honest with you. I headed south and crawled into a bottle of tequila, and that's where I stayed. You'd be surprised how fast the years fly by when you're retired."

Dickie shook his head, and Josie could see the disgust on his face. She didn't blame him. It was difficult to fathom holding on to that money all this time if Jerry wasn't dirty himself.

"I want the information about your box and a key for it."

Jerry cocked his head as he seemed to consider Dickie's request.

"Something happens to you," Dickie continued, "there's only one way to put this case together and clear your name. And now that you've told the cartel you have their money, there's a good chance something could happen to you. It wasn't the smartest move, Captain, telling the cartel you've got a stash of their money."

For the first time since Jerry appeared at Josie's side on *Revolución*, a mere shadow of the man she had known and no longer the cocky former SWAT cop who'd been battle-tested, Jerry displayed some fortitude. He pointed a finger at Dickie and said, "Not a smart move? We're surrounded by armed men, and I'm not sure we're going to get out of there alive. You think I give a fuck about that money? I was a step ahead of him on that,

Detective. I knew we'd walk out of there if he thought there was something to gain from keeping us alive."

Dickie stepped into his space. "She never would have been there if not for you, *Captain*. You got my partner into some shit she doesn't need any part of, and *you're* lucky they didn't touch her."

Jerry inched closer, the two now nose to nose. "Or what?"

Josie stepped in and gently nudged Dickie back. Now she stood between them, her hands out toward each of them as if she were Big John McCarthy getting ready to say, "Let's get it on!" to two fighters in a UFC ring. But the last thing she wanted was for these two Neanderthals to go at it—none of them needed that.

"Enough, you two!"

Dickie and Jerry continued to stare each other down, but now Josie held her ground until she saw each of them soften their stances and take a few breaths.

"I'll give you the fucking money," Jerry said. "What do I care? I'm a dead man walking; it's just a matter of time. I'll be taken out by one of those dirty coppers or by some asshole with gold teeth and a silk shirt in a Tijuana alley. Either way, my days are numbered. I just want my name cleared, and I want someone to be held responsible for killing my wife."

Dickie took two more steps back and leaned against Josie's car, looking off to the south, maybe trying to see in his mind the ordeal that had taken place in Campo's office. Or maybe he was seeing Jerry on his knees in an alley, an enforcer for the cartel looking down the barrel of his pistol at the former cop. He said, "I wouldn't go back down there."

"I have to," Jerry replied. "I have to find Mina."

"No, you don't," Josie said. "I'm with my partner on this—nothing good can come from you returning to Mexico. We work the case from this side of the border from here out."

"I'm going to find her and bring her back."

Josie stepped away, ran her fingers through her hair, and let her hand rest on the back of her head to keep from blowing her stack. She huffed out a big breath. "What can Mina add to what we already know, Jerry? What did the doctor tell you about her? You never told me that part."

"The doctor?" Dickie said.

Josie dropped her hand, stepped away, and then turned back—nervous energy being expended in San Ysidro. "Tell him about the doctor, Jerry."

Jerry shoved his hands into his pants pockets and looked down at his feet for a moment. He met Dickie's expectant gaze and said, "There's a cosmetic surgeon who has an office somewhere in L.A., maybe Beverly Hills, and another down in TJ. He and I have become friends, and when I confided in him about my wife's death and about Mina seeming to know something, he told me a story."

"How much did you tell him?" Dickie wanted to know.

"Everything. The drug raids, the stolen money, the murder —everything."

Dickie nodded. "Okay, go on."

"Anyway, he did surgery on Mina, breast augmentation. They became friends, maybe dated, I don't know. He's single, never married. He favors Mexican women and spends most of his free time in Tijuana. Has a house on the beach. So he knows Mina well, and when I told him about how she seemed to pull away from me after I told her my story, he pondered it for a while and said he thought she might have some connections to the cartel. I hadn't even considered that, and once he said it, I sort of panicked. I mean, if she took that information to the cartel about department members ripping off those drug dealers, and if she told them she knew a guy who could give them names, well, shit, where would that leave me? On my knees in some warehouse, begging for my life? Giving up names of people I once called friends, knowing they'd be dead not long after I was gone? So I tried to get in touch with her, talk to her about it, and ask her not to betray me. She kind of blew me off."

Josie had paid close attention to everything Jerry said, and one thing didn't make sense to her. She said, "Jerry, I thought you wanted me to come down to talk to her, to hear her side of something that would prove your case, like you had a meeting with her arranged. Now you're telling me you had me come down here not even knowing if she would talk to us? Never mind us not even finding her."

His eyes were on his shoes again, worn-out leather loafers beneath his chinos. She could see how he had fit in with the masses in Mexico. He was one of those guys who tanned well; clearly, he spent a lot of time in the sun. With his long hair streaked gray and worn in a ponytail, a matching, straggly beard, and a sinewy body, he could easily give one the impression that he was just an old Mexican. Only his eyes would betray him—he still had the look of a cop in his steely eyes.

Finally, he said, "Doc had spoken with her and set up the meeting. She agreed. I figured it might be my last chance to talk to her, and I really wanted you to be part of that, to be a witness to whatever she told me. Doc said she was reluctant to see me again because she had learned some things about my past that hit too close to home for her. He didn't know for sure what that was, but he thinks she knew the other side of the story—the cartel's side."

"Because dope busts impact cartels," Dickie said.

He nodded. "Yeah, their bottom line. And people get killed over losing drugs and money. Chances are, someone on their side of the deal got whacked for losing that load. Then to find out that the cops also skimmed some of the money, which they would view as stealing from the cartel, would also have consequences. Maybe Mina thought I'd be the one held responsible, and that's why she ghosted me. Either way, she must have known about the busts and seizures that were taking place in L.A. Maybe she even knew what the cartels were saying or doing about it. I'm thinking there must have been some inside information for the team to be cleaning up as well as they were, and I suspect the cartels would have been thinking the same."

"Someone on the other side informing the cops, you mean," Josie said.

"Yeah, one of my investigators' informants, maybe. And if the cartels never figured out who was giving up their loads, that's something they would really like to discover. Don't ya think? Or maybe they already found out, and that person is dead." He shrugged. Life was cheap in Mexico.

Dickie said, "What happened to the Narco brass?"

He shook his head. "I know Benny retired, and I think the commander did also—Don Wilkins."

"We need to look at them," Dickie said, "see how they're living."

He nodded. "Quite well, I imagine."

Dickie looked at Josie. "Well?"

She shrugged.

Jerry turned his head and looked to the south, contemplating. He said, "Okay, I've got to go now."

"Where are you going?" Josie asked.

He looked at her. "Back across. It's home for me now. I realize it's dangerous for me to be there, but I could make an argument that it's more dangerous for me to be seen in L.A. now. *Especially* now. Plus, I still have half a mil the cartel would like to get their hands on. They're not going to kill me before they do."

Josie said, "They might torture you until you wished you were dead."

He raised his brows. "There's that."

She stepped into him and hugged him. As they pulled apart, Jerry took her hands in his and gave her something small. He leaned in to hug her again and whispered, "Safekeeping."

They separated, and Jerry turned to Dickie and nodded. "I appreciate what you're doing."

Dickie didn't respond.

Jerry held the cool gaze momentarily, then turned on his heel and started south, down the concrete path to Mexico, as alone as anyone could ever be.

17

"IT WAS BIZARRE, PARTNER. THIS BOSS MAN, CAMPO, SEEMED TO KNOW everything about us. How can that be? What do you think? I mean, I literally crossed with a fake ID, yet this guy knew me—knew my name, knew I was from L.A. Knew I was a cop."

They were headed north, Dickie behind the wheel. Josie had asked that he drive because she felt herself shaking by the time they left the parking lot, likely the result of an adrenaline dump that would soon level out. Still, she had no interest in focusing on the road for two hours while her head was whirring with reflection and contemplation.

Dickie said, "Cartel, no doubt. Dude runs a brothel, he's either part of the cartel or they own his ass. And the cartels have their people embedded everywhere—their government, our government, DMV, law enforcement, at the border… Buddy of mine, worked Dope his whole career—you know Banuelos—he said the cartels have profilers, people who go out and find weak or vulnerable people and put them on the payroll. You're making twenty bucks an hour or whatever, watching the border, filing records at the DMV, inputting data for the L.A. County Sheriff's Department—that's who they target. You're in a dead-end job and barely getting by, and someone offers to put an extra grand or two in your pocket every few weeks, what do you do? All they ask of you is to answer a question now and then, look something up on your computer here and there, or—in the case of the dude at the border—look the other way when someone or something needs to come across. I can see where a lot of people would be tempted to be on the payroll."

"I guess some people will do anything for money."

Dickie glanced over at Josie, the soft glow from dash lights reflecting off his glasses. Beyond him, through the driver's window, Josie could see the lights of million-dollar coastal homes and businesses scattered along the beachfront. Beyond it, nothing—a vast emptiness she knew was the Pacific Ocean. They were traveling north on the I-5 along the coast, past Del Mar and Encinitas, coming up on Carlsbad and then Oceanside, still an hour and a half from the office, maybe less if Dickie kept his foot on it. She leaned over and saw the speedo showing 82. "Better watch out for the chippies."

He checked his mirrors and shrugged. "This time of night, we should be fine."

"You hate him."

"Jerry?"

"Mm-hmm."

"I don't hate him—I don't even know him. I know he was a good cop, had a good reputation. Guess I'm just a little put off that we're in this situation now. That and I don't know how much I trust him yet. How do you sit on all that money and never say anything? That's the part that really makes him look dirty."

"I don't disagree—it looks bad. But I can also see where you're not sure what to do with it, so you let it sit until you figure something out."

"Ten years."

"I know it looks bad. I agree with you."

"And now we're in the middle of it. I wish we didn't know about the money."

"*I'm* in the middle of it, partner—not you. The truth of it is, I never should've told you I was going down there to meet him. Then you wouldn't have felt so obligated to accompany me, and I wouldn't have dragged you into this mess. From here on, I'll work on this case to whatever degree I'm able, and you can stick to working our unsolveds."

"This *is* an unsolved."

"Yeah, but we're not assigned to it."

Dickie shot her another look. "We're partners. If you're working it, I'm working it. That's the end of the conversation."

She contemplated that for a moment, the throaty rumble of horsepower and the whir of the road beneath their car filling the void of conversation. Finally, she said, "Emily's going to want to know why I'm keeping you out all night."

"Trust me, she's not even a little worried."

"She trusts you."

He smiled. "Well, yeah, of course. Don't you?"

Josie grinned and looked out her window, seeing the city lights on the inland side and then signs for Camp Pendleton. She pictured Marines out doing their thing in the middle of the night, creeping around with their faces painted black and green while they trained in the dark, unloaded rifles cradled in their arms. Or the others who had gone to town and were drinking themselves blind and raising hell. She said, "Jerry was a Marine. Did you know that?"

Dickie shrugged.

"Just thinking about it after seeing the sign, Camp Pendleton."

"And?"

"Nothing, really. Just sort of heartbreaking how this man who served his country honorably his entire life, the Marines and then the department, narrowly escaping death countless times, how his life seemed to get upended through no fault of his own. I mean, the man is honestly a hero. Pulled his dead partner from a house during a gun battle, getting shot in the process, then going in alone and smoking the bad guy."

Dickie didn't respond.

She watched him, waiting, her gaze lingering on Dickie in his ball cap and conservative eyewear, his focus on the road but his mind clearly on Townsend. His mustache was unruly and could use a trim. She usually preferred the clean-shaven look on men, but she couldn't see Dickie without a mustache. He was one of those guys who, if he shaved it, you'd beg him to grow it back. Like Sam Elliott. Josie had had a fit when she saw a clean-shaven Elliott in *Justified,* a TV series based on the Raylan Givens novels by Elmore Leonard, Dickie's favorite author. Some men could pull off facial hair like some women could wear their hair super short, and there was nothing dikey about it. Fact, sometimes it was sexy as hell.

He finally said, "I want to take the files home, go through everything over the next couple of days."

She considered saying no, telling him again he needn't stay involved, but she knew what a waste of oxygen that would be. You couldn't win an argument like that with Dickie. She said, "Okay."

"Give me a few days to do that and come up with a plan. This is dangerous territory we're treading through, and I'm not quite sure how to proceed. My instinct is we're going to have to go straight to the sheriff with it—if we put enough of the pieces together so that we don't look crazy. It's that, or we go to the feds with it, one of the two."

"What a mess."

"Uh-huh, that it is," he said. "I don't know, maybe we keep it in-house."

Josie thought about it for a minute. "As far as Stover, I'd be fine with that. It's Neely I don't trust—especially now that here we are with another case her ex fucked up."

"Maybe."

"Maybe what? That we can't trust her, or that her ex fucked it up?"

Dickie grinned, his eyes on the road. "Yes."

She pondered it a moment. "Or was he a dirty cop?"

"You never know, I guess. Again, this whole thing is a huge mess."

"I'm sorry, partner."

Dickie looked over at her. "It's why they pay us the big bucks, partner."

18

A STORY ABOUT VIOLENCE SOUTH OF THE BORDER DISRUPTED JOSIE'S serenity.

She was sitting on the patio at her local coffee house, sipping on an iced caramel macchiato with whipped cream, indulging this morning after last night's ordeal. She had hoped to sleep until noon, but her mother decided that today would be the day for housekeeping. Esmeralda had likely heard Josie roar into the driveway at three in the morning and assumed that she had stayed out late partying and should be punished for doing so. She had run the vacuum up and down the hall, banging its head against the baseboards and Josie's door while whistling some tune—yes, Esmeralda whistled while she worked, or at least she did this morning. Josie didn't know if her mother was jealous that Josie lived much larger than she ever had or if it bothered her that Josie hadn't popped out a bambino or two for Esmeralda to raise. There seemed to be an insatiable maternal need with her mother's generation of Mexican women, and Josie's mother probably knew there was little hope for her being an *abuela* anytime soon.

Josie looked at her phone through oversized Pradas, the midmorning sun behind her warming her shoulders and soaking into her hair. Josie, dressed this morning in shorts and a T-shirt, sandals on her feet, searched the internet for news about the Mexican cartels, her interest renewed after the bizarre evening she'd spent at a brothel.

She looked up and took in her surroundings: a mother with a toddler on a chair next to her and a baby in a stroller beside them, the woman busy on her phone while enjoying some type of coffee drink herself. A man in running attire just beyond her, a newspaper in his hand, his salt and pepper hair betraying his age. The executive type, probably now retired, does his five miles in the morning and has the rest of the day to himself. Josie could see him hitting the links with his former colleagues after a cocktail luncheon at the country club, a team of Mexicans taking care of his lawn for him while he was gone, another one inside keeping house while the missus enjoyed brunch with other kept women, foregoing the coffee for mimosas.

Josie's eyes returned to her phone as she enjoyed the quiet morning alone in her thoughts, which was what she preferred after traumatic or chaotic events. She had noticed that many of her male colleagues needed to be with their counterparts at work, almost clinging to them. She had seen guys involved in shootings who would stay at the station, toss and turn a few hours in the bunk room and then be at the front desk or in a chair back in the detective bureau, chugging coffee and repeating their story to anyone who would listen. Or they'd go home but be back in hours, saying they couldn't sleep and didn't know what else to do. Lost because department policy dictated that they weren't allowed to return to duty for a couple of days and until they saw the shrink. Josie was the opposite; she didn't want to talk to anyone, not even her partners. She needed time by herself to contemplate all that had happened and reconcile those things in her mind. Generally, she liked to blend into the public as she did on the patio this morning, appearing normal and tranquil, though she was anything other than that inside. Maybe that was part of her desire to flee from the safe confines of her law enforcement family after a traumatic event. She was aware of how different she was from the rest of society, but at times, she longed to be unnoticed, to just fit in with the regular people, average citizens who would be shocked to hear some of her stories that other cops would shrug off as if they were no big deal. *Oh, Josie smoked some dude last night. Did you guys catch Yellowstone?*

Josie imagined how the "normal" people around her would respond if she told them about parts of her professional life. Clear her throat to get everyone's attention and announce: "I was kidnapped last night by the cartel while enjoying the company of an old friend and a naked angel in a Tijuana whorehouse." See if that livened up the setting. Watch people gather their children and belongings and slither away, frightened or disgusted with the crazy broad in designer eyewear.

She'd had similar thoughts after being involved in shooting incidents and trying to resume life during the following days as if nothing had happened. Sitting at the coffee house, the café, or the bar, and listening to the idle chitchat of others. People lamenting the hectic schedules of their children's activities or complaining about how long it takes to get in at the salon. She'd imagine saying to the woman who was irate because her child spilled a drink—tell her, I shot a man last night, had to watch him gurgle his last bloody breath while waiting for the paramedics to get there. Shrug and say, Your baby is adorable. You're so fortunate. Give her some perspective to work with.

But she never told others about the extraordinary things she saw because she believed she'd be a leper among these Southern California socialites. Josie kept things to herself, for better or worse. There was always tequila.

She tuned out her surroundings and replayed last night, the *Caballo Loco* scene a continuous loop in her mind. She could smell the stale air and see the hordes of young girls baring all for feverish men whose eyes darted from one woman to another, one body part to another, frantic like famished little boys in a candy store. The executive who sat across the patio from her wouldn't have had a bored expression with his nose in the business section while in a joint like that.

She wondered how many girls there had been. More than twenty for sure, probably closer to fifty. Where did they find so many young women willing to sell their bodies so cheaply? Josie saw Angel's dreamy, faraway eyes, and again, she imagined that many of the girls must have been groomed for their trade through a process of fear and abuse followed by the comfort of mind-numbing drugs. Then, a facade of love, or the closest thing to it they would ever know. Taken from their broken homes or off the streets, given everything they would need for the paltry price of their souls.

A chair scraped against the concrete patio, and Josie looked up to see two young women taking the table next to her. One of them met her gaze and smiled. Josie smiled back. Two strangers exchanging silent pleasantries on the outskirts of Los Angeles, just a half-hour's drive from Skid Row and two hours from a wall that separates one society from another—one where there was at least a pretense of civility, the other that flaunts its lawlessness like glittering bare women twirling on brass poles under strobing lights.

Back to her phone, Josie read about four Americans who crossed the border in Brownsville, Texas, and who were fired upon and kidnapped. Two of them were murdered. The attorney general of Tamaulipas, Mexico, declared the incident "a misunderstanding." Innocent Americans gunned down in broad daylight, and this moron says it's a misunderstanding. Five cartel members had been charged in the slaying after they were turned over to authorities in a markedly Mexican way: bound and left for the authorities with a note, apparently written by a cartel representative—their way of making amends for the misunderstanding. *We're sorry. Is okay?*

According to family members, one of the victims, a mother of five, had traveled from South Carolina to Mexico for a cosmetic medical procedure. Josie thought about Dr. Fleming, this friend of Jerry's who performed such surgeries in Beverly Hills and Tijuana—apparently billing the former enough to pay for the latter, his own little socialist experiment. Mina, the missing girl, was one of his pro bono clients. Josie didn't think that Angel had partaken in any augmentation—at least, there had been no apparent signs that she had. There was no question about it with some of the girls she had seen last night, the ones with conspicuous scars and gravity-defying breasts or their ballooning lips and Kardashian asses. Josie wondered if this doctor believed he was making life better for these young women, enhancing their lives and providing them with tools for their trade.

She pictured Campo behind his desk, the small man mighty in the company of his armed and formidable goons—a well-spoken businessman, cunning and knowledgeable. Josie wondered how much he really knew about her. About Jerry. About the theft of drug money in L.A.

County and the players involved. She had to consider that there was more to all of it, that it wasn't as simple as Jerry had portrayed it. Not that he was lying, necessarily, but maybe there were things he didn't know himself. Or maybe he was lying. Josie had learned long ago to be slow to trust, steady to verify. Right now, her partner was the only person she trusted in any of this, but that was no surprise; Dickie was unwavering and transparent. She wondered what he was doing now while she enjoyed her peaceful morning on a patio with a caramel macchiato that was nearly finished. Emily would be gone to work, and Dickie would be home with Angelo and their nanny, Rosalva. He was probably trying to balance spending time with his son and jumping into the murder case of Laura Townsend, the files he had taken home last night. She wondered if he had read or seen on the news the story about the Americans who were killed by the cartel south of Texas. If so, he would use it to reinforce his position that they should never go south again. Rather, *she* should never go south again. Because God knew that if she did, he would go with her or, at the very least, be standing by at the border, ready for a rescue mission.

But she wouldn't worry him with her thoughts now. They had agreed to take a day to decompress from their trip south and evaluate the case and facts as they knew them now. Josie would see how things played out here at home before she thought about going south again—and certainly before she mentioned to Dickie that she saw another excursion as a strong possibility as Angel weighed on her mind.

Josie looked up from her phone and noticed the executive had gone. So had the mother with her two children. The two young ladies were alternately chatting with one another and focusing on their phones. People passed by on foot, walkers and a few joggers, several people out exercising their dogs: Labradors, golden retrievers, cockers… some of them pulling their owners along, others that had been properly trained.

A woman wearing an apron exited the shop and began cleaning up behind those who left without bothering to pick up their empty paper cups and throwing them into the trash can ten feet away. The employee was in her fifties, an unglamorous sturdy woman who likely had spent the bulk of her adult life raising children. Now she worked a low-wage job to make ends meet or maybe to have something to do while her husband worked fifty hours a week at the office, selling insurance or programming computers. She caught Josie's gaze and held it. Josie smiled and said, "Good morning."

The woman smiled back. "Good morning. How was your coffee?"

"Fabulous," she said.

The woman paused, an empty cup for the trash in one hand, a damp towel in the other. She seemed to consider something for a moment before speaking again. She glanced at the two young ladies lost in their worlds and met Josie's eyes again. "You're a cop, right?"

How would she have known? It always surprised Josie when someone guessed correctly that she was, in fact, a cop. Depending on the person, place, and situation, she might deny it, feign surprise at the question. There were a number of stories she would tell those she didn't want to confide in, everything from being in real estate to being a commercial pilot. She used to say flight attendant, but at some point, she had realized she wasn't the type to bump her hips across a thousand elbows a day, that she would be more apt to sit up front and control their destiny.

But this woman's eyes told Josie she already knew that Josie was a cop and that her question had been more of a statement.

Josie glanced at the girls chatting and checked her surroundings before answering. "Yes, I am. How did you know?"

She nodded toward Josie's Charger parked at the curb. "The car."

Josie looked over her shoulder, saw the sun glinting off the hood and windshield of her county car, looked hard to see the lights concealed behind the dash, and noted that they weren't easy to spot even when you knew they were there. She was a little surprised that this woman had noticed.

Smiling, she said, "You're good. You either run drugs for the cartel, or you're from a law enforcement family."

The woman stepped over, tossed the empty cup into a nearby trash can, turned back, and met Josie's gaze again. "My husband was a cop."

Josie nodded her understanding. The spouses of cops were often more observant and aware of their surroundings than the average citizen. "Retired now?" Josie guessed.

"He's dead." Turning away, she said, "Have a nice day, and be safe."

Josie watched her walk away and saw the door close behind the woman as she returned to the shop. Josie continued staring at the door while her mind raced to make sense of the brief and awkward conversation. What was its purpose? Because it *was* purposeful, she thought. And who was this woman? Who was her husband, and how had he died?

And it occurred to Josie that it wasn't just she who had her secrets and stories; everyone had their own.

19

Dickie put Angelo down for his nap after lunch, cuddled next to him and read *Night Night, Dino-Snores* twice, as requested. Read to him through an onslaught of laughter, the kid cracking himself up with his impressions of dinosaurs snoring, Angelo saying that's how his dad sounds when he falls asleep in his chair. He finished the book and told Angelo to close his eyes and go to sleep—issuing the standard warning that he was not to get out of bed and leave his room until he had taken his nap. Angelo pouted, turned onto his side, and buried his face in his pillow —sad boy.

Dickie cleaned up the mess he'd made in the kitchen, poured himself an iced tea, and spread the contents of the Laura Townsend murder file out on the table. Rosalva was washing blinds, and he cautioned her against entering the kitchen while he worked, letting her know he'd have some unpleasant photographs on display while he reviewed a case. She clicked her teeth, shook her head, and went about her cleaning.

Before he read anything Victor Robles had written in his reports or jotted in his notebook, Dickie wanted to view the scene and autopsy photographs. He wanted to study these things and draw his own conclusions before considering those of the former disgraced homicide cop who had been known for being a drunk who produced sloppy work and ultimately ate his gun. The latter had occurred a year or so after the Townsend murder case, and Dickie had to consider that it wasn't a coincidence. Though it could have been nothing more than that—it wasn't as if Robles hadn't worked a dozen other murders in that same year—but it was something to contemplate as Dickie took a deep dive into this unsolved murder of a cop's wife. Wild speculation throughout the department held that this was a domestic murder staged by one of their own, Captain Jerry Townsend. But nothing had ever come close to being proven.

It was quiet. The only sounds in their suburban home were the faint clattering of wooden blinds and a distant leaf blower—background noises of others also at work. At the office, there would be chatter, phones ringing, and, worse yet, well-intentioned colleagues stopping by to ask what he was working on. This was why sometimes it paid to work from home, which was one benefit to being assigned to Homicide—nobody ever expected you to be in the office nor worried about what you were doing when you were gone.

The scene photos showed a tidy home of two professional adults with no children. It was well-appointed with luxurious décor, an elegant bar in the living area, and a view of an unguarded swimming pool just a few steps out the back slider, which was open. The front entry door stood open as well, and Laura Townsend's body was only a few feet inside it. She was sprawled face down on the Spanish-tiled floor, dressed in business attire suitable for casual evening wear: a light-colored pantsuit and beige block-heeled booties with straps. One arm was outstretched, pale fingers with manicured nails clutching a handbag, silver bracelets wrapped around the wrist. If not for the small volume of blood leaking from beneath her, you'd think someone captured a picture of a woman who fell to the floor after consuming too many cocktails at happy hour or was knocked down from behind after walking through the door. But there was no evidence of violence beyond the dead woman on the floor. There were paintings on the walls, photographs on shelves, figurines and bronze statues of horses and their riders on a mantle—none of which had been disturbed. A glass-topped corner table held a vase of fresh flowers and not so much as a speck of dust. The place appeared immaculate, other than the unfortunate corpse.

Dickie moved the photographs around on his table like puzzle pieces until he could see the entirety of the scene as he might if he were there. Visiting the site would be helpful, even all these years later, and asking the current residents if he could walk through their home might be an option. Take Josie with him and significantly increase the odds of the homeowners saying yes.

As he viewed it through the photographs, most of the scene was unremarkable. However, he was bothered that he didn't see a safe. Half a mil, where would he have kept it? Hadn't he said it was in a safe back then, moved to a safe deposit box since Laura's death? Yes, Dickie recalled, that's exactly what he had said: that envelopes of cash had appeared in his desk drawer, and he had taken them home and put them in the safe. Told Laura the story behind the money and said don't touch it.

And what cop didn't have a safe in his home?

He browsed through the photographs again, those he had chosen for the display on his table and the remainder of the large stack he had set aside, pictures of areas beyond the immediate scene: bedrooms, bathrooms, an office area, the garage...

Along one side of the garage were shelves and cabinets, the shelves stacked with boxes and plastic totes. The cabinets were enclosed, and Dickie guessed they would hold canned goods and tools. On the opposite side of the garage was a long workbench with a pegboard on the wall behind it that was meticulously organized with hand tools hanging from hooks. To each side of the workbench were two large cabinets with doors, each large enough to contain a full-size gun safe. Dickie knew of several cops who kept their gun safes in their garages in Southern California, where temperature controls were unnecessary and humidity never an issue. He thumbed through the reports until he found the crime scene description and scanned it a second time. There was no mention of the contents of anything in the garage. Other than a notation that the home was equipped with an attached three-car garage, there was no mention of any contents.

Dickie leaned back in his chair and took a long drink of his iced tea, his eyes fixed on the garage photos. The fact that Robles hadn't described the interior of the garage or its contents didn't surprise him at all. The crime scene was the interior residence, and nothing Dickie saw in the photographs would compel him to think that the burglar-turned-killer had even entered the garage. Yet, to be thorough—which a homicide detective would do when a cop's wife was killed, whether or not it was his or her standard practice—the compartments of the garage and their contents should have at least been noted, if not photographed for future reference.

He reflected on a past murder scene wherein a locking two-drawer file cabinet in a garage was found with the top drawer open, and Dickie had argued with his partner about its significance. The partner said the garage was sloppy and unorganized, and there was an even chance that the open drawer had nothing to do with the murder. But the victim had likely opened the drawer, Dickie argued, noting specks of blood on the concrete floor beneath it. Samples were taken, and it was later learned that the blood on the floor was the victim's, who had sustained injuries to his head. That evidence would suggest that the victim had opened the drawer, presumably for the killer—presumably after being threatened with bodily injury or death—and the killer had taken something of value from it. The victim had been shot execution-style a short distance from the file cabinet. The victim's associates would later reveal that the victim had kept his cache of drugs and money in that drawer. That information, coupled with the victim's blood being found beneath the opened drawer, not only provided Dickie and his partner with a motive but also allowed them to charge the case as a special circumstance murder. The special circumstance being that the murder was committed during the commission of a robbery. This meant that, theoretically, the prosecutor could seek the death penalty or life without the possibility of parole.

Dickie retrieved a yellow notepad from his briefcase and wrote across the top of a blank page: *Questions for Jerry*. Below it, he wrote: *#1 – Where was the safe?*

He set his pen down, leaned back in his chair with his glass of iced tea, and took two long sips. Something bothered him about the safe, but he couldn't grasp what it was.

Rosalva passed through the dining area. "Do you need anything, Mr. Dickie?"

He loved that she called him that. In the beginning, she would call him Mr. Jones. He didn't like that, so he asked her to call him Dickie instead. Mr. Dickie was the result. "No, thank you, Rosalva. I'm good."

She continued into the kitchen, picked up a glass she had set on the counter earlier—tucked away at the back so as not to be in anyone's way —filled it halfway with water from the faucet, and began drinking it.

Dickie shook his head. "Use the good water, Rosalva." He pointed at the refrigerator. "It's filtered and cold."

She waved him off. "Is okay, Mr. Dickie, is good water."

It amazed him at times how selfless and thrifty she was. Rosalva had come into their home as a nanny, but soon, she was cleaning the house also. They would tell her she didn't need to clean and only needed to care for their son. She would argue that she had nothing to do when Angelo was sleeping or quietly playing, and what was she to do, sit around and do nothing? So they paid her extra for the housework and only had to argue with her about the bonus pay the first couple of times.

Dickie thought about Jerry and other Americans who had moved south and lived in Mexico. He could see the draw to doing so, knowing there was a large population of decent, hardworking people who lived there very modestly. But he also knew there was an element of simplification with that thought process—a bit of *the grass is greener* syndrome that factored into it. After all, the Mexicans weren't flooding into the United States just for the drinking water. There was widespread poverty, unchecked violence, blatant corruption…

It made him consider the doctor—what was his name, Fleming? Why would a man of stature and wealth risk everything by spending time in Tijuana and working for far less or no money? He jotted a note to research the doctor and put an asterisk next to it since it wasn't a question for Jerry but something to remember to do. He might also need to start a shit-to-do list, but for now, the one list would suffice. Maybe that would be how his research of the doctor would start, by asking Jerry a few questions about him.

Movement caught Dickie's eye, and he looked up to see his son standing at the threshold of the hallway to his room, a stuffed green dinosaur in one hand, a yellow metal backhoe in the other. He smiled at the boy and asked how his nap had been while quickly gathering the photographs and documents scattered about the table before him. It was early afternoon, and he had finished his work for the day. It was time to work on his life balance.

20

SOUTH OF THE BORDER, JERRY TOWNSEND SAT ON CONCRETE STEPS painted red and splashed by gray-brown sand that bare feet and cheap sandals had tracked from the beach to the sidewalk. Seagulls circled and cawed while gentle waves crashed on the shore, the water dark but still inviting as the sun beat down on his head. A gentle breeze carried hints of raw sewage, one of several constant reminders that he had sought refuge in a third-world country. Another was his view of the fence that separated Tijuana from Imperial Beach, California, and jutted a football field's length into the Pacific. Some might wonder what kept the *desperados* from swimming out and around the end of the fence, but Jerry knew from conversations with the locals that it was a nearly impossible task, though it wouldn't appear so from the comforts of the shore. The water was cold, the riptides relentless, and if one could survive the unlikely swim out and around the end of the fence, the border patrol would be waiting on the other side. The security of a physical barrier was enhanced by electronic surveillance and continuous monitoring by border patrol agents who scoured the beaches in their trucks and ATVs. There were also eyes in the sky: cops in helicopters and planes, as well as high-def cameras affixed to drones. The few who had made the swim around the barrier were quickly apprehended in most cases. Occasionally, the would-be migrants would organize a blitz—a coordinated beach assault where scores of them would charge into the water and do their best to swim out and around the barrier into the United States. In a recent case, about half of the seventy who had started the journey didn't make it and returned to the beaches of Mexico, some of them rescued by Tijuana lifeguards. A couple of them drowned. And of the thirty or so who made it across, only a few escaped the waiting arms of U.S. border patrol agents, the Coast Guard, customs officers, and local police.

The most pressing reminders of Jerry's locale and predicament, though, were the loosened teeth, the taste of blood in his swollen mouth, the excruciating pain in his ribs, and the whirr of a tuning fork echoing in his head—the haze from his beating just starting to clear. The three young men who had used him for a *peñata* and relieved him of his car, wallet, and phones—his own and the burner that Campo had provided—had also left him with a message, which Jerry loosely translated to mean: *fuck around and find out.*

Perhaps a message from the cartel?

But that didn't make sense to him. Why would Campo give him a burner to stay in touch, then send out goons to kick his ass and take it from him? In fact, why would he have sent kids rather than the heavy hitters he had on hand?

Jerry watched the seagulls diving for food, desperate for any scraps. If he had wings, he'd fly his ass over that wall and never return to this godforsaken land. The pickings would be better anywhere north, even on Imperial Beach next door. Before he did—if he could fly back to the U.S. by some miracle or another—he would find Mina and take her with him. But he wasn't a seagull, and he didn't have wings. He couldn't hire a coyote to smuggle him because not even the dumbest of them would believe he had half a million in cash from which he could pay them. Josie had been right: he shouldn't have returned to Mexico.

A helicopter moved slowly along the border on the other side of the fence. Jerry thought to wave at it like a castaway signaling Search and Rescue. Maybe dig an SOS into the dirty sand and start a smoky fire on the beach. But he knew it would all be in vain; his government didn't rescue expatriates from themselves.

A lone surfer waded in the water, bobbing up and down. Jerry didn't think the hopeful youth could do much with the small waves of the afternoon, even with the gigantic board on which he sat. Perhaps he was a beginner, and he was taking things slowly. Californians had started the craze of surfing in Mexico back in the sixties and seventies when it was a relatively safe and simple drive south for a day in the sun and surf. Locals caught on to the sport, and when the surf was up, Baja beaches could be littered with locals and *Californios* alike. But times had changed, and not many Californians ventured south with waxed boards on the tops of their Beetles to risk being robbed and murdered while pursuing the perfect wave.

Jerry pondered the idea of using a longboard similar to the one on which the lone surfer sat to paddle around the point himself. He would welcome the apprehension that would surely await him. Another option would be trying to walk across the border without his ID. Surely, the cops there would be able to verify his citizenship, and they would allow him to cross back. Wouldn't they? Or he could go to the U.S. consulate in Tijuana and ask for their help. He wouldn't be the first American to lose his ID in Tijuana by being drunk, getting mugged, or both.

He could go to Campo.

And what, ask the man for a loan? Tell him he'd been robbed and had no means to survive or return to the States. Maybe ask Campo if he would get him back to the U.S. for a cut of Jerry's money—the money that had been stolen from Campo or someone just like him, perhaps an associate of his. Or ask him to take him out back and shoot him in the head as Campo had previously joked he would do. At this point, maybe that would be the best resolution. Put an end to his own life and let Josie and her partner go on with theirs. They could close the books on Laura's murder and let it go rather than risking their careers or worse to find the answers.

Now he wished he had never called her. He could have left it alone and lived with the injustices and guilt that plagued him. Gone back for the money and vanished for good—much farther south. It would have been better for everyone.

But he didn't want to give up just yet. If Mina knew something about his wife's murder, she was the key to solving it, and he needed to find her. That took him back to Campo. Campo or Dr. Fleming.

Fleming was the safer choice. After all, Jerry had just been beaten and robbed by three Mexican nationals, so he wasn't exactly feeling embraced by the locals currently.

21

THE BUREAU PHONES WERE QUIET WHEN DICKIE ARRIVED AT THE OFFICE early the following day. Beating most everyone else in at just after seven o'clock, he hoped to catch the captain's secretary, Martina, in her office before the other admins arrived. She was usually in at seven, followed by Neely at around half past seven. The captain usually came in around eight, but you couldn't count on it. Sometimes, he'd surprise you and be in at six; other times, he'd show up at nine. Dickie always figured it depended on how much the man drank the night before or whether he had driven home or stayed locally. The captain lived up in Santa Clarita—a forty-five-minute (in light traffic) drive from the office—but it was rumored that he spent some nights in East Los Angeles with a waitress from Corina's.

She was at her desk, and there were no lights on yet in the offices across the hall from hers where Stover and Neely would be found.

"Mornin', Marti."

She looked up from her computer screen, a soft blue glow reflecting on her glasses. She smiled. "Dickie, you're bright and early this morning. What's going on?"

"Got a favor to ask."

She leaned forward as if it were top secret. It was, but how would she know? He moved closer to the edge of her desk, reinforcing the confidentiality of their impending conversation.

He smiled. "It's not a big deal. I need to get a phone number for one of our guys who's retired."

Marti's eyes moved back to the screen, and she moved her right hand to the mouse that sat on a plain rubber pad next to the keyboard. "Who're we looking for, hon?"

Though she was certainly no receptionist, her desk was designed in a similar fashion, with a countertop enclosing the front and one side of her workspace, separating her from the hallway and visitors. It was the height that allowed you to stand and fill out papers without having to stoop or sit in a chair to be comfortable. And there were no chairs to sit in, which perhaps was part of the design: handle your business and move along; this was a no-loitering section. Dickie rested his arm on the countertop and leaned against it, casual and relaxed. He said, "Walker. Brett Walker."

She shot him a look but said nothing while her fingers drummed a riff on the keyboard and stopped. She returned her attention to the work before her but not before Dickie caught something in her eyes.

"What are you up to now?" she asked, still looking at the screen.

"Oh, just following up on an old case of his. Need to get in touch with him."

Marti looked up at him again. "Victor Robles's partner."

He nodded. "That's right, they were teamed up for a while, weren't they?"

"You finished the councilman case." Again, another statement, not a question.

"Yeah, it's all wrapped up," Dickie said, scrambling to come up with something to keep her suspicions to a minimum. He knew Marti had her finger on the pulse of the bureau, more so than did the captain for whom she worked. But now she seemed to be questioning the reason Dickie would have to contact Robles's old partner. "But the DA had something he wanted us to follow up on."

"McKnight," she said matter-of-factly.

Dickie nodded, pondering how she would know who the district attorney was on any given case.

"Isn't Josie dating him?" she asked next, the interrogation continuing.

He frowned. Dickie liked Marti, but while this was a simple request for a retired member's contact information, it felt more like an inquest. "I think so, why?"

"Mmmm," was her response as she scanned the monitor again.

Dickie knew it wouldn't take but an instant for her to come up with the information he needed, and now he was becoming more agitated with the process than concerned about Marti's meddling. She might have been the captain's secretary, but she *was* a secretary—Dickie didn't answer to her. He said, "How about that number, Marti… I have things to do."

She glanced at him with surprise in her eyes, how she might respond if her captain sauntered in wearing lingerie. Dickie pictured that scene as Marti jotted the name "Brett Walker" on a sticky note and a phone number with a 208 area code. She handed it to him without comment and turned in her chair as if she was now busy with other matters.

Dickie turned on his heel, busy with other matters himself, and silently cursed the information on the two-by-two pale blue sticky: an Idaho phone number. Like so many other retired cops, Brett had fled the state of California with his pension and sought refuge in a red state. Idaho, Texas, and Arizona had been the Big Three for years, but now Arizona had turned blue, and Idaho was overcrowded, so some retirees were getting creative, moving to Tennessee, Arkansas, and Florida. Even those who weren't necessarily politically aligned with the ideology of the right knew, as cops, that the blue states were becoming meccas for the lawless and were not the types of places they wanted to live out their lives—not after everything they had seen and done during their careers. Dickie couldn't blame them, but it was challenging to work unsolved murders when many retired investigators were scattered across fifty states and beyond. At least Brett Walker was in Idaho, not Florida. If Dickie had to visit him, it was a two-hour direct flight to Idaho rather than an all-day flight to the Sunshine State.

Idaho was an hour ahead, so when Dickie returned to his desk, he made the call. His window of time alone in Unsolveds was limited—maybe he had half an hour before others began filing in. The call went to voicemail, but Dickie hung up without leaving a message. What would he have said? Hi, just wanted to ask you a few things about a case you and that idiot Robles fucked up. *Ciao.*

Getting him on the line, exchanging some small talk, and working his way toward the conversation would be better.

Or maybe fly up and surprise him.

He picked up his coffee-stained bulldog mug and went to the break room. A television hung above a cluster of empty tables, left on though nobody was there to watch it. The set seemed to run continuously, the channels varying throughout the day. Currently, a local news station reported the weather: dry and hot. How much skill did it take to be a meteorologist in Southern California? And when they got it wrong, who even cared? Near lunchtime, the channel might be switched to soaps by the secretaries, and then someone would inevitably put it back on the news for the afternoon and evening. It was uncanny how often you could be in the break room and see your colleagues on the news, in the background of a breaking story—beyond the yellow tape. Dickie turned to the coffee machine and found it empty and off. At least someone had cleaned the carafes. There were three: two for regular coffee and one with an orange handle used for decaf. Nobody working cases drank the latter. Dickie placed a filter in the basket and scooped a generous amount of Kirkland coffee into it, filled the coffeemaker with water, and turned it on. The news had moved on to the traffic now, reporting that the morning commute was slow and there were accidents everywhere. Again, this was Southern California—was it ever anything but heavy and congested? Weather and traffic were two consistent things in L.A., and crime was a third.

As the coffee brewed, Dickie sat on a plastic chair beside one of the tables and checked his phone. There were no text messages, so he went through his emails, deleting the spam and anything forwarded to him by friends and colleagues meant to entertain or enlighten him. He didn't bother opening any business emails, either. Those he would leave unread and open on his computer once he returned to his office with a fresh cup of strong joe. Reading your email on the phone was convenient but not practical—not for Dickie. Not now that he needed readers to see small print.

Never known for patience, Dickie removed the carafe when it was less than half full, placed his mug under the stream of freshly brewed coffee, and filled it to the brim. He replaced the pot with the precision of a practiced coffeeholic, not a single drop spilled during the operation.

Back in his office, he found an unexpected guest waiting.

"Good morning, Captain."

22

───────

HE SAT IN THE GUEST CHAIR NEXT TO DICKIE'S DESK, HIS BLOND HAIR combed back and his paisley tie knotted in a perfect Windsor. He had likely just arrived at the office, hung his jacket on a coat tree, and placed his briefcase beside his desk. Then he would have spoken with his secretary, if only briefly. Had she already informed him of Dickie's request?

Stover didn't bother returning Dickie's greeting. He was all business; nothing warm or fuzzy about the man this morning. To be fair, this was his baseline disposition. Josie would refer to it as his RBF—resting bitch face.

The scene was set, and it gave Dickie a clue about what to expect of the impending conversation—the captain hadn't stopped in to ask about his health or his family. This was unfortunate because Dickie had just had his annual checkup and was given a clean bill of health, with the standard cautions to watch his glucose and maybe drop a few pounds. And the family had never been better. Emily was content with her work as a federal prosecutor, and their son, Angelo, was the light of Dickie's world—a charming and happy child with a wild imagination and seemingly endless energy. Dickie hadn't known what to expect when his life changed so dramatically four years ago, and now he wouldn't trade his little family for anything. Sure, being a father had its challenges for a homicide detective nearing fifty, but it also filled a void that Dickie hadn't even realized was there. These were the things he could tell his captain if the man was even slightly interested, but he wasn't.

The captain hadn't dropped into Unsolveds to exchange pleasantries, and Dickie was braced for either an interrogation or lecture. He sat down behind his desk and took a long sip from his steaming mug of coffee while composing his thoughts. Then he set it down and said, "What's up, boss?"

Stover drummed his fingers on the edge of Dickie's desk. "What's up with you?"

Dickie shook his head and shrugged as if he had no clue what the skipper could be talking about. "*Nada.*"

"Working on anything interesting?"

Another shrug. "Not really."

Stover's lips drew tight as he nodded, his pale blue eyes telling Dickie he didn't believe him, revealing that he knew something about what Dickie and Josie were up to, and that's what he was there to discuss. But how much might he have known?

Dickie sipped his coffee again. "I mean, we're still trying to put the councilman case to bed. McKnight asked us to tie up a few loose ends—"

"Such as?"

"Oh, you know, crime lab stuff, mostly. DNA reports, firearms reports —just some of the things that haven't yet been finalized. The DA's office is braced for a shitstorm on the civil side now that Anthony Macias has been exonerated. Two decades in prison has a price tag."

"What else?"

"Let's see… what else? Oh, Josie's sniper case, the fourteen-year-old who was shot out in Baldwin Park. Potter—Rusty Potter. And a couple'a DNA cases—that's about it. Everything else we're looking at is still in the review stage. Fact, yesterday, I worked from home, read through some of the files that've been piling up. I can get more reading done at home than I can here. That's about it, boss."

Stover regarded Dickie for a long moment. Dickie didn't know what was coming, but he knew the captain had aces in his hand—Dickie knew he'd been caught bluffing and was about to pay the price. But what could the skipper know? That they had gone to Mexico? That they were working with the disgraced Jerry Townsend while looking into his wife's murder? Dickie didn't think so. He didn't think the captain would know about any of that. The only thing he could know was that Dickie had asked Marti for Brett Walker's contact information, and Dickie had already covered his bases with that by bringing up the councilman murder case.

Stover said, "So you're not looking into the Townsend case?" and grinned a little. Not a grin that might suggest he thought something was funny, but a grin like what you might see on the face of your chess opponent after you clumsily moved your queen into the kill zone.

Dickie's mind raced. How would he know that they had opened the Townsend case? Could he have known that Dickie pulled the case from the library without officially checking it out? Or did he know that he and Josie had been to Mexico? Suddenly Dickie had a sinking feeling in his gut that *America's Finest* had made some inquiries about who he was and why he had been down at the border. The two patrol officers or the sergeant? The two cops? Not likely—Dickie had lied to them about his name. Maybe the sergeant—what was his name, Johnson?—could he have made a call? Dickie didn't think so. He had been straightforward with Dickie, and the two of them had built somewhat of a rapport. Or maybe Josie's crossing had raised a red flag with Customs.

Either way, the captain wasn't the one bluffing here. He knew enough to come into Dickie's office and confront him with it, so there was no way out now. The first rule of survival was to stop digging when you found yourself in a hole.

Dickie nodded, holding the captain's gaze. "Yeah, boss, we are. We're poking around a bit but haven't technically reopened it."

Neither blinked in the prolonged moment that followed. Stover raised his brows, encouraging Dickie to expound. The tables were turned, and Dickie didn't like being the one with something to hide when the other one seemed to know the truth and appeared to be able to see through you. Dickie was better on the other side of that table.

Dickie came clean. "Townsend reached out and asked for our help. He thinks he knows why his wife was murdered and wants us to find the killer and clear his name." He left it there, hoping that was enough to satisfy the captain. Okay, fine, you got a call and were looking into it. You should have asked permission. Put the case away, carry on, and go through the proper channels next time. That was what he hoped the captain would say in response to Dickie's partial confession. And Dickie would be happy to comply, say yessir, and be done with Townsend's bullshit. When Josie came in, he'd tell her to close her file, let it go, and not even bother speaking with her old mentor again. He's bad news—this whole thing was terrible from the start.

But instead, Captain Stover said, "Find your partner and Lopes and meet me in the conference room"—he glanced at the Rolex on his wrist—"let's say ten."

The captain and who else, Internal Affairs? Dickie had a hunch the skipper wouldn't be alone, or else why the conference room and not his office?

Dickie said, "Lopes isn't involved in it, skipper. He doesn't even know we were looking at it. This is all on me and my partner."

Stover nodded. "Yeah, I know. But I want him there." He pushed out of his chair and started for the door.

Dickie said to his back, "Can I ask what the meeting's about?"

The captain stopped in the doorway and turned to look at him. "You'll know soon enough. Don't mention any of this to anyone other than Lopes and Sanchez. Got it?"

"Yessir."

Dickie sat staring at the doorway long after Stover was gone and until Lopes's large frame filled the void. Unlike the captain, Lopes didn't appear fresh from the shower after a good night's sleep. His tie was loosened, his cuffs turned up, and his eyes looked like two pissholes in the snow.

"The hell happened to you last night?"

"Your friend, Floyd, happened to me last night. Hits me up on my way out the door, tells me about this happy hour thing he goes to over in Lakewood, some Mexican joint with decent food and great drinks. You ever have a Cadillac margarita?"

Dickie shook his head. "I don't do tequila."

"They're pretty fucking good. I'm not sure what makes 'em different than a regular margarita, but they're better and more potent. All I know is dumbass kept ordering more, and by the time I left, I was in no shape to drive home."

"What'd you do?"

"Slept in the bunk room at Lakewood station. It wasn't like I could leave a county car in the parking lot and take an Uber home."

Dickie nodded just as Josie pushed in behind Lopes, telling him, "You look like shit, dude."

Lopes stepped aside and grinned. "Thanks, Sanchez. Right back atcha."

Dickie said, "You guys just missed the skipper. We've got to talk."

The smirk on Lopes's face disappeared. "What's up?"

Josie closed the door. "Yeah, what now?"

"Not here. Let's go get a coffee somewhere."

23

They sat at Manny's in East L.A., sipping strong coffee and breathing in the aromas of *chorizo* and fresh tortillas. Mariachi music filled the air: the polka-like beat with its high-pitched trumpets and violins, the *thump-thump* of an acoustic bass, and the melodic strum of a five-stringed guitar. Dishes clanged while the door chimed steadily, and locals chatted among themselves as they came and went, contented.

Coffee was served, and Dickie began by telling Lopes about the Townsend case and how *they* ended up in the middle of it. Josie, browsing a menu, offered a few details about her trip to TJ but was otherwise uncharacteristically subdued. Lopes watched Dickie with squinty eyes that would dart toward Josie and come back filled with intrigue. Or question. Dickie wondered if Lopes knew something about the Narco scandal or had more information about the murder of Laura Townsend. Maybe Lopes knew some things that he and Josie didn't. Or perhaps it was something else altogether that enthralled the former Marine captain. Dickie encouraged him with a nod. "Well?"

After a moment, he said, "What happened to the painting?"

Josie looked up and frowned. "The angel?"

"Yeah."

She rolled her eyes and shook her head. "Men."

"I'd like to see it."

"You can have it," she said, "if you're that desperate to have a naked woman in your home. It's under my desk currently—I'll be sure to give it to you when we get back."

"Perfect. I'll hang it in my living room."

"You would."

Lopes snickered, and Dickie tried to steer him back on topic. "What do you know about the narco scandal?"

He lifted his chin at Dickie. "Wha'd'ya mean?"

"There's something you're not telling us."

Lopes sipped his coffee and held Dickie's gaze as he pondered the question. Dickie waited, the proverbial ball now in his opponent's court. He could see the wheels spinning behind Lopes's watchful eyes.

After a moment, Lopes set his coffee down and looked from Dickie to Josie and back. "We looked into the narco connection after Townsend's wife was killed."

"And?" Dickie encouraged.

He shrugged. "And what? We didn't find anything to connect the murder to anything related to dope. The feds ultimately charged a few deputies with an assortment of crimes related to some ripoffs, but we never came up with anything on Townsend. Some of the cops were convicted, and a few took plea bargains."

Dickie chimed in. "I remember."

"The sergeant of the crew cut a deal to save his ass, and he testified against the others. He's the only one charged that didn't do any time."

"Who was that?" Josie wanted to know.

Dickie shook his head. He recalled that some went to prison, and at least one rolled against the others, but he couldn't remember the names of any of them. He knew that a task force had been formed after the Townsend murder and that Lopes had been one of about half a dozen Homicide detectives assigned to it, the murder cops joining forces with Internal Affairs to investigate corruption within the Major Narcotics unit. Though at the time, none of the homicide guys admitted they were involved in a criminal investigation focused on deputies. The word around the bureau had been that the task force was formed to investigate the murder of Laura Townsend, the wife of a sheriff's captain, and that was what the masses believed for a time. Eventually, though, the catchy name of the newly formed team, *Arco Narco*, gave pause to anyone paying attention. The temporary offices for these reassigned detectives were offsite, downtown in the Arco Towers. That told part of the story. The "Narco" part of their title told the rest of it. There was more to the task force than solving the case of a cop's slain spouse.

"The sergeant's name was Perry, something-or-other Perry..."

Dickie snapped his fingers in an *ah-hah* moment and aimed his index finger at Lopes, holding it there while trying to put a first name to the face he now recalled. The sergeant had been a deputy at Lynwood back when Dickie and Lopes worked at Firestone, and there had been some other controversies associated with his name. "Mike," he said, the loaded finger still trained on Lopes. "Mike Perry."

Lopes nodded. "Yep, that's it."

"They cut him a deal, uh?"

"Yeah, they did. And I didn't agree with it. In my opinion, they didn't need Perry to make their case against the others, so I have no idea why he got a break. He should've gone to prison right alongside his boys."

"And they didn't look at anyone above the rank of sergeant," Dickie said, a statement more than a question.

Josie shook her head and huffed. "Of course they didn't."

"Which means they didn't look at Jerry," Dickie said.

Josie shot him a look.

Lopes said, "No, they didn't. Not really, anyway—not as far as the ripoffs. As far as his wife's murder, we never came up with anything for a motive. No affairs, no money trouble, nothing."

Josie sat with her arms crossed, giving Dickie a clear signal of her irritation. Loyalty was one of her strongest traits, and Dickie knew that. Her need to defend an old partner and friend came naturally, and Dickie knew he'd have to tread lightly on the topic going forward. He said, "Okay, good. So, who would have had a motive to kill her?"

Lopes shrugged.

"I say either the cartel or one of his deputies," Dickie said, "someone who thought Jerry was about to roll over on them. Everyone knows most cops will do anything to stay out of prison."

"So they kill his wife?" Lopes asked.

Josie shook her head. "I don't think they killed her to shut him up. I think someone was there that night looking for something."

"Like?"

"Jerry thinks that whoever broke into his house was there looking for evidence of him informing, and the murder came from the would-be burglar panicking when they came home early."

Dickie nodded his agreement, adding, "Which takes you back to the dinner date with the chief—Benny Carmen—and the commander."

"Wilkins," Josie said, "and also Supervisor Anderson."

Lopes leaned forward in his chair. "You think a county supervisor is a part of this?"

Now it was Josie who shrugged. "Follow the money, honey."

Lopes seemed to ponder the idea of it for a moment, then looked at Dickie. "Did the captain say anything about the feds joining us for this meeting today?"

Dickie shook his head. "Why?"

"Well, you're talking about Arco Narco now, which means you're talking feds. If someone's found out you two are looking into Townsend, there's a good chance that the feds are going to get involved."

Dickie and Josie exchanged glances. Dickie let out a breath and turned his gaze to Lopes, who sat across the table from him taking large gulps of water to supplement the coffee and replenish his bodily fluids. "Okay, so generally speaking, what was the consensus of the task force about the *who and why* of the Townsend murder at that time?"

Lopes pushed back from the table and crossed one leg over the other. "Some guys thought Jerry might have had something to do with it. Others thought Laura was killed because of the ripoffs." He shrugged.

"What do you think?"

"I think Jerry should have never gone to Narco. That unit was dirty long before he arrived."

"But was *he*?" Josie asked.

"There's no evidence of it," Lopes said. "But why would he be put in that position unless whoever made the appointment either thought he'd play nice or they were ignorant about what was going on in the unit."

"Benny Carmen," Josie said.

Lopes shrugged. "Maybe. They never pointed any fingers at him."

Dickie huffed, and then silence hung in the air for a long moment before Dickie asked the half-million-dollar question: "Okay, so someone wanted Townsend dirty. They planted stolen money in his desk and watched to see what he would do. He took the envelopes of cash without comment, so wouldn't they figure he was in? If that were the case, why would the killer have been a cop in his unit? Could this burglar have been there for something else?"

"Like?" Lopes asked.

Dickie shook his head. "I don't know."

"Maybe it was the cartel trying to recover some of their losses," Josie offered.

"I don't know," Dickie said. "That doesn't feel right to me. How would they know to hit his place? Why would they assume he had the money?"

Josie shook her head. "No, it doesn't feel right to me either. Jerry thinks it was someone in his unit and that they were searching for evidence that he was turning on them. Nobody was supposed to be home, and the murder doesn't really fit the cartel M.O."

"That was the problem with the investigation," Lopes said. "It was hard to believe that the cartel would go after a cop—not in America. And the idea of cops killing cops is just too over-the-top to consider, even if it was a panic situation. It's easier to swallow the idea that the marriage was bad, that there was infidelity, and that an insurance payoff was part of the equation."

"But you found no evidence of any of those things," Dickie said.

Lopes shook his head and then drained his glass of water. He set the glass on the table and glanced around the room. Dickie could tell he was ready to go.

"That's what pushed Jerry out of the department and into hiding," Josie said. "Those rumors. And why would he need any insurance payout if he's sitting on half a million in cash and would be retiring on a captain's salary?"

Dickie said, "Not like it hasn't happened before, cops killing their spouses."

"Or cops killing other cops," Josie said. "We've seen that too."

Dickie nodded. "Greed is a funny thing. People get money, and they want more money. Money is power, and power is a drug. I think there are a few plausible motives there."

Lopes glanced at his watch. "You guys ready?"

Dickie tossed a twenty on the table for their three cups, and they filed out silently.

SHORTLY BEFORE TEN, THEY ROLLED INTO THE BUREAU PARKING LOT IN Dickie's Crown Vic. Lopes sat up front with Dickie. Josie was in the back seat, uncharacteristically quiet during the return trip.

Dickie put the car in park and looked over his shoulder. "You good?"

Josie's expression said it all: she wasn't good. She likely felt responsible for whatever wrath they were about to receive because of their unsanctioned work on the Townsend case, and Dickie could see it was weighing on her.

She said, "We'll probably be rolled up over this fiasco, partner. I'm sorry."

Dickie shook his head. "I don't think so."

"If they know we went to Mexico—"

"I don't think so, Josie. If they were rolling anyone up, why a meeting in the conference room? Wouldn't Stover just call us into his office for that? And why is Lopes included in this meeting? I think there's something else in the works."

She looked through the passenger window for a moment, contemplating. When her gaze came back to Dickie, still watching her over his shoulder, Josie said, "I don't know. Maybe they want Lopes there as a witness to our termination."

Lopes chuckled and popped his door open. "Come on, it's not going to be that bad. You know Stover. He'll piss and moan and chew your asses, but then he'll forget about it, and we'll be back to chasing killers and solving murders an hour later."

"When's the last time you chased a killer?" Dickie asked.

Lopes grinned. "About a week ago, right after I finished with your mom."

Dickie grinned and shook his head as he unfolded himself from the front seat.

Josie popped out of her seat and started for the back door. "Okay, boys, let's do this. If I'm getting fired, I don't want to waste the whole day here."

Inside, they headed straight for the conference room. Lopes led the way, followed by Josie, with Dickie bringing up the rear. Stover was waiting for them. Stover and two suits Dickie had never seen before but immediately recognized.

Feds.

There is as much difference between cops and federal agents as between cops and convicts, cowboys and Indians. Ford and Chevy, crunchy and creamy peanut butter. The vast majority of federal agents are college-educated and classroom-trained. They don't patrol dangerous neighborhoods where one miscalculation could get someone killed. They don't interact with gangsters and killers in dark, graffiti-covered alleys that smell of rotten food and piss, nor are they sent into cockroach-infested homes to quell violent arguments between drunken and drug-crazed adults or to remove neglected and abused children from their families. They don't walk up on a thousand cars a year, knowing that every contact is potentially a deadly encounter.

These were feds.

Dickie had been the subject of a civil rights violation investigation during his patrol days. There had been a gang fight, and while breaking it up, he and his partner used force to restrain and arrest one of the combatants. There was a complaint that excessive force had been used, even though their supervisor witnessed the incident and stated that everything they had done was within policy. The department's Internal Affairs Bureau investigated the case, and the allegations were unfounded. Nonetheless, Dickie and his partner were sued in federal court and lost. Shortly after the trial, and before the Ninth Circuit Court of Appeals would overturn the verdict, the FBI notified Dickie that he and his partner were the subjects of a federal criminal investigation. When the agents requested an interview, Dickie told them as politely as possible that they could fornicate themselves, and he exercised his right to remain silent. For the next year and a half, the criminal case against them remained open, and every time Dickie saw a fed around the station, he wondered if that was the day he would be arrested. Eventually, the feds closed their case, citing insufficient evidence to prosecute. But the ordeal left Dickie with distrust and a helping of contempt for the FBI.

And here they were, in *his* house, a pair of college kids with guns in their gray Brooks Brothers and dull black loafers.

In the doorway, Josie turned and looked at Dickie. Her intense stare told him she shared his concern about the direction of this meeting. Was it a meeting, or was it an inquest? Maybe the feds were here to arrest them.

Stover motioned for the three of them to come in and take their seats at the table. That was a good sign, Dickie thought, that they weren't being arrested. At least not yet. But a line of questioning surely awaited them. Maybe Dickie would invoke his right to remain silent again.

They went to the far side of the table and sat together. The two suits and Stover took their seats across from them. There were no introductions.

Stover said, "These gentlemen are with the bureau—"

Dickie bit his tongue. *No shit.*

"—and they're working a task force involving cartels. They have some questions for you two," he said, his eyes darting from Josie to Dickie and back, clarifying for anyone who wasn't sure to whom exactly he referred.

But why was Lopes there? That was the question that lingered in Dickie's mind.

The two suits were nearly indistinguishable with their boyish haircuts, clean-shaven faces, and expressionless faces you only saw on poorly drawn cartoon characters. Other than the fact that one was white, the other black, that is.

The black guy said, "I'm Special Agent Williams. This is my partner, Special Agent Jaworski. As your captain informed you, we are assigned to investigate Mexican cartels, specifically the Arellano-Félix Cartel, most often referred to as the Tijuana Cartel."

Silence from Dickie's side of the table.

Jaworski opened a briefcase on the table before him as Williams continued. "We have a few operatives across the border who diligently provide us with activity reports, and recently we learned that Detective Sanchez"—he said this without looking at her—"went to Tijuana and met with a close associate of the cartel, Mr. Juan Ricardo Campo, the proprietor of a gentleman's club on Revolution Boulevard."

"Not a gentleman's club," Josie interjected, "it's a whorehouse."

Oh shit, Dickie thought, *here we go.*

The captain frowned at her.

Williams nodded, "Be that as it may…"

Jaworski removed a photograph from his briefcase and maneuvered it toward the opposite side of the table with his professionally manicured hands, orienting the glossy 8x10s for Dickie, Josie, and Lopes to view. The first was a picture of a thin man with slick hair wearing an open-collar shirt and a suit jacket, gold jewelry around his neck draping onto his hairy chest. He bore the look of a man with either money or power, which in Mexico was the same.

Josie said, "Campo."

Jaworski nodded as he placed a second photograph alongside the first, this one of a much larger man with a thick neck and bulging traps and shoulders beneath a floral-printed silk shirt. He was clean-shaven, and his skin was dark from the sun or maybe a tanning bed.

"Carlos," Josie said flatly. "Campo's bodyguard."

Again, Jaworski nodded.

Williams said, "Juan Carlos Serrano Medrano. He's Mr. Campo's right-hand man, an El Salvadoran Death Squad enthusiast who filled a number of contracts for the cartel before he was assigned to Campo."

Josie said, "Hmpf. I would have thought Fur Face was the killer among them."

Williams tilted his head in question as Jaworski placed another photo on the table.

Josie reached over and pointed her finger. "That's Fur Face."

"Ah," Williams said, now understanding Josie's nickname for the bearded man. "That's Hector Vasquez Romero." He glanced at his partner, and they seemed to exchange telepathic signals before Williams continued. "He's one of our informants."

Josie reached and pulled the photo closer. "No shit? I figured him to be the one that would shoot me in the head."

Dickie watched his captain's reaction, but he was difficult to read, the skipper leaning back in his black leather chair and biting at the end of a pen. He must've already known that not only had Josie gone to Tijuana but also the details of what went down at the club. After all, these feds apparently had inside information.

Williams shook his head. "He may have intervened if it came to that."

Josie leaned back in her chair. "I'll be damned."

Dickie didn't disagree with her assessment. They probably both would be, but he didn't say so.

They showed one more photo, a clean-shaven, soft-appearing Hispanic man that Josie referred to as Baby Face. Williams identified him as Arturo Beltran, another killer. And Josie seemed surprised that she had misjudged the killers among them.

When the photo display ended, Dickie said, "So why are we here? What's the purpose of all this?"

Stover leaned forward and put his elbows on the table. "The purpose of this is to let the two of you know how stupid it was for you to go to Mexico on your own and without going through channels. Do you not think we'd consider reopening the Townsend case if you came to me with a good argument about why we should?"

Dickie shrugged. "I don't know, boss."

"I honestly felt we just needed to speak with Jerry and find out what he had to say before we came to you. It's my fault, not his," Josie said, indicating her partner.

The captain looked at Lopes. "Consider the case officially reopened. Lopes will be working it with you." He pointed his Bic at Dickie and Josie alternately. "You two are on thin ice after that Mexico stunt. Don't make me regret this. You run this thing out, but keep these guys in the loop."

The stuffy room fell silent.

Stover pushed out of his chair. "I've got things to do. You'll not do anything on the Townsend case without notifying me first, and again, everything goes through them," he said, gesturing toward the two suits next to him.

Josie said, "Yessir," and the skipper was gone.

After a long moment, Special Agent Williams said, "We have an idea of who killed Laura Townsend."

24

"Fucking feds."

Dickie sat down in the chair next to Lopes's desk. "Yep."

Lopes leaned back in his seat and pulled the knot of his tie loose. "Dude says they know who killed Townsend, then backs away from it when you pushed him for a name."

"He said they *might* know who did it… they don't have anything more than we have, which at this point is just a theory as to why she was killed and a guess at who might have been involved. These college boys think they're smarter than everyone."

"We need to talk to Walker," said Dickie.

Dickie swiveled his chair to see Josie in the doorway, eating a yogurt. She had her shoulder against the doorjamb and legs crossed, relaxed in her pinstriped suit. Given her pose, Dickie assumed she'd been there a minute.

He asked her, "How about a trip to Idaho?"

Lopes said, "Who the hell is Walker?"

Dickie turned back to face him. "Brett Walker."

"Ah."

"You know him? He was Robles's partner in the Townsend murder case. Retired to Idaho."

"Like everyone else," Lopes said. "Yeah, I know him. He was an okay cop, I guess…. He wasn't ever going to set the world on fire, but he showed up to his scenes half-sober, and every once in a while, he'd put a case together. Kind of a weird dude, though, you know? Had those crazy eyes and a permanent smirk—you never knew if he was happy to see you or about to gleefully kill somebody."

Josie crossed the room and tossed an empty yogurt container and a plastic spoon into the trash beside her desk. She pulled her chair out and stooped down to retrieve something. It was the angel painting. She held it up for Lopes to see and carried it to him while he admired it. Lopes said, "Damn, that's nice."

Josie handed it to him. "It's all yours."

He studied it while Josie went back to her desk and grabbed her chair. She wheeled it over to Lopes's desk and lowered herself into it. Now the three of them were in a semi-circle, close enough to speak freely without being overheard by anyone passing by in the hallway.

Lopes finished admiring the naked angel and set the framed portrait next to his desk.

Dickie was reflecting on the meeting, thinking about these two feds they now were supposed to work with. He looked at Josie. "So this dude they say's their informant down there…"

"Fur Face," Josie said.

Dickie glanced at his notes from the meeting. "Hector Vasquez Romero."

"What about him?" she asked.

"Maybe we should see if he would work directly with us."

Lopes chimed in. "They were hesitant to even tell us this guy was their informant. I doubt they'd share him with us."

"I was just thinking," Dickie said, "if he knew where Mina was, we might be able to save ourselves a lot of work. If she knows anything about the Townsend murder, we need to talk to her."

"Jerry thinks she does," Josie said, "but who knows? I mean, even if she knew about that case and knew the players, what's to say she'd tell us? We've got no leverage on her, and she has to live her life down there. Best way to do that is to keep your mouth shut. Surely she knows that, and it's probably why she was nowhere to be found."

"I think we have to go through the feds," Lopes said. "I don't see any other way to do it. But I do agree with Dickie that we need to talk to her."

Dickie nodded. "You're probably right about going through the feds. So hit 'em up, see if they'll work with us."

Lopes squinted. "Oh, okay, I get to deal with the feds, uh?"

"Dickie doesn't play well with feds," Josie said. "So either you can hit them up, or I will."

Lopes shrugged.

"Back to Walker," Dickie said, "I think we need to make that a priority. Just like any other unsolved, you know? We review the case, then talk to those who were initially involved in it."

Josie said, "Why can't we just call him?"

Lopes chuckled. "Dude never answered his phone when we were paying him five grand a month to do so—what makes you think he'll answer it now?"

"So, what, just fly up there and knock on his door?" Josie asked.

"Probably find him in a bar," Dickie said, "from what I remember of him."

Lopes grinned. "Dude's probably sitting in a treehouse smoking weed, weird little fucker." He looked at Josie. "Did you know him?"

She shook her head. "I don't think so."

"Little guy with Manson lanterns, a goofy-ass grin on his face. He was a chain smoker, so he was always outside the back door and spent half his shifts there. If you'd met him, you'd remember him."

"He was gone before she got to Homicide," Dickie said. "Hey, we can give Farris a call, maybe have him look Walker up. He's in Boise now running a PI business."

Lopes smiled. "Rich Farris. Wonder how he's doing."

"The thing about it is," Dickie said, "Farris is one of those guys everyone likes, no matter where he goes."

Lopes was grinning now. "Even in Idaho, ya think?"

Dickie nodded. "I worked a case with him up in Lancaster involving skinheads. Of course, our victim's family was drawn to him, obviously pleased to have a black detective working the case, but I swear the skinheads we dealt with liked him too. One of 'em we caught trying to escape through a back window of his house when we went to talk to him. Farris grabbed him, pulled him out, and dropped him on his head. He was crying about being injured and saying he was going to file a complaint, yada yada, and five minutes later, Farris has the dude smiling and thanking him like he'd never sworn an oath to hating people of color. Farris just has that way about him."

Lopes shook his head. "Fucking skinheads."

"But how's he going to help us with this? Farris," Josie clarified.

Lopes raised his brows and lifted his chin toward Dickie, apparently seconding the question. Josie's office phone rang, but other than a glance in that direction, she ignored it.

"If nothing else," Dickie said, "he can show us around town. I think he'd be a good connection to have up there. Maybe we have him track Walker down before we make the trip. Make sure the dude's available."

"In his treehouse," Lopes said.

Josie looked at her cell phone, and Dickie saw there was a call coming in on silent. She ignored the call and looked up to meet his gaze. "Give Farris a call, partner. Meanwhile, what else do we have going on this afternoon?"

Dickie shrugged. "Nothing pressing. You have something to do?"

She stood up from her chair. "Not really, but I need to make a call."

Dickie glanced at Lopes and saw an expression that matched Dickie's response to the sudden shift in Josie's demeanor: curiosity with a helping of concern. As Josie gathered her things from her desk, Dickie asked, "Everything okay, partner?"

She didn't look at him. "Yeah, I'm good," she said and walked out.

Dickie and Lopes sat in silence and watched her go. After a long moment, Lopes said, "The fuck was that about?"

Dickie's gaze remained on the empty doorway as he pushed out of his chair and adjusted his fedora. "Who knows? ... *Women.*"

25

"WHAT HAPPENED?"

Josie looked out over the bureau parking lot from the shade of the building, her cell phone at her ear. With two missed calls, a text from a number she didn't recognize, and a message saying it was Jerry and he needed to talk to her, she could only imagine something was wrong.

The sounds of chatter and music filled the background. Jerry said, "I need another favor."

He told her about the robbery, said he'd been beaten and left with what he believed to be a broken rib or two. If they weren't broken, they were severely bruised. No, he wasn't going to the hospital. It's fucking Tijuana, he said. Why bother? The thugs had taken his cell phone and his wallet containing cash, credit cards, and identification. Without these things, he couldn't survive in Mexico or get back into the U.S. A broken rib or two was the least of his concerns.

"So, what can I do, Jerry?"

"The safe deposit box. I need the money and my passport."

She pictured a bank vault where the money was stashed, saw herself being escorted into the private room by a rotund man with a bad comb-over, or maybe a studious woman with specs on a chain around her neck, a ring of keys on a colorful spiral wristband. Her host would direct her to

133

the box in question and leave her alone in the room with instructions on how to notify someone when she was finished. Soon after, she'd be walking out of the bank with a bag of cash that some very bad people might claim as their own and be ready to recover. The thought crossed her mind that she needed to ramp up her off-duty officer safety vigilance— double-check to ensure she wasn't being tailed by anyone when she left the office and keep an even closer eye on any activity near her home. Tell her mother not to answer the door for anyone she didn't know.

She said, "You want me to cross over again."

He was silent for a moment, and Josie heard the voice of a woman speaking Spanish. Josie pictured him at a bar. Not the *Caballo*—no, it was too quiet for him to be there—but likely at some other Tijuana pub where beady eyes no doubt surveyed him. She said, "Jerry, where are you?"

"I'm at a little place near the beach. I know the woman who runs it, and I came here to get a drink and borrow her cell phone."

"Get a drink."

"Yeah, I needed a drink, Josie. It's been a while since I've had my ass kicked, ya know?"

"But you have no money."

"The woman here, Lucinda, knows I'm good for it. Fact, if you need to leave me a message, get ahold of her. It's the *Puesta del Sol cantina.*"

"The Sunset bar, uh?"

"It's a dive, but it's near the beach and not far from my apartment."

Josie pictured a brightly colored ramshackle hovel, sheets of hinged-plywood window coverings raised to shield beachfront boozers in their flip flops, their skin leathery from the afternoon sun. Lucinda would be a voluminous woman stuffed into a frilly white top and counterfeit designer jeans. Or maybe she was young and hot like many of the Latinas at the Crazy Horse, and she wondered just how much Jerry should trust this *señorita* who was serving him drinks.

"You didn't have anything stashed at your apartment?" she asked. "Some cash or another ID?"

"Nothing. And I've lost the apartment."

"Because you don't have money for rent," she guessed.

He cleared his throat. "No, because someone told the manager to lock me out."

"The cartel."

"Yeah, I'm sure."

She paused as a pair of young detectives, two men, both Hispanic, walked past her on their way into the office. She recognized one from East L.A., a young patrol deputy when she was there in the gang unit. No pleasantries were exchanged; she barely got a nod of acknowledgment. The door closed behind them, and she said into the phone, "So you want me to come across again? That's what you're asking? Bring you some of the cash and your passport, and then what?"

"All of it," he said.

"All the cash!"

"Josie, it's that, or they're going to kill me."

"Who's going to kill you, Jerry?"

The bureau door popped open, and Dickie poked his head out. "Everything okay, partner?"

She nodded and turned her back to him.

Jerry was saying, "The cartel—who do you think? They've got me by the balls now and want their money. I'm sure this beating was a message."

Sounds of laughter and Spanish voices rose in the background.

She said, "I don't know—"

"Josie, it's the only way."

"They'll kill you anyway. Go to the border. I'll meet you there with your passport and get you back across."

"And what? Live happily ever after, waiting for the day they come up behind me again? You can't beat the cartel. You can pay them and hope they don't kill you, but you can't keep their money and expect to live long after."

The door closed behind her, and Josie glanced over her shoulder to make sure her partner had gone back inside and wasn't standing behind her listening. She was alone. "You told them you had two hundred thousand. Why would you want all of it? Didn't you say there was half a mill?"

"Nearly, not quite. Maybe four and a half."

"Okay, but why would you want all of it?"

Jerry sighed into the phone. "Because I'm not coming back. I'll have to disappear. Drop two hundred on Campo and split with the rest."

"This is stupid, Jerry. You can't disappear. In fact, if I brought you all that money, you'd never make it out of TJ. You're not thinking."

Jerry said something in Spanish, but Josie couldn't hear him clearly enough to decipher his words. She pictured him covering the phone with his hand while he spoke to someone there, likely the barkeep. She thought maybe he had asked for another minute or said he'd only be a minute.

She said, "Jerry?"

"I'm here. It's the bartender's phone, and she's asking me to finish."

"Jerry, it's dirty money. You take it and disappear—*again*—you're a dirty cop. The fact is, I bring it to you, I'm dirty too. Know what I mean?"

"Look, I've got to get off the phone, Josie. I hear you—I do. But I'm running low on great ideas at the moment, and I'm not sure what to do. Give me some time to think this through."

"I say get out."

"I'll call you back tonight," he said. "*Adios.*"

The call ended, and Josie stared at her phone. She had a bad feeling about this. She had learned to trust her instincts on matters of officer safety and survival, and she knew the danger of returning to Mexico to help Jerry. There was more to consider than just the potential for violence and deadly encounters—she would also be risking her career. Unless there was a way to do this through the two feds she'd just met, the salt and pepper dynamic duo—what were their names? Jaworski and Williams. Josie felt she'd connect better with Williams. Jaworski seemed a bit uptight, even for a fed. But what could they do for her? Help get Jerry back? Jerry said he didn't want to return and wanted to disappear. The feds wouldn't be willing or able to assist him with that, and chances were they wouldn't know about his stash of dirty cash, either.

As Josie contemplated that, she realized what a tangled mess Jerry had gotten them involved in. Without the money, it was a simple matter of looking into an unsolved murder. No problem, that's what they did. But the money muddied the waters, and the problem with muddy water was you didn't see the snakes until after you'd been bitten. And now she faced a moral dilemma: be committed to helping her friend and mentor or march into the captain's office with an addendum to the scenario. *Hey, skipper, I forgot to mention that we're sitting on a half million cash for Jerry.* He would insist that the money be confiscated immediately and booked as evidence, which could seal Jerry's fate with the cartel.

The door opened again, and Josie glanced over her shoulder to see that Dickie had returned. He was empty-handed, so she knew he wasn't on his way out. He had come to check on her again. She was no longer on the phone, so there would be questions. How much did she want to tell her partner about the latest developments in Jerry's world? Not much, she quickly determined. Not yet, anyway.

26

———————

JERRY ORDERED ANOTHER DRINK AND CONTEMPLATED HIS NEXT MOVE: FIND the good doctor and see what, if anything, James Fleming, M.D. knew about Mina and the rest of everything that had happened. Fleming seemed to have his finger on the pulse of the TJ underground, which was to say he had his finger on the pulse of Tijuana. Jerry wondered if Fleming would have heard about Josie's visit and their "meeting" with Mr. Campo. There was only one way to find out. Track the doctor down and ask him.

Jerry asked Lucinda for the time. She picked her cell phone up from the counter where she had plugged it in after he finished his call with Josie.

"*Son casi las tres*," she said and set the phone back down on the countertop behind her, ignoring the patchwork of sticky wet rings, the fallout of haphazardly mixed cocktails.

Almost about three, Jerry translated easily—which he knew could be anything from 2:15 to 3:30 in Mexican Standard Time. There was no need for anything more precise in Tijuana. If Doc was in town, he'd likely be at his office, seeing patients. It was too late in the day for surgery. Cosmetic enhancements were rarely emergencies, and Jerry knew that most doctors preferred to do their operations early in the day when they were refreshed and sharply focused. And it was too early for Doc to be at the *Caballo*

Loco. Not too early for many—including Jerry—but he'd never seen Fleming in that club or any other in the afternoon.

He'd finish his drink and work on Lucinda about his transportation problem.

PABLO, LUCINDA'S *PRIMO*, SHOWED UP A HALF HOUR LATER IN A BEAT-UP white Crown Victoria with tinted windows, spotlights, black-wall tires, and antennae on the trunk lid and top of the car. There was no doubt that the tortured Ford had been a cop car in its better days, and the irony of it didn't escape Jerry. In fact, the retired cruiser might have been his kindred spirit. The kid, Pablo, might have been fifteen, and he might have been twenty-three. It was difficult to tell sometimes with the baby-faced, sinewy Hispanics who lived in poverty and resembled the desperate and starving coyotes who roamed the Mexico deserts—the four-legged ones, not the chrome-plated pistol-carrying predators who made their fortunes trafficking humans.

The window rolled down as Jerry approached, and he bent down to speak to the kid behind the wheel, see if he was to ride up front with him or sit in the back like he was in a cab or an Uber. He did it with gestures and simple words, pointing at the front seat. "*Aquí?*" he asked. Then he turned his eyes to the empty back seat. "*O allí?*"

Pablo replied in English. "Wherever you want."

Jerry got in the front passenger seat and offered his hand. "Jerry Townsend."

They shook. "Pablo Quintana. Call me Pablo or Q."

"Okay, Pablo. It's good to meet you, my friend, and thank you for helping me out."

"My *prima* said take good care of you, that you are a good American."

"That's debatable."

"She likes you," he said, pulling away from the curb and glancing from Jerry to the bumpy, half-paved road they traveled. "Where am I taking you, my frien'?"

Jerry told him the name of Dr. Fleming's medical office and said it was next to the pharmacy across from the plaza, up near the border. Pablo nodded, said he knew the place, and said, "Is where the *señoritas* go for the *tetas grandes*," momentarily taking his hands off the wheel and cupping them far from his chest to make his point.

"*Las tetas grandes son muy buenas*," Jerry said, a smile spread across his face, and a pain shot through his jaw, reminding him of the beating he had received just a few hours before.

Pablo returned the smile. "I wait for you while you do your business, then bring you back or take you wherever you need to go."

Jerry gently moved his jaw from side to side and wondered if anything was broken. Probably not, he concluded, though he could wiggle a couple of his teeth with his tongue. At least none had been knocked out. He knew from experience that the teeth would tighten up over time. "Listen, Pablo, I was robbed and beaten a few hours ago. I have no money. But I will pay you when I do, which will be soon enough. Okay?"

"Is no problem, *señor*."

They rode along in silence for a while, bumping along the roads and ignoring the sounds of horns, which were constant. Finally, Jerry asked, "So, Pablo, where did you get this nice car?"

Pablo smiled again. "Is not so nice, but was cheap. I think it comes from America. Was a *policía*, no?"

Jerry nodded. "I think so, yes."

Pablo said, "There is a *pistola* under the back seat. You have to lift it up to get it—lift the bottom part." He shrugged. "I don't know anything about it because I'm afraid of guns, so I left it there. Lucinda said you are *policía*?"

Jerry frowned. How would Lucinda have known he had been a cop? Sometimes Tijuana felt like a small town in the south, where everyone knew everyone else's business. "Long time ago, my friend. The gun, it was there when you bought the car?"

"*Sí.* I found it when I took the back seat out to run wires from the radio to speakers in the back."

"Where did you get the car?"

"From the *subasta*," he said, nodding in the direction they were traveling, "on *Revolución*. Was eight thousand, but I make payments."

"*Pesos*," Jerry confirmed.

"*Sí, los pesos*."

Jerry figured it to be around five hundred dollars for the car and silently questioned whether it was worth it. It depended on what type of *pistola* was beneath the back seat, he reasoned. And then he contemplated the firearm, something that would put him in the *cárcel* here in Mexico, likely without a trial or any recognizable system of justice. But he also considered that arming himself could be a necessary risk, depending on how things played out over the next few hours or days. The fact was, having a piece handy might be his only chance of survival.

He watched the decrepit buildings pass by and noticed the children playing on the sidewalks and on the streets, the youngsters in shorts and T-shirts in the heat of the day, their faces as dirty as their feet. Women watched from the shade of buildings, lingering in doorways, wary of passersby. There were no men to be seen, and Jerry wondered if they were working or inside having their *siestas.* Or maybe some were lounging at their preferred watering holes, maybe the *Caballo Loco* where the *señoritas* with their *tetas grandes* slinked around on elevated stages in pumps and gogos and not much more—or nothing else at all. He thought of Angel and then of Mina. He saw Angel nearly naked in the VIP room with him and Josie, and then he saw Mina completely naked—in VIP rooms, on stages, in her private room above the club…

When they were only a few blocks from the medical office, Jerry said, "Pablo, do me a favor, *por favor*… Pull into an alley over there, or find me an empty parking lot."

Pablo grinned. *"El baño?"*

He shook his head. "I want to see that *pistola*, Pablo. I might need it depending on how things go here."

"Yes, Mister Jerry, is no problem."

Pablo jerked the wheel to the right, and they bounced into a dirt alley littered with junk and debris on both sides, a narrow path just wide enough for a car to pass through the center. He drove about halfway into the alley and stopped, and a cloud of dust washed over them. Jerry stepped out onto piles of cardboard and an old rug, flies rising from the stench and swarming around him. He opened the back door and lifted the seat cushion to find a Glock wrapped in a blue shop rag. The chamber was empty, but the magazine was full of 9mm hollow points. He wiped the parts of the gun he had handled, returned it to its original place beneath the seat, pushed the cushion back, and carefully stepped through the debris to reenter Pablo's car.

Inside, Jerry said, "Not a bad piece."

Pablo looked at him but didn't respond.

Jerry nodded, signaling for him to drive on. "Let's get out of here."

They turned out of the alley and circled back to resume the route they had been traveling, Jerry quietly contemplating the pistol beneath the back seat. He thought about Campo and his goons, and he thought about the kids who had jumped him, and he began embracing the idea of packing heat even though it came with significant risk.

They arrived at the clinic, and Jerry pointed to the far side of the parking lot where fewer cars meant less congestion in this overpopulated city. "Somewhere over there."

Pablo pulled into a space with room on both sides. He parked and turned in his seat to look at Jerry. "I wait here?"

Jerry nodded. "If you don't mind. I shouldn't be long." He popped his door open and stepped out, hearing Pablo behind him now asking if he wanted the gun and if he needed to take it with him. He told the kid, "Not on this stop. Maybe the next one."

27

Dickie would say, What the hell are you thinking, partner? He'd say, Josie, no way I'm letting you go back across—did you listen to your captain this morning? He'd say, Are you trying to get us both fired?

He wouldn't be wrong.

But how could she tell Jerry she wasn't going to help him? Sorry, partner, you're on your own down there. Good luck.

Well, it was his own doing. That was something else Dickie would say to her if he had even an inkling about the actions she was considering. But he didn't, and she thought it might be best to keep him in the dark about it, at least for now. As far as she was concerned, Jerry—for all his flaws and shortcomings—was still a friend, a former partner, and a mentor. Josie didn't walk away from those relationships lightly, and unless something steered the Laura Townsend murder in another direction, one that focused on Jerry, she would remain loyal to him. She wasn't sure about bringing him the money. Doing so would cross a more definitive line than the gray one she had stepped over on her previous trip. Technically, at this point, that money could be considered evidence in the corruption case against the Majors Narcotics team that Jerry had supervised. Although they hadn't yet revealed to the captain or his fed buddies the existence of any such cache, primarily because they had yet to confirm that it did, in fact, exist. And Josie knew it was stolen money that needed to be turned in as evidence.

Unless it was the only way to get Jerry out of Mexico alive. Then she might have to consider another course of action, something one might consider to be an even darker gray area. She'd have to think about it when her partner wasn't ten feet away, staring at her expectantly.

Finally, he spoke. "That was Jerry."

Not a question.

She nodded.

"What now?"

She turned and looked out across the parking lot. Two more detectives were coming away from a dark sedan, one male, the other female. The male carried a poor-boy folder, likely the case file of their latest murder, and had a backpack over his shoulder. The woman carried a purse in one hand and a coffee in the other. Each was smiling as they chatted while heading toward her—toward the back door where she stood, actually—and for a moment, Josie longed for the days when she first came to the bureau. She remembered her elation at being selected to go to Homicide and the nervousness and excitement of being called out in the middle of the night to handle murder cases. She wondered if she and Dickie, the man assigned to train her at the bureau, had appeared as young and fresh as the pair of detectives crossing the lot with the carefree appearance of undergrads on their way to a pep rally. Maybe she had, but Dickie had never looked fresh in the years she knew him. He probably looked like a twenty-year veteran cop when he graduated from the academy sometime before cell phones and email, a time when police reports were written with Number 2 pencils by street cops and typewritten by detectives.

The pair passed by with casual greetings and went through the door that Dickie held open for them while waiting for Josie to respond.

"What now, *what*?"

"What's he asking you to do now? You wouldn't slip outside for a private conversation unless there was something you didn't want to share with the class."

"The class."

"Yeah," Dickie said, "me and Lopes, a couple of honor students."

She looked out over the parking lot again but saw in her peripheral vision that Dickie had stepped the rest of the way out and let the door close behind him. It clicked closed, and she heard him say, "There's no more Lone Ranger shit on this deal, partner. Whatever you're contemplating, we need to run it by the boss and get blessings from the feds. I'm too close to retirement to take a chance of losing everything for the likes of Jerry Townsend."

Josie turned to meet his gaze. The Windsor knot in his tie had been loosened and his collar unbuttoned. His shirt sleeves were turned up, and his fedora was set high on his head, exposing a robust forehead damp with perspiration. She thought about when she first arrived at Homicide, and Dickie had been none too happy about having her assigned as his trainee. Later, he admitted to her that he had been apprehensive about her background, citing a few rumors he had heard about her legacy: running over a bum in an alley was one; participating in a controversial beating caught on video, another. The former was a mishap, and the latter turned out to be a justified yet unsightly use of force. It hadn't taken long for her to win him over with her work ethic and keen investigative mind. Still, the experience taught her something that she had witnessed repeatedly over the ensuing years: Dickie's baseline was contempt and distrust. He started off hating everyone and waited for them to prove him wrong. She had asked him about it once over drinks, long after their partnership had developed into the close friendship they now enjoyed, and he had said, "I don't waste time getting to know people before I hate them."

She said to him now, the sounds of chatter spilling out of the office as Lopes popped out with a questioning look on his face, "Let's be honest, partner, you've hated Jerry from the start, and you're not going to change your opinion about him unless and until he is proven innocent of killing his wife."

"And taking dope money," he said.

Lopes said, "I hate to break up this little lovefest, kids, but who wants to go to Idaho? Skipper approved a trip for two."

Josie didn't hesitate. "You two go."

Dickie frowned. "Why?"

"Because you both know this Walker guy—it only makes sense. Besides," Josie started, thinking she needed to make sure this happened, that the two of them got out of town for a couple of days so she could figure out what to do about Jerry, "my mom's not been feeling well, and I shouldn't leave her alone right now."

Her partner gave her the *I-don't-believe-you* glare she'd seen on his face a hundred times. Usually, this untrusting look of his would be directed toward someone they were interviewing who seemed to have trouble with the truth. Or when the brass had an idea or agenda that differed from his own. But now those daggers were boring into Josie's stoic exterior, Dickie trying to read her thoughts and examine her conflicted heart.

On the one hand, she had known Jerry longer, and he had been a significant part of her professional life, guiding and mentoring her during her early years in the department. But on the other hand, Dickie was her partner, and he had been for many years now. They had been through a lot together, from tragic cases to deadly encounters and even the most terrifying time of her life, the days and nights she had spent captive on a mountain, alone, cold, badly injured, and, at times, hopeless. It had been Dickie who never gave up searching for her and, through his relentless determination, ultimately found her and saved her life. She owed him everything.

But her loyalty to Dickie notwithstanding, she couldn't just turn her back on Jerry.

Could she?

No, she didn't think she could. There was much to contemplate, and Dickie and Lopes being out of the picture for a few days would at least give her breathing room while she navigated this delicate situation. After all, it wasn't just friendships on the line this time—her career hung in the balance.

Josie, her serenity a pretense to mask her internal conflict, put her hand on Dickie's arm and held his gaze with reassuring eyes. "Seriously, you guys go. I'll stay here and follow some leads."

"You'll stay here," Dickie said.

She nodded. "Yeah."

He nodded along with her. "Here, as in north of the border."

"Of course," she said, knowing it might not be the truth.

28

THE DOCTOR WASN'T IN.

Jerry scanned his surroundings as he left Fleming's office and started across the congested parking lot to where his driver and car awaited him. He was accustomed to counter-surveillance and felt sure he hadn't been followed, but his meeting with Campo the other day and now a seaside beating by a gang of young thugs left him with a heightened sense of situational awareness. He didn't see anything that concerned him.

Pablo was leaning against the side of his car smoking a cigarette, the sun gleaming against his black-framed knockoff Ray-Bans that were too big for his narrow face. He looked like a kid who'd stolen his father's cigarettes and glasses and was trying to look cool while posing at the side of his faux cop car. Jerry saw him in a black suit and fedora, a Mexican remake of the Blues Brothers. *Hermanos del Blues*. Pablo would be Elwood, the skinny one, and it wouldn't be challenging to find a heavyset *hombre* who'd just gotten out of jail to play the role of Jake. He had the cop car and the shades; all he needed now was a fat partner with a mission. Although Jerry had one of his own, it wasn't a mission from God, and he certainly had no intention of putting the band back together.

"I may start calling you 'Elwood.'"

Pablo tilted his head in the universally recognized sign of question.

"Never mind," Jerry said. "Do you have anything planned for the rest of the day?"

He shook his head. Time seemed meaningless in TJ.

"Could you drive me down to Rosarito?"

"Of course, my frien'."

They loaded up, and Pablo navigated through the parking lot, avoiding wandering pedestrians and a rooster that seemed lost but determined as it strutted in the center of the narrow lane that led to the street. The scene reminded Jerry of East L.A. with its narrow roads that were overcrowded with cars, kids on bikes, and the occasional roaming chicken.

Jerry felt himself grinning at a memory of a wild chase that had taken him and other pursuing deputies through the same alley three times, the suspect inexplicably stuck on a loop around the block and through the alley. During the first pass, a chicken flew into the air with the dust and debris of the speeding car ahead of them, and Jerry's partner yelled for him to watch the chicken, as if Jerry, driving, was going to risk their lives by swerving to avoid hitting the resident yard bird while pursuing a felon. A rotund Hispanic woman with a broom entered the fray on the second pass. She had wrangled the chicken and had it clutched beneath one arm while swinging her broom with the other, first at the speeding miscreant ahead of them and then at Jerry's patrol car, too. Though Jerry couldn't hear her over the racing motor, the siren, and a squawking police radio— and by then, a helicopter whirring above them—he could see that the woman was yelling at them, her wrinkled face twisted into a mask of anger. When the suspect turned into the alley the third time, Jerry hoped the woman and her chicken would be gone, but now she was in the center of the alley, facing them down, still clutching her chicken and broom, determined. The suspect swerved to avoid her and ran his car through a pair of metal trash containers and into a fence, the front end of the compact foreign car folding like an accordion, steam shooting into the air. Jerry slammed on his brakes and instinctively swerved in the opposite direction to avoid running directly into the suspect's vehicle, resulting in them bearing down on the chicken woman. She jumped back, and her chicken flapped violently, trying to break out of her grasp. The woman fell backward, and her chicken flew straight into their windshield, bouncing off it with a thud and landing among the piles of trash that had spilled from the smashed containers. Chicken Lady had fallen against the fence on the other side and returned like a pro wrestler who had been hurled against the ropes. Her arms were outstretched as she ran to her fowl, shrieking, "*Mi pollo! Mi pollo!*" The chicken must have broken a wing because it was now running and trying to take flight but was stuck in a circular pattern and unable to gain altitude. At the same time, Jerry and his partner bailed out of their patrol car and ran toward the suspect's smashed-up car. The suspect crawled through the passenger side window and landed on the ground among the debris and not far from the wounded fowl. As he tried to get up, the irate woman began beating him with her broom, landing several solid blows to his head. The man wilted, and Jerry and his partner carefully approached him, not for fear of this fleeing felon but in all due caution of the furious woman.

As Pablo turned onto the street, Jerry, looking out his window at the people of Tijuana, poor people who might kill you for stealing or injuring their chicken, said, "*Mi pollo. Mi pollo.*"

Pablo looked at him questioningly.

Jerry shook his head. "Long story, my friend."

They snaked south through the city in the Blues Mobile and soon were picking up speed on the *Transpeninsular/México* 1, or what Jerry and other *gringos* might call Highway 1. Pablo explained that there was a scenic route that was more enjoyable, a winding highway that often hugged the cliffs along the coast and offered spectacular views of the Pacific Coast of Mexico and its rolling waves crashing onto crowded beaches. He referred to this bypass as the *autopista,* which Jerry knew meant a toll road. However, Pablo and some locals had avoided the scenic route since the landslide of 2013, triggered by a series of earthquakes resulting in 300 meters of highway falling a hundred meters into the ocean. Besides, he said, there were checkpoints and patrols along the way, so it would be best to take the longer, less scenic route and avoid any potential trouble.

The drive took less than a half hour, even with Pablo's meandering way of driving. As they drew nearer, Jerry took in the sights: the high-rise hotels overlooking the Pacific, endless rows of apartments and condos or perhaps timeshare rentals, and structures of nonconforming design, audaciously decorated in shades of turquoise, purple, yellow, red, and all the other colors you'd find in a box of Crayolas.

He pictured Dr. Fleming in one of the more subtle affairs, something unpretentious that blended with the natural landscape, a modest condo with a balcony that offered a view of the ocean, potted plants marking the corners. A nice bar inside, maybe leather sofas and glass tables. More plants. Jerry didn't know if Fleming lived alone when he stayed in town or had a Mexican girlfriend who stayed there too, taking care of the place when he was in L.A. and taking care of him when he was here. It was indeed a possibility. Maybe a former patient who was now perfectly proportioned. He wondered if a doctor who created aftermarket body parts for ladies had an appreciation for the natural look—Jerry certainly did.

As they entered the city, Pablo slowed and asked, "Where to?"

That was a good question. Jerry didn't know where in Rosarita Beach the doctor lived—or vacationed, as it were—but he knew two things and thought he could easily find him if they got close: The doc had mentioned the name of his street was *Mexicali*, and that it was a newer construction that had a community pool. These things came out in casual conversation, and Jerry still had a knack for storing details when they were presented. A sickness, even. He said to his young chauffeur, "Do you know where *Mexicali* Street is?"

Pablo glanced over and shook his head behind the dark shades. "No, but we can find it. I'll ask around."

"If you get me to *Mexicali* Street, Boulevard, or whatever it is—maybe *Calle Mexicali*—I think we can figure it out from there."

"Is no problem, my frien'."

They passed a McDonald's, and Jerry turned his head, looking back, thinking that would have been a good place to stop and ask someone for directions. Maybe get a milkshake or even a burger while you're at it. But he didn't say so, and shortly after, Pablo turned right into the parking lot of a taco stand where a small crowd of patrons gathered around tables and stood in one of two lines to order food at a small window. In Mexico, tacos were always on the menu, and Jerry could always have a couple, regardless of the time of day or night.

"You want a taco?"
Jerry nodded. "Are they good here? You know the place?"
"*Sí, muy bueno.*"
"*Muy bueno,*" Jerry agreed.

29

—————

The boys were catching an early flight to Boise the next day.
Rich Farris was set to pick them up and chauffeur them around—he told
them not to bother with a rental car, that he had nothing better to do than
hang out with a couple of his favorite white boys. He'd said—Josie heard
it for herself, Dickie and Lopes having a conversation with him on the
speakerphone a few hours ago—"It won't cost you anything but a steak
and however many beers it takes to wash it down." They'd probably grab
breakfast and catch up on the latest department happenings and rumors,
then reminisce about times past the way old partners do. Then they'd find
Brett Walker and try to get some answers about the Townsend case. Hopefully, he wouldn't be sitting in a treehouse smoking dope as Lopes insinu-
ated he might. Josie was pretty sure he had been joking about that, but you
never knew. It would be a delicate process to coax from this former detective information that should have been documented in the case without
making it clear that he and his partner Victor Robles screwed up a cop's
wife's murder case. When they finished with Walker, the boys would grab
a late lunch or early dinner, consume some adult beverages, and check into
their hotel for the night. When traveling for investigations, you always
allowed extra time—in this case, a second day—just in case something
else came up or, for whatever reason, they couldn't speak with Walker the

first day. They were scheduled to fly home the following afternoon. By then, Josie estimated, she would have figured out what to do with Jerry and the situation south of the border and resolved it one way or the other.

Jerry had said he'd call her back tonight, but he didn't say when. She had the key to his safe deposit box—he had slipped it to her before they parted ways at the border—but she had no idea where the box was located. Even though she was struggling still with the idea of taking him the money, she knew she'd at least need to get him the passport he said was there too, if he ever hoped to return to the States—or to flee to some other country, for that matter.

She thought a compromise might be in order. Tell him, Jerry, I can't bring you that money—you know that. But I can get you the passport so you can leave. He'd say he wasn't coming back, that he needed the money, and then he'd say something that would leave her feeling guilty and torn between two forces. But she couldn't allow him to persuade her to do something that could cost her her job—maybe her freedom.

Josie also thought about revealing to Jerry that Fur Face was an informant, but she wasn't sure how much good that would do him. Jerry was no longer a cop, and she had to be careful about how much she told him. After all, at this point, he was still technically a suspect in his wife's murder. And at the very least, he was sitting on money he had no business having. A lot can happen in ten years, and although she felt she still knew Jerry and that she could trust him, she knew deep down that she had to remain cautious.

Josie sat in bumper-to-bumper traffic on the Hollywood Freeway, the guttural purr of her Charger and the whirring of its air conditioner the only sounds in her car. Her meditations effectively muted the sounds of the city around her, the occasional angry blasts of a horn, the rumble of after-market exhaust systems designed to be loud and throaty, and the tinny whine of Japanese crotch rockets while their leather-clad riders gunned their throttles while splitting traffic, an often-ineffective manner of alerting daydreaming drivers of their presence. She was on her way to the courthouse where Justin McKnight would be waiting out front, having taken her up on the offer of an afternoon cocktail. McKnight, the charming and handsome prosecutor she'd been dating for a year but still didn't consider her boyfriend, had just wrapped up a trial and awaited the jury's verdict. There was no way they'd be back this afternoon, he had said, but just in case, they should go somewhere that wasn't far away. Perfect, Josie had said, seeing the pirate-themed interior of the Redwood not far from the courthouse. It was a dark and dingy bar that she had come to enjoy, where few from her department would ever be found. LAPD, yes—they were there occasionally—mostly the downtown crowd, detectives and some administrators. There were usually some city workers too, a smattering of lawyers—defense attorneys and prosecutors alike—and the occasional hipster. But it wasn't a cop bar, per se, so Josie felt anonymous there, just another downtown worker with a thirst.

She hadn't decided how much to tell McKnight about the Jerry Townsend situation. He'd been out of the loop the last couple of weeks, immersed in his murder trial that was now in the hands of the jury. Like Josie, McKnight poured himself into his work—which might be one of the reasons their relationship had lasted much longer than Josie's average fling —and during the times he was in trial, she barely spoke to him. He'd be in court all day and going over evidence and testimony late into each evening while preparing for the next day and the next witness. So Josie hadn't told him a thing about Townsend or her trip to Mexico, and she didn't think now was the time to burden him with her dilemma. Like Dickie, he would be skeptical about Jerry and his story, and he would certainly advise against going back to Mexico. Maybe she'd just mention the case they were working on—of course, he'd likely ask at some point—in generic terms: a former cop's wife was murdered, and the case was never solved, so they're looking into it. It's what they did in Unsolveds, so there wouldn't be much question about it from her lawyer friend.

At the Redwood, they slid into a booth with a heavy, dark wood table, red vinyl-covered seats, and a glowing candle that sat between them, the reflection of its small flickering flame dancing in McKnight's dark eyes, an instrumental jazz number playing low in the background. A waitress took their orders, a twenty-something dark-haired woman with tattoos and piercings—saying, "Yeah, sure, uh-huh," never "thank you"—and Josie waited until she walked away to continue the conversation they had had from the drive over and their short walk from the paid parking lot around the corner to the bar. She answered the question she had hoped he wouldn't ask, but dating a prosecutor was like marrying a cop: every conversation has tones of interrogation, no matter how unintentional. "Yeah, I did know him on the job. I met him when I was working patrol in East L.A., and he's the one who got me to Gangs and became somewhat of a mentor to me."

He held her gaze a long moment. "Was he a suspect in his wife's murder?"

Josie's eyes flicked toward the bar, her thirst suddenly unbearable. The waitress was looking at her phone while the bartender scooped ice and turned bottles upside down over two highball glasses, presumably mixing her Tito's and cranberry and McKnight's scotch and soda. Josie used the manufactured moment to consider her answer. "There was widespread speculation, but you know cops; everyone's guilty until proven innocent."

McKnight grinned, but his eyes bore into her, searching for the truth. The drinks arrived, and they clicked their glasses and took their time with the first sips of the afternoon. Josie was thinking, Here comes the direct examination, while McKnight was likely trying to figure out how to get more information from her about this former mentor without being too lawyerly about it.

"What do you think?"

She shrugged as if she had no stake in the matter. "I don't think there's anything to it. Jerry was a good cop and a great guy."

He nodded. "O.J. was a great guy, too, as far as anyone knew. So was Robert Blake and Phil Spector."

"Spector was a freak."

McKnight shrugged. "You get the point."

Josie took another sip, set her glass down but kept hold of it. "Jerry Townsend didn't kill his wife."

He now took a sip of his cocktail and rattled the ice around before setting it on the table. "I believe you."

Josie didn't think he did. The counselor was smart enough not to treat this witness as a hostile one—not if he ever hoped to hold her in his arms again. But it was a great segue to a new conversation. "How do you feel about your case? Will they find him guilty?"

McKnight drew a breath. "I think we have a good chance, but I'm a little concerned because the foreman, Juror Number Three, is a retired schoolteacher who seems to have a chip on his shoulder toward cops."

"Why do you say that?"

"Just his mannerisms whenever a cop was on the stand. He seemed to have some inherent mistrust of them, from the patrol cop who found the body to the lead detective."

"Maybe one of those guys who got a ticket once, and the cop had an attitude. I swear traffic cops can be our worst enemies sometimes, pissing off our future jurors."

"This one, he seems to be the type who has to be the smartest person in the room. Know what I mean?"

She nodded, seeing the unidentified retired schoolteacher as a bald white man with eyeglasses and a sweater over a button-up plaid shirt, a double chin when he drops his head to glare over his specs at witnesses on the stand or the attorney asking questions. Or maybe he was a tall, thin black man in a jogging suit, the former schoolteacher also the basketball coach whose life experiences made him wary of the police. Or a radical Hispanic who taught civics in East L.A. but also partook in the Chicano movement of the seventies, marching alongside Ruben Salazar up until the moment he was struck in the head and killed by a tear gas canister as he sat sipping a beer in the Silver Dollar Saloon and the protests outside escalated into riots.

"The kind of foreman who might overanalyze and overthink the evidence and push his agenda onto the others."

She lifted her glass, not quite a toast but a silent agreement. "You never know about a jury, do you?"

"You don't," he agreed. "But sometimes you have a feeling. Where's your partner today?"

"He and Lopes are flying to Boise tomorrow to do some follow-up on the case—"

"This Townsend murder?"

She nodded. "Yeah, they're going to interview one of the two primary detectives who investigated it. The other is dead—well, you know of him, Victor Robles."

"Ah," he said, his eyes and a smirk betraying his thoughts, "so you think maybe the case wasn't handled so well."

McKnight knew well how badly Robles and another partner screwed up the murder of a city councilman, their work locking up the wrong man for two decades.

"Let's just say there are some holes in the case."

The tattooed waitress appeared and eyeballed their glasses. McKnight held up two fingers and said, "Might as well bring us another round." Then to Josie: "Where's Townsend now? He still around?"

She dropped her eyes to focus on stirring her drink, which was no more than half-finished. She said, "Mexico," and raised the glass to her lips and took a long pull on its contents. How did they end up back on Townsend after she had successfully steered him away from it?

He said, "Uh-huh, and what are you not telling me?"

She finished her cocktail and moved the glass toward the edge of their table, looking forward to another round. "What do you mean?"

"You know what I mean. There's more to all this than you're letting on."

"He was just a friend, Justin."

"When was the last time you saw him? Have you seen him or talked to him since his wife was killed?"

Fresh drinks arrived and not a moment too soon. Josie reached for hers and brought it to her mouth but stopped and held it there as she studied McKnight over the rim of it. There had never been any signs of jealousy since they'd been dating, but there seemed to be a hint of it now. She took a sip of her fresh cocktail, and he had a gulp of his. She reached for his hand across the table. "What's bothering you?"

McKnight glanced toward the bar while he seemed to consider his response. Josie pulled her hand back and waited. After a moment, he leaned back against the cushioned seat and met her gaze. Josie wondered what he was thinking or what he knew—what was he about to say? He'd been busy with court. They hadn't seen each other for weeks nor had they spoken much either. A few texts each day, and that was about it. Maybe that was all there was to this; Justin McKnight needed some Josie time.

Before he answered, she said, "Hey, counselor… How about we celebrate your victory tonight after that verdict comes back."

A nearly imperceptible smile cracked his face, and his eyes softened. "What if there's nothing to celebrate?"

"When's the last time you lost a trial?"

"What if it doesn't come back for days, say until next week?"

"Why are you arguing, counselor? I'm asking you to dinner. Are you interested?"

His smile spread across his face. "Dinner sounds lovely."

They finished their drinks, and Josie drove McKnight back to the courthouse on Temple. He leaned in for a kiss, and after a moment, she pushed him away. "Get your tongue out of my mouth, McKnight... I'm kissing you goodbye."

He smiled and said, "I'll text you when the verdict's in," and then he was gone.

Josie merged onto Temple and gunned it to get ahead of a lumbering bus spewing black smoke and to position herself for a left turn on Los Angeles Street. A moment later, she was on the Hollywood Freeway headed south in typical L.A. stop-and-go traffic. Her phone rang, the caller ID showing +52 preceding a string of numbers. It was a call from Mexico.

She pushed a button on her steering wheel and said, "Hi, Jerry."

His tone was dark, subdued. "She's gone."

30

WHO WAS GONE?

The angel? Mina? And by gone, did he mean missing or dead? Or was Jerry lamenting about the loss of his wife as if the reality of her death had just now struck him during a drunken afternoon in Mexico surrounded by his Latina friends? Josie didn't think so; he didn't sound drunk. His voice was melancholy, but his words weren't sloppy or slurred.

"Who's gone, Jerry?"

While awaiting his response, letting him take his time, Josie listened to the background noises for a hint of where he might be and whom he might be with. There were sounds of papers being shuffled and the scrape of a chair—now a muted voice, the murmurs of a younger man, maybe an adolescent.

"Mina," he finally managed.

"Where are you, Jerry? And who are you with?"

"I'm with my friend Pablo. He's been helping me out, driving me around. We're down at Fleming's apartment in Rosarita Beach."

"Is he there?"

"Doctor Fleming?"

"Yes."

"Yeah, he's here."

"So what happened to Mina?"

"She's dead."

She waited in the ensuing silence, considering the possibilities: Mina was murdered; she overdosed on pills and booze; it was a case of suicide…

He said, "I'll call you back in a bit."

PABLO HAD EXCUSED HIMSELF AND WAS SITTING ON THE PATIO SMOKING A cigarette while Jerry and Dr. Fleming sat at the breakfast bar inside, each of them sipping from bottles of water as they discussed the particulars about Mina. Fleming told Jerry, "The other night, I went by the *Caballo*. One of the goons came and got me and took me to Campo's office. He questioned me about my relationship with Mina. I told them she was a friend and also a former patient."

"Campo already knew that."

Fleming nodded. "That's what I believe as well, so it seemed a bit contrived, honestly. Then they asked about you, how close we were, what did I know about your wife being killed, if I knew about the money—"

"They asked you about the money?"

"Just if you'd ever told me about it, which of course, you hadn't. That's all I told them."

Jerry stroked his beard as he thought about this, finding it interesting that Campo was homed in on the money part of what they had told him the night the man had entertained him and Josie.

Fleming said, "And they asked if I knew the woman cop you were there with the other night, which of course, I didn't."

"Who all was in the room?" Jerry wanted to know.

Fleming shrugged and shook his head, and he seemed to see the scene again in his mind as he gazed up at the ceiling. "It was Campo and his bodyguard, the buff guy who's always with him—I think they call him Carlos—and the big dude who came to me at the bar and asked me to go with him to see Campo. He stayed the whole time and then saw me out after."

"Just one guy, or were there two?"

"Who came and got me from the bar?"

Jerry nodded.

"Just the one."

Jerry was picturing the two goons Josie had referred to as Fur Face and Baby Face, certain that one of the two was who Fleming described. He said, "The clean-shaven guy or the dude with the scraggly beard?"

"The clean-shaven one," Fleming said. "I know who you're talking about, though, the ugly man with his hairy face. Yes, the two of them are usually together, but I didn't see him that night."

"But Campo didn't say anything else about Mina, that he had seen her, or talked to her, or anything?"

He shook his head. "No, he didn't say much about her at all. Just that she was no longer an employee there."

Jerry looked through the sliding glass door and across the patio where Pablo sat smoking. Beyond him, a hazy sky hung above Rosarita Beach, and an afternoon breeze blew in from the ocean. The fronds of a dozen palm trees fluttered softly like the wings of giant seagulls drifting above the sea. He wondered why Campo would question Fleming's relationships with him and Mina and even Josie, and he wondered if Campo knew that Mina was dead.

Jerry told Fleming about being jumped by the young men, losing his wallet and cell, and even the burner that Campo had provided him.

Fleming said, "Why would he give you a burner?"

"Because he wants the money, obviously."

"Then he probably didn't have anything to do with you being mugged."

Jerry shook his head. "I don't think so. But I need to go see him."

"What are your thoughts on Mina?" the doctor asked, a nod in the direction of the guest room. "Was she murdered?"

They had only peeked in on the scene—his guest room where Mina was found dead on the bed—and Jerry had closed the door and walked away in disbelief. Fleming tried to console him, and then they had come out to the dining area where they'd been trying to make sense of her death and trying to decide what to do about it.

"If they killed her," Jerry said, "they did it because I said too much, told them I thought she might be able to shed light on my wife's murder."

"You think all of this is related to your wife's death?"

Jerry nodded. "I think so. I need to go see him," he said again, but this time he was picturing the Glock beneath Pablo's back seat as he said it.

"*Ten cuidado*, my friend. He's a very dangerous man."

"I'll be careful. But before anything else, we need to figure out what to do about her," Jerry said, his gaze drifting toward the guest room door across the living room. He took a deep breath. "I need to go back in there and take a better look."

Fleming pushed off his stool with his bottle of water in hand. "I'm going to pour a drink. Would you like one?"

"Not yet," Jerry said. "Soon."

31

Josie gathered her purse and a few files she was working on and stood behind her desk, contemplating the call she needed to make before she joined McKnight for a celebratory dinner and drinks at Bottega Louie's downtown. She'd already decided on which fed she would call—Williams, the black one—but she dreaded the idea of speaking to either of them, truthfully. Especially given the topic she intended to address, a highly unlikely request for her and her partners to be able to contact their informant, Fur Face, directly. Cops were very territorial when it came to informants and food spots, and she expected some pushback from any such request. But she and Lopes had flipped a coin—a challenge coin with the sheriff's star on one side (heads) and the bureau's bulldog mascot on the other (tails)—and Josie had lost the toss.

Lopes and Dickie had left the office, and she wouldn't see them for a couple more days if all went well. They were headed to Idaho, and Josie was manning the phones, so to speak. And she had promised Dickie she wouldn't be going south in his absence. She intended to keep that promise, but she knew Jerry was going to be pulling her in another direction when he called back to give her the details of Mina's death. Hopefully, he wouldn't call during dinner—that was all she needed after her awkward conversation with McKnight about Jerry and the case she was working on.

She remembered that Lopes had the business cards of the two feds on his desk, so she took a seat in his chair, picked up his desk phone, and dialed Williams's office number. She rocked back and forth in Lopes's chair waiting for her call to be answered. After four rings, the call went to voicemail, and Williams's voice announced that he was on the other line or out of the office and to leave a message and he would get back to you. Josie left a brief message and her cell phone number and hung up. The framed angel remained at the side of Lopes's desk, and Josie stared at it for a moment before turning it so that she could see the painting again. As she studied it, she was more convinced than before that their angel had been the model for this heavenly masterpiece. It made her sick to think about it, and she hoped that nothing had happened to the angel after they had left the club in Tijuana that night.

Josie thought about taking the painting into the captain's office and hanging it on his wall. She smiled at the idea of it, but instead of going through with the prank, she returned the painting to the side of Lopes's desk facing inward so passersby wouldn't notice it. Someone would surely find it to be offensive in today's department climate, and they'd file a complaint.

She gathered her things and left.

ALL THROUGH DINNER AND DESSERT AND COCKTAILS AFTERWARD, JOSIE had anticipated receiving a call. She wasn't surprised that Williams hadn't called her back since she'd left the message on his office phone. She could've called his cell—the number was right there on his business card beneath the office number—but she hadn't really cared to speak with him anyway. Leaving the message was the first step in doing as she had been tasked to do after losing the coin toss to Lopes, and now she could say that she had tried. If she never heard back from him, it would be okay with her. She personally believed it was a waste of time asking a fed to put her in direct contact with their informant.

The fact that Jerry hadn't called was something that weighed heavily on her mind as she held the gaze of the lawyer across from her, McKnight full of himself as he recounted the parts of the trial and his guilty verdict.

Josie may have been there physically, but her mind was somewhere other than Bottega Louie's—in fact, it was currently somewhere far south of it. She knew Jerry would be reeling with guilt, certain that their botched meeting with Mina must have factored into her death, and he would undoubtedly be blaming himself. She wondered how much he had learned about Mina's passing, and she pondered his next set of actions given the turn of events. Hopefully, he would remain levelheaded and not do anything stupid. But that was a lot to hope for at this point.

"You're still distracted."

She blinked. "No, not at all, babe," she said, giving him a nice smile.

McKnight didn't buy it. He signaled for the waiter and asked for the check when he arrived at their table.

"I guess we're finished," Josie said, the smile no longer there.

He was fishing in his wallet for a credit card, saying to Josie, "I know you have a lot going on…" as the waiter returned with the check.

Josie beat him to the punch, handing the waiter a card of her own. "I've got dinner."

He looked at her while putting his wallet away. "You don't have to do that."

She smiled at him. "I know, but I want to."

"Thank you."

"You're welcome. I'm sorry I wasn't better company. I guess there's just a lot going on in my head right now."

"Townsend," he guessed.

She nodded, her eyes fixed on the glass of ice water she cupped in her hand. "Jerry found out today his informant is dead."

"Murdered?"

She shrugged. "I don't have any details yet, and I guess that's why my thoughts are all over the place. I have a bad feeling about it, and I hope Jerry doesn't do anything stupid down there."

The waiter returned with Josie's card and the bill with her receipt. She did her usual quick math for the tip: ten percent of the total, times it by two, and then round it up to the nearest dollar or nice round number. The only time she varied from this method was when the service or food was lousy, and then she'd just forego the times two part of it—ten percent sent a message that it wasn't great, whereas no tip meant you were a cheapskate. They walked out of Bottega Louie's hand in hand and waited at the corner of 7th Street and Grand Avenue for the light. Traffic was heavy in the Financial District with its Restaurant Row, the sounds of motors and squeaky brakes, and the occasional toot of a horn as motorists jockeyed to get somewhere else now that the workday was behind them. Men and women in business attire crowded the sidewalks, many of whom would wait out traffic in one of the many downtown restaurants or cocktail lounges—let the happy hour begin! Josie was glad they had made it an early dinner and mostly avoided the crush of thirsty Angelenos.

The late afternoon sun reflected off a towering glass building that sat kitty-corner from where they stood outside of Bottega Louie's, beyond the Chipotle and the Karl Strauss Brewing Company. McKnight shielded his eyes from the glare, looking in that direction, and said, "You want to get a beer before we go? Strauss has an incredible selection of craft beers: IPAs, lagers, ales… What do you think? Wanna have a brew or two and let traffic die down?"

No, she didn't. Josie knew the popular pub would be brimming with the happy hour crowd, and she wasn't in the mood to deal with it. She was expecting that call at any moment with more information about Mina's death and hopefully an idea of what Jerry planned to do next. Josie worried about how Jerry was handling the death. He obviously cared for Mina, and he also felt she had information about his wife's murder. Now she was gone, and Josie couldn't help but think it was their fault that she was.

She didn't want to use the worn-out excuse of having a headache, but the sensation of tiny needles pricking her brain couldn't be ignored. A doctor had told her these occasional headaches she suffered were likely related to the stress in her life. "What stress?" she had said rhetorically while the man in the white coat scrawled a nearly illegible prescription for Rizatriptan. Though the headaches now came with increasing regularity, she hadn't experienced the debilitating, migraine-like pain that she had had the day before that appointment and hadn't yet taken the prescribed pain reliever. Usually, a hot bath and glass of wine would work well enough, and Josie saw the home remedy in her immediate future.

"I'll have to pass on the beer, Justin," she said. "I've got a headache coming on, and I'd rather get home before it takes me down."

He turned his head to meet her gaze in a silent cross-examination. Josie forced a tight smile. "I'm sorry."

"Hey, no worries," he said, turning and taking her hand again, leading the way across the street now that the signal had changed. "The truth is, I'm beat anyway—it's been a long couple of weeks."

They continued down Grand to the LAZ parking structure where each had left their cars, bounded up the steps to the third floor, and walked together to Josie's county car. They turned to face each other, and Josie stepped into him and put her head on his chest. She could feel his warmth and hear his heart beating while the structure moved under their feet as a stream of cars corkscrewed its way toward the street-level exit, tires squealing against the concrete. Josie said she'd call him tomorrow, and they parted ways with a light kiss and strained smiles.

Josie started her car and then checked her silenced phone for missed calls or text messages she might have received. There were several text messages, some from friends, one from her partner, Dickie, and two from her mother asking that she stop on her way home to pick up some groceries: tortillas, *queso*, and some peppers, adding in the next text a package of Double Stuf vanilla Oreos. How the woman didn't have diabetes Josie would never know. Dickie's text was short and sweet: *See ya in a couple days, partner*. And a blue heart emoji. A series of dressing room selfies from a girlfriend who needed fashion advice, and several follow-up texts emphasizing the urgency of Josie's counsel, the last being, Bitch why are you ignoring me? But nothing from Jerry. No texts, no missed calls. Not from the barmaid's phone—which Josie had programmed into her contacts as "Jerry's Hoochie Friend," just in case she would end up needing to find him—and no random foreign numbers that could be Mexico burners.

Josie motored out of the parking structure and crept through downtown traffic toward the freeway, continuing to glance at her phone, willing it to ring. She needed to know what happened. Had Mina been murdered, run over by a Tijuana taxi, or had she taken a handful of sleeping pills or Valium and washed them down with a fifth of tequila? Anything was possible, Josie knew, but she had a feeling that Mina's manner of death was not a fortuitous event.

She had just pulled into the market parking lot to pick up the things her mother needed for dinner and dessert when her phone came to life from an incoming call, the caller ID "Unknown." Josie drew in a breath and pushed the button to answer.

"Detective Sanchez, this is Special Agent Williams."

"Sergeant Sanchez," she corrected.

"Yes, Sergeant, of course… I got your message, and I'm glad you called. I needed to speak with you as well. Are you still at your office by chance?"

Josie glanced at the clock on her dash. "No, I'm not. Can it wait until tomorrow?"

"I'm afraid not."

Thoughts of Jerry flashed with images of worst-case scenarios: Jerry locked up in Mexico, his clothing sullied by blood, mud, and beer; Jerry dead in Tijuana, two gunshot wounds to his head—a neat hole in the crown with a sticky black circle against matted gray hair, and a bloody gaping cavern where his mouth and nose had been until the expanding hollow point bullet tore through his flesh—and a cop with a pistol in his hand and extra cash in his pocket standing over the expatriate's contorted body; Jerry in the back of a fed's car, stainless steel bracelets digging crevices into his wrists.

Williams wasn't calling her to deliver good news—of that she was certain.

"I can be back to my office in half an hour."

"We'll see you there," he said.

She hung up and drove out of the parking lot and onto the freeway, reversing her previous direction in order to head back to the office. Assuming that "we" meant Williams was bringing his partner with him, Josie considered calling Dickie for reinforcements. She didn't know what the urgency of this meeting with Williams might be, but clearly, there was some degree of importance, and she didn't have a good feeling about it.

Josie cued Siri to call Dickie, and a moment later, she heard half a ring before his voicemail picked up. She frowned and pushed the button to disconnect the call. Like Jerry, she was on her own now. At least this time she was on American soil.

32

COPS ARE VERSED IN DEATH. NO MATTER THE JURISDICTION, COPS ARE routinely sent to deal with the remains of the deceased, whether they are found at a crime scene, at the scene of a traffic collision, in the bedroom of someone who had lived a full life, or in the crib of another who never had the chance.

In major metropolitan areas, cops see death more regularly as countless men, women, and children die prematurely and unexpectedly at the hands of others in acts of violence: shootings, stabbings, beatings, strangulations, and even drownings. In most of those cases, it didn't take a highly skilled homicide detective, a team of forensic specialists, and a medical examiner to determine the manner of death. Though to bring a killer to justice, it is exactly such a team effort that is required. When a gangster lies on the street leaking from multiple gunshot wounds, it is no mystery how (and in most cases, why) he was killed. The only real question was, who did it, or, as some cops might say, whodunnit. Same for those found slashed or hacked or choked to death and dumped in alleys. And when an old person is found in their bed, lifeless and at peace, a homicide detective is seldom even summoned. But when it comes to the young and healthy who die without violence, an experienced homicide detective and a competent coroner are essential in determining the manner and mode of death.

Jerry had known of cases that turned out differently than how they appeared to the untrained eye. A man had been hanged, and it appeared to the patrol deputies who had been dispatched to the scene to be a case of murder. Jerry had gone by, as had others, while the handling crew awaited the arrival of Homicide. There was some speculation about the possibility of it being a suicide, but most agreed it had to be a murder. After all, the man's hands were bound together by a length of rope. The detectives arrived and, after only a few moments, boldly stated that it was a suicide. One detective explained to the confounded cops at the scene that the way the hands were tied together was a commonly used method of tying oneself. He'd seen it used in other cases of suicide, once by a man who tied himself to a chair and secured a plastic bag over his head. If it hadn't been for the suicide note and a secure residence, the detective would have sworn it was a homicide. He went on to explain that if someone else had hanged the man, they likely would have secured his hands behind his back rather than in front of him. He also pointed out that the noose was at the side of the man's head, not behind it, which was common in cases of suicide.

Jerry recalled another case where a man was found dead in his garage with a single gunshot to his head. The gun was nowhere to be found by the investigating deputies, and they were certain that a murder had occurred. When a detective arrived, he studied the body and the wound, then seemed to ponder the scene for a while, his squinty gaze roaming the room until he focused on the rafters above the decedent. He then retrieved a ladder from the back of the garage, climbed up its steps, and said, "Got it." The gun was attached to a bungee so that it was retracted into the attic once it was released from the dead man's hand. In response to the accolades of those watching, he simply said, "Must've wanted the wife to get an insurance check," a reference to the suicide clauses in most life insurance policies. Jerry realized then that some detectives possessed an uncanny ability to reconstruct a crime scene. Whether it was instinctive or learned—or a little of each—it was amazing at times how clever some detectives could be.

He needed Josie and her partner to see this scene. Jerry thought about asking Fleming for the use of his cell phone and taking pictures to send her. He could show how Mina appeared comfortable on the bed, lying on top of the comforter and resting against a mountain of pillows, dressed in shorts and a light blue T-shirt with a graphic showing a shark wearing a Hawaiian shirt and sunglasses, holding a surfboard, *Cozumel* printed above the design. A dark red ring encircled a small, perfect hole that had torn through the shark's teeth and into the center of Mina's chest. A rifle lay on the bed next to her, parallel to her body, the muzzle beneath her splayed right arm, the butt of the gun below her knees. The question was, of course, had it been a case of suicide, or was it a cleverly disguised homicide?

Fleming, sitting at the dining room table drinking bourbon from a glass that held a large spherical ice cube, called out from behind Jerry, who remained on the threshold of Mina's room. "You ready for that drink?"

Jerry didn't answer right away as he continued to stare at the young woman on the bed, someone he had considered a friend and occasional lover. Someone he cared for deeply and felt sorry for at the same time, which, during times of reflection, he felt was patronizing and shallow of him. His deliberations now, however, had little to do with past feelings of love or pity; he could only dwell on purpose and fault. He had little doubt that this young Mexican woman was dead because of him, but had she taken her own life, or had she been murdered due to their association? Either way, he had no way to place the blame anywhere but at his own feet, and he knew this would be his burden to carry, just as he carried the weight of Laura's murder.

Finally, he retreated. "Yeah, I would love a drink. And pour it strong."

"Bourbon okay? I stock a nice supply of it here because a guy can only drink so much tequila."

"Anything's fine."

Fleming left his drink on the table and went into the kitchen. He took a glass from the cupboard and poured a drink, then poured a little more. He looked over at Jerry expectantly, and Jerry nodded.

"Ice?"

"Yeah, sure."

He brought the drink over, and the two of them settled at the table. Fleming said, "Four Roses, nothing fancy. It's a reasonably priced bourbon that's pretty nice to sip with an ice cube or a dash of water.

Really good in an old-fashioned or manhattan if you'd like me to mix a drink."

Jerry shook his head. "This will be fine." He didn't bother to toast as he took one sip and then another before setting down his glass.

"Is it a suicide?"

His eyes were fixed on the drink that remained in his grasp. "I don't know," Jerry said, then he took another drink. "I'm torn."

"Where did your friend go?"

"Pablo? I assume he's waiting in his car. I guess I should check on him."

"I'll do it if you would like. I need to get some air."

As Fleming pushed out of his chair, Jerry said, "Can I use your phone? I lost mine earlier."

"You were robbed," Fleming said, "that's different than losing something." He raised a finger to his own eye and said, "It's swollen and starting to darken. Gonna be a purple shiner."

Jerry felt the bump rising at the side of his eye socket. "Isn't my first, and it probably won't be my last."

Fleming took a phone from his pocket and slid it across the table. "Do you need anything else? I can give you some cash to help you get by."

"I appreciate it, *amigo*. I could use a few bucks probably."

Fleming took a money clip from his pocket and peeled off three twenties. "How's that? Or do you need more?"

"Perfect," Jerry said, knowing sixty bucks would go a long way in Mexico. It was plenty to get him through the next day or so, which was as far in the future as he cared to consider. For that matter, he might not need to worry about tomorrow, given the thoughts he now entertained about the rest of his day.

Fleming left, and Jerry took three more pulls from his bourbon while contemplating how he'd broach the topic of Mina's death with Josie. He had already asked too much of her, but there was a dead woman in the other room, and he certainly didn't trust the local cops to get to the bottom of it. They wouldn't likely possess the skills to determine whether Mina had shot herself or was the victim of a homicide, and they probably wouldn't care enough to even try. Moreover, he had no confidence that they wouldn't arrest him on a trumped-up charge and lock him away to never see the light of day again. His earlier thought to summon Josie's help now left him with no choice but to beg for her assistance again. How would he ever repay her?

He finished the drink and rattled the ice around in the glass, slurped the remaining drops, and then refreshed his drink before he made the call.

Josie scrunched her brows as she studied the number displayed on her phone. "Who the hell," she muttered while deciding if she wanted to answer it or let it go to voicemail. She drew a breath, pushed the button on her phone to connect the call, and said into the quiet interior of her car, "This is Josie."

In the moment of silence, she contemplated how she had answered the call, realizing that somehow, she had suddenly taken the more casual approach that her partner used when answering unknown numbers rather than the more formal address she would typically use, citing her rank and last name and unit of assignment. God help her if she was turning into a female version of Dickie.

It was Jerry.

She listened as he filled her in on what they knew, which wasn't much. He told her Dr. Fleming was there with him, but currently outside with Pablo, and it was the doctor's phone he was using. He finally got around to providing a few details about Mina's death, telling Josie that Mina was found dead in the guest room at Dr. Fleming's Rosarito home. He sounded sober, but she heard the rattling of ice in the background and pictured him working on a stiff drink to settle his nerves.

"Is it a suicide, Jerry?"

"That's the thing, Jose"—she hadn't heard him call her that for years, his taking the "y" sound off the end of her name so that it rhymed with gross or grandiose or glucose—"I'm not sure."

She thought of asking if they had called the cops but knew instinctively that he hadn't. But maybe Fleming had, she considered. Instead, she asked if Mina was still there and if anyone had disturbed the scene. He said that she was still there, and he didn't think anyone had disturbed anything in the room where she died. That told Josie what she needed to know—the authorities had not been called. She pictured Mina in the bed as Jerry described the scene, and she knew this was the type of case that could easily be mistakenly categorized as something it wasn't. It could have been a suicide, and it could have been a murder. She wished she could see the scene herself.

Jerry said, "Who shoots themselves in the heart, Josie?"

"Women do, Jerry. It's a vanity thing. Where was your friend, Dr. Fleming, when it happened? Do you know?"

"When I got here, he was pale and clearly frightened. He said he just got home moments before and found her. The thing is, he wasn't here overnight, and when he came by yesterday afternoon, it was a brief stop, and he hadn't even gone into that room. She could have been in there dead even then."

Josie pulled to the curb a block from the office. The last thing she needed was to have Williams approach her car in the parking lot while she finished this call. With that thought, she wondered again why he needed to see her, what the urgency might have been, and for a fleeting moment, she considered that maybe the news she was receiving from Jerry had something to do with her impending meeting with the feds. She left her car idling and said to Jerry, "Have you checked her for rigor mortis by chance?"

"You're kidding."

"No, Jerry, I'm not kidding. It might be important to have an idea of when she died."

"I'm not a homicide detective, Jose—I don't know how to do that."

"Okay, listen. Check her fingers and hands. If they're stiff, then check her arms and legs. If she's in full rigor, it's been at least twelve hours and could be as much as twenty-four. After that, the rigor dissipates. While you're checking, see if you see any postmortem lividity. You know what that is, right?"

"Kinda, yeah. The blood settling, right?"

"Yeah, make sure if there's lividity that it's consistent with how you found her. In other words, if she's on her back, make sure that lividity is on her back and the backs of her legs, et cetera. Otherwise, she's been moved. That make sense?"

"Yeah, I've got it."

"Jerry?"

"Yeah?"

"Has Fleming said anything about the gun?"

"No—no, he hasn't. What do you mean?"

"Where would she get a gun? You need to explore that. And find out when Fleming last saw her alive."

"I wish you were here."

She let that hang in the air a moment, having had the same thought herself but knowing it was the last place she should be. She disregarded the comment and asked about a suicide note, had anyone looked for one? What about her phone? Can you get into it and check the activity? That might give an idea of the time of death. For that matter, her messages might give some insight as to what happened and why. She rattled off these questions and a few others without a response from Jerry. When she finished, he repeated himself. "I really wish you were here."

"Jerry, I can't be there. Can you check those things and call me back? Also, take some photos and text them to me. Take more than you think you need, and not just of the body. Get pictures of everything in that room."

He was silent, and it occurred to Josie he was reluctant to go back into the room. Jerry was no stranger to death—what cop was?—which told her there was more to it. More to his feelings for Mina than she knew. Maybe he even had loved her, Josie considered. In a soft, low tone, she said, "You can handle it, Jerry, and it's important that you do. Shoot me the photos, and I'll call you in a bit. I have to meet with some feds now."

"You're meeting with feds? Is it about all this?"

"No," she lied, "something else. I'll call you in a while. Will you be available on this phone?"

"Yeah, I'll let James know you'll be calling."

"James?"

"Dr. Fleming."

She said okay and goodbye and they disconnected. In the parking lot, Williams stood outside a dark sedan waiting. His partner, Jaworski, wasn't with him but someone else was. A large man in slacks and a short-sleeve silk shirt that hung untucked. His back was to her, and she wondered who this man was. Her first instinct was this person wasn't a cop. No cop dressed in that fashion. Maybe New York mafia cops did in the eighties, but not any L.A. cop, and not any fed she had ever met.

The lights of her Charger washed over the two men as she wheeled into a parking space a few spots over even though the lot was otherwise empty now that it was after five. The stranger turned and met her gaze. She couldn't believe it: Fur Face.

What was he doing here?

Josie had feared this man more than all the other thugs surrounding Campos down in T.J. There was Baby Face and Fur Face, who had brought her and Jerry the angel and then later escorted them to the boss's office. That was where they met Campos and his bodyguard, the buff pretty boy named Carlos. But it was Fur Face she had assessed to be the most dangerous of all of them. There was something about his eyes that told her he was the one to watch, the one who would put them on their knees in an alley and pop a cap in each of their heads. Then, after meeting Williams and his partner, she learned that this Fur Face was an informant for the feds. It didn't mean he wasn't also a killer.

The two men waited near their car, watching. Good. She had parked at a distance as a matter of practice, giving her time and distance to exit her car and be on her feet before they approached her, assuming they might meander toward her as she parked. Josie never wanted anyone lingering outside her door when she was trying to get out of her car. It was a matter of officer safety and a practice that had been ingrained in her from her early days on the job. And though there surely was no potential threat of danger in this encounter, and although she now knew that Fur Face was technically on their side, Josie had felt vulnerable in his presence down in Mexico, and she had a lingering hostility toward him.

But they remained at their car, and it was she who approached them, her shoulders back and head held high, confident and determined to be the one in charge this time. Now this big hairy thug was on *her* turf.

"Oh look," she said, holding the gaze of the man in his silk shirt, "it's my old friend, Fur Face."

He scrunched his brows and glanced at Williams, his handler. Josie shrugged. "I didn't know your names, so you became Fur Face and your partner is Baby Face. Where's that asshole, anyway?"

"This is Hector," Williams said, making the formal introduction now. "I told you he's working with us."

Josie didn't respond, nor did she offer her hand or even a nod of acknowledgment. Informants weren't recruited from college campuses or law enforcement academies and implanted in the criminal world. They were not the brethren of cops. Rather, they were criminals in their elements who, for a variety of self-serving reasons, had chosen to provide information about the illegal activities of their colleagues and associates. Informants, like politicians, had to be kept at safe distances and treated like pet rattlesnakes.

After a moment, Josie broke her stare and shifted her eyes to Williams, the dapper black fed who had insisted on this impromptu after-hours meeting. "What's up?" she asked, sounding practically disinterested.

But it wasn't Agent Williams who answered her. "The woman you and your friend wanted to meet with, Mina, she is in danger," Fur Face said, his accent less prominent than she had remembered it being south of the border. "You need to find her and get her out of Mexico if possible."

Josie pictured Mina on the bed in Dr. Fleming's guest bedroom, a bullet hole in her chest, the manner of death yet a question. Yeah, she was certainly in danger—or she had been, anyway. But Josie would hold those cards close to her vest for now. "Oh?" she said, feigning surprise. "And why is that?"

"I don't know the reason, but Mr. Campo ordered her found and brought to him."

"When was this?" Josie asked.

"Yesterday."

"How do you know she's in danger? Might Campo only want to speak with her?"

"Believe me," he said, "she's in danger."

Josie cut her eyes to the handler. "It seems to me you could have told me this over the phone. Is there another reason we had to meet?"

"Detective Lopes said you wanted to work with Mr. Romero," indicating Fur Face next to him in the event she didn't know his last name, "so I brought him here. He has to return to Tijuana this evening, so if you have questions you think he can answer, now is the time. I tried calling Lopes, but he didn't answer his phone."

"Well then," she said, "shall we go inside?"

34

The office stood virtually empty at nine that night. Most of the lights were dimmed, and the usual constant ringing of phones had all but ceased. The sound of TV news emanated from the front desk area, and Dickie, at his own desk now in Unsolveds, pictured Miguel up front manning the phones, his feet propped up and his eyes fixed on his phone as he scrolled through Facebook or Instagram or Elon Musk's X, formerly known as Twitter, Miguel a part of the generation whose eyes are glued to their electronic devices. Dickie didn't do social media, but he knew enough about the various platforms from the investigations he'd been a part of where digital footprints added value to a case. Miguel, on the other hand—the overweight overnight civilian employee assigned to the front desk—was clearly addicted to the primary source of entertainment in this twenty-first century: social media, YouTube, various word games, and puzzles. All of that was fine with Dickie— to each their own—but he wished Miguel would at least lower the volume on the TV since he really didn't pay attention to it anyway. The wall that separated the front desk from Unsolveds did little to silence the blaring voices of evening newscasters and the annoying commercials that accompanied the broadcast.

Lopes sat at his own desk across the room from Dickie, his focus on the computer screen before him, blue tint of light reflecting off his eyeglasses. His shirtsleeves were rolled up, his tie hung loose around his open collar, and Dickie could smell beer on him from ten feet away. He said, "Where were you when you got the call? Corina's?"

His eyes remained fixed on the computer screen. "No, I met a friend at a place downtown."

"A friend."

Lopes looked over at him. "Yeah, I have three or four of them—five if I count your mom. You should try finding one for yourself."

"Overrated," Dickie said, leaning back in his chair now, his gaze set on the ceiling beyond Lopes's desk. There was a cobweb strewn from a light fixture to a corner, and Dickie found himself searching the region for spiders. He wasn't afraid of them, but as with flies, mice, snakes, and Internal Affairs, he preferred that they remained in their own pathetic worlds and didn't encroach on his.

Lopes tried to follow Dickie's gaze, then frowned at him. "What the fuck are you looking at?"

Dickie grinned. "The Brown Recluse that's getting ready to drop down on your head."

Lopes whirled around, rolling his chair away from his desk and distancing himself from the corner behind him while reaching for the gun on his hip. Dickie laughed at the sight of it, Lopes ready to defend the office from insects by use of deadly force. In his defense, detectives were not issued nor trained in the use of less-than-lethal weaponry.

Still chuckling, Dickie said, "There's no spider, dumbass."

"Not funny, man. I hate spiders."

Dickie put his feet up on his desk, comfortable this evening in his jeans and untucked short-sleeve button-up, not having bothered to put on a suit when he'd gotten Josie's call a few hours ago asking him to come into the office. He checked his watch and said to Lopes, "How long do we give her?"

Lopes looked at him with no expression on his face.

Dickie said, "I mean, she's upset. I get that. But it's late, and we have a flight to catch in the morning."

"Not anymore, we don't."

Dickie frowned. "We don't?"

"I just canceled our trip. Is she still in the little girls' room, or did she split?"

"Her purse is under her desk—she didn't split. But wait, aren't we still going to Idaho to see Walker and hang out with Farris?"

He shook his head. "I don't see a reason to now—not yet anyway."

"Do you believe him?"

Lopes shrugged.

Dickie said, "I'm not convinced. Dude's a cartel member who happens to be an FBI informant. Doesn't mean he's not full of shit."

"What does he have to gain by lying to us? Nothing as far as I can see. He came in, went to his handler and told him he had some information that would interest us. It's not as if we pinched the guy and he's trying to get out of something. At the very least I think we need to put Idaho on hold until we follow up on some of this information."

Josie appeared in the doorway and struck a pose there, her shoulder braced against the doorframe and her arms folded across her chest, bunching her jacket in the front against the beige blouse she wore beneath it. Dickie watched her closely, hoping to get a read on her disposition, but Josie's eyes were cast downward, and her face betrayed nothing about her emotional state. Dickie figured she might waver between bitter disappointment and raging anger, but she showed neither on the surface. He watched her quietly and gave her the time she needed to organize her thoughts—it was clear she had something to say to the two of them, something to say about the implications that had been made about Jerry's involvement in the drug busts rip-off scheme.

After a long moment, Lopes broke the ice. "First thing we need to do is verify this informant's story, just as we would any other. Williams says he's reliable, but I'm not taking his word for it."

Josie glanced his way but didn't respond.

Dickie said, "How do we verify what he told us? Ask Jerry?"

Josie went to her desk, moving through the office with purpose, and settled into her chair while abruptly moving the computer's mouse to bring it to life. Moments later, her fingers blazed across the keyboard as she typed in her password. She moved the mouse, typed, then clicked the mouse, and typed some more.

Lopes said, "Yeah, sure, tell him an informant for the feds says he's dirty on the dope rips, and ask him if it's true. What do you think he's going to say?"

Josie, jotting a note on a piece of scratch paper next to her keyboard, said, "No, we don't ask Jerry anything. Not yet, anyway."

Dickie and Lopes exchanged glances and waited. Dickie tried to identify the tone of her statement. Anger and frustration, or simply resolve? Clearly, she was suddenly driven by some kind of emotion, and in the way a man knows to shut his mouth and allow his wife or significant other to vent, rant, or stew, Dickie instinctively clammed up and waited. Lopes seemed to be on the same page—they were two men whose life experiences with the fairer sex had left them wiser than their youthful selves had been. Sometimes the safe bet was to shut up every chance you had.

Josie finished whatever she was doing on her computer, then turned in her chair to face them. "I'm going to see Perry."

Dickie frowned. "Perry?"

"Yeah, Mike Perry, the Narco sergeant who cooperated and testified against the deputies who were charged. I've got his address," she said, with a glance toward her computer screen, "and I'm going to drop in on him and ask a few questions."

"What makes you think he's going to talk to you?" Lopes asked.

"Oh, he'll talk."

Lopes grinned. "I'd be surprised."

"Would you like to make a wager on that, Detective?"

Whatever Josie's emotional state had been following the meeting with Williams and his informant, this man she called Fur Face, had apparently turned to resolve. Josie had a plan and wouldn't be deterred.

Lopes gave her a "Whatever," and Josie shot back at him. "Whatever your ass. This furry-faced moron says Jerry was a dirty cop based on what Campo told him after our meeting. Give me a break. It's all speculation and innuendo and certainly not anything that should compel us to throw a former cop under the bus."

"Okay, but again," Lopes persisted, "what makes you think Perry's going to talk to you—that's A—and B, if he does talk to you, what makes you so sure you're going to get the truth out of him?"

Josie gathered her belongings now, ready to go—Josie set on a mission. "Because he has immunity and that means he has nothing to lose."

"But if Perry had information that Townsend was dirty, wouldn't he have already provided that information?" Dickie asked. "I mean, he wasn't shy about giving up all these other Narco guys to save his ass."

"They weren't going after the brass, for whatever reason. You know that. They didn't go after anyone over the rank of sergeant, and the one sergeant they targeted, Perry, they offered him a deal. You know there was brass involved."

"Well, that's what Jerry said. I know that. But where's the evidence?"

Lopes chimed in. "She's right that they never looked at anyone above the rank of sergeant. That was something many of us wondered about back then."

Josie looked at him and nodded, apparently glad to see Lopes in her corner. Dickie considered it for a moment while the sounds of late-night news persisted from the front desk area. The whole thing had him irritated —the call to come back in for this meeting with the fed and his informant, Josie's steadfast loyalty to Townsend despite evidence that he might have been dirty, and Miguel with his goddam blaring television. He could walk up to the front desk and shoot the TV, walk out without a word while Miguel sat there with his jaw on the desk. A John Belushi moment, a favorite scene of Dickie's in Animal House, when Belushi took a guitar from a flower child and bashed it against the wall, irked by the man's cheerful melody.

Dickie's impish daydream ended when Josie started for the door, her purse over her shoulder and a file case tucked under the opposite arm. He said, "Where are you going?"

"I told you. To see Perry."

"Right, but where is that?"

She glanced back at her computer screen which had gone dark but had swirls of colorful shapes fading in and out. "According to DMV, he's in Long Beach."

"Want some company?"

"Suit yourself," she said, still peeved by the whole ordeal.

Dickie pushed out of his chair and looked at Lopes, who sat silently at his desk, suddenly the spectator and innocent bystander. "Come on, let's go for a ride with Josie, keep her out of trouble."

Josie turned on her heel and said over her shoulder, "Good luck with that."

Lopes, gathering his coat and briefcase, said, "Yeah, good luck is right."

35

Dr. Fleming told Jerry, "You were never here," as he walked him out to the car and the driver who awaited him—Pablo—and his recycled cop car with the gun under the back seat. The Blues Mobile. They had agreed it would be best for Jerry to be gone before Fleming called the cops, though Jerry worried that the Mexican authorities would mishandle the case. Perhaps they'd even presume it to be a murder and lock up the American doctor for an indeterminate sentence, perhaps forever. Fleming assured him he'd be fine, telling Jerry that he had come to know many of the local officials and politicians, and he had taken care of some of their spouses and girlfriends when they came for his services, discounting his fees substantially and in some cases, not even charging them.

In the car, Pablo said, "Where to?" He fired the ignition and gunned the motor for effect as a young driver might, his dark oversized sunglasses aimed at his passenger. Jerry, thinking there was no way Mina's death was suicide—but not certain because, for some reason, Josie hadn't gotten back to him after he sent her the crime scene photos from Fleming's phone —was deliberating about his next move. His options were few since he'd now lost everything: his apartment, his wallet containing his ID, credit cards, and cash, his cell phone, and now Mina, the young woman with whom he had become enamored, was gone. What did he really have left?

His pride? Not even close—he'd left that north of the border years ago when he became a whoremongering expatriate. His freedom? Not any longer—not after the beating he'd taken earlier today. True, when he first came to Mexico, he had felt free to sleep off last night's bender and then spend the remainder of the day with his feet in the sand while the balmy rays of the sun caressed his ever-darkening skin, and free-spirited seagulls circled lazily (and noisily) above him, embodying the essence of liberty. But freedom is relative. In the joint, some prisoners were free to roam the halls and walk the yard, hit the weight pile, or throw hoops. They were relatively free compared to others who spent 23 hours a day in a box and were shackled and escorted wherever they went. Jerry had felt free after walking away from his structured life in middle-class America, but now he felt more like a runaway, a fugitive, a man with a dark past and few allies remaining. Pablo was now one of them. Pablo waiting behind the wheel, his gaze set on Jerry, the old Crown Vic rumbling at an idle, ready to go.

But where would he go? The idea to go see Campo was one he couldn't shake. It had come to him as he stood in that room looking at Mina's lifeless body. The scenario in his mind: Pablo drives him to the *Caballo Loco*, drops him in the front, and then drives around to the back to wait for him in the alley. Jerry offers the doorman a warm smile and a cool twenty in the palm of his hand, slides in uncontested, and moves through the crowd with the Glock from Pablo's back seat concealed in his waistband, his shirt untucked. He bumps along through the sweaty crowd and barges into Campo's office. Maybe he sticks the gun in the bodyguard's mouth—what was his name, Carlos?—and walks him back to a chair, shoves him into it while asking if he'd like some 9mm dental work or could he behave himself. Turns to Campo, who would surely be frozen behind his desk, and asks a few pointed questions: Who killed Mina and why? What do you know about the death of my wife?

And then what? Kill both and walk out back, tell Pablo, Let's go!?

But Jerry didn't think he could do it; he wasn't a cold-blooded killer. He was not going to shoot a man in the face who wasn't trying to kill him at the same moment.

Same plan, different approach. Leave the gun behind—nothing good could come from using it, and he certainly couldn't afford to be caught with it by the local law or *federales*. Tell Campo he'd been mugged and he lost the phone that had been provided to him, see if his reaction betrayed his involvement in the beating. Then tell him about Mina. Or maybe ask him first. Ask when he last spoke with her and if he knew of any reason someone might want her dead. Gauge his reaction.

The problem, though, was Jerry knew that Campo wouldn't tell him the truth if he'd entertain him at all. In fact, he might not be so lucky as to leave there alive again—he had to seriously consider that. Maybe Plan A was the only option. Bring the heat even though it could be the beginning of the end, the proverbial loose thread being yanked with no regard to the fabric's structure.

Pablo waited patiently, his young face showing neither intrigue nor worry. He was a young man who seemed to have a zest for life and a curious nature. Jerry said, "Tell me, my friend, what do you know about the cartels?"

Without much thought, he said, "They are bad. Very dangerous, *señior*, and must be—how do you say, aboid?"

"Avoided?"

"*Sí*, aboid. Stay away."

"Uh-huh," Jerry agreed, "I would think that's best. What about Mr. Campo? He runs the *Caballo Loco* in town."

"Yes, I know thees one."

"Is he with the cartel?"

Pablo shrugged. "Is possible, but I no' too sure. He for sure pay them taxes. Tha's how TJ works."

Jerry stared out the window, watching two kids playing fetch with a mongrel dog on the side of the road, the kids throwing sticks and giggling as the dog retrieved them one at a time, the mutt wagging his tail and limping along. He'd probably been hit by a car and left to heal on his own or not make it at all. It wasn't a society of 24-hour emergency vet clinics and thousand-dollar pets who received their shots and went to the spa to be groomed and pampered. But that didn't seem to matter to the kids or the dog, epitomizing the universal love language between the two factions. There was also a universal language of outlaws, and that language was violence. That was a truth that many facets of the community didn't understand, including those self-appointed law enforcement watch groups. Or maybe they understood it but refused to acknowledge it. Some of those people hated law enforcement more than they embraced a safe and civil society, and the results could now be seen in many large cities. The cops backed off, and the criminals took over. The sheepdogs pulled back, and the wolves came in unchallenged, licking their chops. Campo and his ilk were no different. The only thing they understood and respected was violence. There was no mercy in their hearts nor pity in their souls. They were wolves. But Jerry was no sheep.

"Take me to the *Caballo Loco*."

36

MIKE PERRY CAME TO THE DOOR IN CARGO SHORTS AND A PLAID BUTTON-up short-sleeve shirt, white socks and Birkenstocks. The top of his head was shiny bald, and the little hair he maintained on the sides was gray, matching his mustache and goatee. He was thin in an unhealthy way, not the way of a runner or someone who watched their calories and macros. And he looked old, Dickie thought, much older than he must have been. Dickie wondered if he was battling cancer or just living with demons. Being a dirty cop and testifying against your colleagues to avoid prison would certainly eat away at a man the way any cancer might.

His narrow, sunken eyes scanned each of them until they settled on Josie as she introduced herself and asked if she could speak with him. As almost an afterthought, she said, "And these are two of my partners, Davey Lopes and Dickie Jones."

Perry nodded, his gaze shifting again from one to the other, and said, "Yeah, I know these two," indicating Lopes and Dickie. "Firestone, right?"

"Back in the day," Lopes said.

"May we come in?" Josie asked.

He took a step back and gestured for the three of them to enter, his

190

expression one of question and concern. Meeting Dickie's gaze as he entered, he said, "You're Homicide now, aren't you?"

Dickie nodded. "Yeah, been there a long time now. We're in Unsolveds."

He closed the door behind him. "Unsolveds, uh? I can't imagine what you want with me."

The room was dark, the blinds all closed, and it smelled musty, like an old basement or the home of a hoarder, but there didn't appear to be any hoarding taking place here. The furniture was simple and from another time, floral patterns showing the wear and tear of decades gone by. They matched the man, Dickie thought. At some point, these pieces had been fresh and welcoming and might have entertained many friends, but now they were old and worn and unwelcoming—lonely and near their end.

Dickie lowered himself onto the sofa along with Josie while Lopes gravitated to the lone chair in the living room, a Queen Anne wingback that was once a vibrant red but now was worn and fading. Perry sat at the edge of the loveseat, which placed him closest to Josie who was perched on the front of her seat.

"I can't imagine why you're here," Perry repeated. "I've been off the job—" he started, but his words faded as he seemed to go back in time with memories he probably tried to leave behind.

"It's about the Narco scandal," Josie said.

He scooted back into his seat, effectively distancing himself from Josie's reach. "Oh?"

She nodded. "I'll get right to it. Jerry Townsend."

"Yeah?"

"He was in your unit."

"He was our captain for a while, right toward the end," he said, casting his eyes downward as if speaking of a lost loved one.

"Did you know him well?"

"Sort of, but as I said, he hadn't been there long when everything went down."

"You didn't know him before he went to Narco?"

"No, ma'am, I did not. I knew of him, but I think most people in the department back then did. He had made a name for himself with a couple of big incidents, one where a partner of his was killed, and then, of course, he worked SWAT for a while, so…"

"Okay, so you knew of him, worked with him for a while at Narco, but didn't really know him well," Josie clarified.

"Correct."

"And at some point, you were given immunity by the feds to testify against some of your team members regarding allegations of theft."

He nodded.

"Was there any question about Townsend being dirty?"

Perry met her gaze, his eyes showing fatigue or maybe sorrow. "Not that I'm aware."

"Did they look at him?"

"The feds?"

"Yes."

"Well, yeah, they looked at everyone who was in the unit at the time. But their focus came down to five players, the ones who were convicted and sent to prison. They were driving new cars, riding Harleys, buying vacation homes at the river so they'd have someplace to keep their new boats and RVs, the fucking idiots."

"Between us—and you have immunity anyway, but I can assure you that we're not looking into the Narco scandal again—were there others in the unit who were dirty that weren't prosecuted?"

His answer was quick and unequivocal. "Well sure, several. Including me."

"But you cut a deal."

"I think others did as well."

Josie glanced at Lopes, whose squinty eyes questioned the statement. Back to Perry, she said, "Explain."

"Well, look at the brass. You had a commander and a chief who most of us knew had skimmed their shares as well, but they were allowed to retire and ride off into the sunset. How do you think that happened?"

Josie shrugged a little in her suit jacket and said, "I don't know. Maybe their names were never mentioned. Did the feds ask you about them?"

"Sure," he said, "they asked about everyone."

"And what did you tell them?"

Perry glanced at Lopes. "Weren't you part of Arco Narco?"

"For a short time," Lopes said.

"So you know how it went down. They were going to hang me and my team, but nobody ever seemed to care about the brass. Sure, they were dirty, too—some of them, anyway—but I don't think the department was going to allow the scandal to reach those heights. They protect their own, you know."

"But did you specifically tell the feds about the commander, Wilkins, and Chief Benny Carmen?"

"They didn't want to hear about any of that."

"But did you tell them?"

He looked down, and the room fell silent. After a moment, he said, "Carmen was like a mafioso, to be honest. Everyone knew it. Nothing was ever said, but two things were clear to me: one, the department was going to protect the upper echelon, and two, Benny Carmen would have me whacked—or maybe do it himself—if I mentioned him or any of the brass to the feds."

"Did he threaten you?"

"Not exactly."

"Then why do you think that?"

"Because they called me in one day and told me as much. Said, 'Look, some of these guys are going down, but not everyone. We made sure they'd work a deal with you. Don't bite the hand that feeds you,' or some such nonsense. Anyway, it was a message that I received clearly, and I took it to heart. Look, they let me walk and keep my retirement. I gave up a few of the dirtier cops in the unit—those idiots that couldn't help but flash their money everywhere—and the stash of cash I'd held onto. I knew what was expected of me, and I did what I had to do and got the hell out."

Dickie waited for a moment, and when Josie seemed to be considering her next question, he said, "Was Townsend in that meeting?"

"The one with Carmen?"

"Yeah."

"No, it was just Carmen and some black guy I'd never seen before and who wasn't introduced."

"A deputy?" Josie asked.

Perry shrugged. "I don't know."

Lopes said, "Maybe his driver?"

Dickie pictured a black deputy driving the chief around and thought, Nah, not today… someone would surely have an issue with that. He tried to think who the black guy might have been, thinking Internal Affairs, Internal Criminal Bureau, a federal agent… He said, "Was he a fed, the black guy?"

Perry shrugged. "Could've been. He dressed spiffy and looked a little uptight if you know what I mean, so I figured he was a prosecutor or another executive or something. But now that you say it, yeah, maybe the guy was a fed. I could see that."

"Describe him."

"I don't know—it's been a while." Perry looked up at the ceiling as he searched his memory. "I just remember he was clean-cut, fit, and wearing a suit, a conservative one."

"Williams?" Josie guessed.

Dickie shrugged, said to Perry, "What'd he have to say during that meeting?"

Perry held Dickie's gaze with interest as if he'd never given that meeting much thought before, or at least he hadn't considered the mystery black man's role in it up until now. He said, "He didn't say a thing. He sat off to the side"—Perry pointed his chin at Lopes who seemed to be outside the circle of conversation—"like this guy here, and just watched and listened." Perry snapped his fingers. "You know, now I remember something that seemed odd that I dismissed then and never gave it another thought. After Chief Carmen gave me his spiel, he glanced over at the black guy, and the black guy nodded as if he were giving him his approval. That mighta been why I thought maybe he was a prosecutor."

Dickie looked at Lopes. "Was Williams a part of Arco Narco?"

He shook his head. "I don't know. I don't remember ever seeing him before he came to our office the other day. I don't think he was."

Josie said, "You think it was Williams."

Dickie shrugged and tilted his head one way and then the other. "I don't know. Could've been."

"If Williams was with Benny Carmen and the commander when they essentially told Perry to roll over on the deputies and shut his mouth about everything else, then there's way more to all of this."

Dickie agreed with her, adding, "And then he shows up at our office with his so-called cartel informant who says—" and stopped himself from saying anything more than that in front of Perry.

Perry asked, "Whose cartel informant?"

Ignoring the question, Dickie asked Lopes, "How do we figure out who the mysterious black man was?"

"I don't know. Maybe they keep a visitor's log at Headquarters."

Dickie turned to Perry. "Is that where the meeting was, Headquarters?"

He nodded. "Of course."

"Even if they do have a log or sign-in sheet for visitors," Josie said, "I doubt they'd keep them ten years."

"Probably not," Dickie agreed. He met Perry's gaze. "Would you happen to know the date? I mean, without that, a log wouldn't even matter."

He shook his head. "I mean, I could give you a month and year, probably."

"Why don't we just show him a picture of Williams?" Lopes suggested.

"Not a bad idea," Josie said, "but where do we get one? It's not like we took a selfie at the office."

"We could get one if we need it," he told her. He said to Dickie, "If it was Williams in the room with Benny Carmen, what does that change? How does that impact our investigation into the death of Laura Townsend?"

Dickie considered the question before answering. If Williams was in cahoots with Carmen—which you would have to assume if he was indeed in the office that day when Perry was given his pardon, so to speak—then they would have to consider that Williams was somehow dirty himself. Why else would a federal agent influence which of the thieves should go to prison and who would walk away unscathed? And if Williams was dirty, how could they trust anything he was feeding them now? Maybe it was time to turn the tables on the fed. Bring him in and let him answer some questions this time. But not yet, he decided, not until they could put a few more of the puzzle pieces together.

He said, "Maybe it's time we talk to Benny Carmen."

37

DICKIE HAD NO QUALMS ABOUT TAKING ON THE BRASS WHEN HE SAW FIT, and his level of respect when doing so was directly related to the respect he believed they had earned. All too often, in these changing times, merit wasn't based so much on performance as it was on appearances. Consequently, at a time when the department had begun to go "woke" and was increasingly considering one's gender, race, and sexual orientation over their qualifications, Dickie's level of respect for some had changed proportionately.

Recently, he had found himself in a pissing contest with a female captain whose initial successes within the department had been aided by her marriage to a high-ranking executive who happened to be quite a bit older than her. That relationship had begun when she was a young, fairly attractive recruit, and he had been the captain of the training bureau. They married, and she found herself going from one coveted assignment to the next until she'd had enough time on the job to start promoting, and she did. But when he retired, her ascension came to an abrupt halt. Undeterred, she was soon divorced from him and had "come out" as a lesbian, being one of the first to do so. Soon thereafter she was promoted to captain. Throughout his career, Dickie had worked with and for people of every race, religion, and sexual orientation with neither bias nor contempt, judging each only by their character and ability to do their jobs. But this particular captain he'd found himself at odds with had done nothing in her career to earn his respect, and he had difficulty disguising his contempt for her. When she decided to win the argument they were having by reminding him that she was three full ranks above him, he told her that regardless of her rank, she still pulled her skirt on one hairy leg at a time, just as he did. Of course, he hadn't meant to imply he wore skirts, but his partner at the time never let him live the comment down, telling everyone about Dickie and his skirts from that day forward. The captain, not at all amused—probably due to the hairy leg part of his comment—had given him a two-day suspension and written reprimand for insubordination. He didn't bother to contest the discipline.

So Josie knew Dickie would pull no punches and offer no favor while interviewing the retired chief, and she had to admit—if only to herself— that she dreaded the impending confrontation. Not that it would start out as one, but it would surely devolve into something close to that if Dickie felt the man was being deceptive, evasive, or worse yet, patronizing. Benny Carmen had been very influential within the department, and she had no doubt that he still had people on his side who were in positions to make their lives miserable. But she also knew that interviewing him was the right thing to do, given this information from Perry and the things Jerry had told her about Carmen's probable involvement in the dope rips.

They were on their way back to the bureau after leaving the disgraced Narco sergeant's home as Josie pondered the impending confrontation with Carmen. "Are you planning to run this by your captain?" she asked.

The mood in the car was subdued and somber, and Dickie seemed to either be contemplating her question or ignoring her. Lopes answered for him. "He'd have a fit."

Dickie nodded his agreement.

Josie said, "And he'll have a fit when Carmen calls him the second we leave his house."

"Yeah, I'm sure he will," Lopes said, "but what's he going to do about it? He'll rant and rave and threaten to put us in Missing Persons or send us back to patrol, and then he'll get over it."

Josie wasn't so sure the captain would get over it so easily. He and Dickie had a contentious relationship at best, and she had done nothing recently to gain his favor. Her trip to Mexico surely hadn't helped. She felt they were on thin ice with him, with this case, with their assignment to Unsolveds. But she also knew that her partners were likely to go with a favorite mantra of theirs: it was easier to ask for forgiveness than permission. They particularly favored that tactic when permission would likely not be given.

She thought back to her conversations with Jerry about Benny Carmen, once his very good friend, perhaps even his rabbi to a degree. Jerry had told her it was Carmen who had him transferred into Narcotics, and it was Carmen and Commander Wilkins who took control of the money seized during the busts. At some point, the money was booked as evidence, but also there was cash doled out among the troops, apparently. Obviously, Jerry wasn't the only one to find an envelope on his desk. Benny Carmen had to be involved in the money skimming, but he was never investigated for it, according to Jerry and now Mike Perry as well. They would be derelict in their duties if they didn't investigate him now. To hell with rank and power, these people were no different than Dickie: they each put their skirts on one hairy leg at a time.

Back at the bureau, they stood in the nearly empty parking lot and debated going for cocktails. Dickie was leaning toward going home. Lopes wanted a drink. Josie could use a cocktail herself. She was bothered that she hadn't heard back from Jerry yet. He was supposed to call her as soon as he knew more about Mina's death. In fact, he was supposed to send some pictures of the scene to her phone. In order to do so, he would have to use someone else's phone, likely Dr. Fleming's. But she hadn't received anything yet, and now she was beginning to worry about what was going on south of the border.

Lopes said to Dickie, "Come on, man, don't be a pussy. One drink, two max."

She could see that Dickie was torn between the camaraderie of choir practice and being home with his family. He looked at his watch and sighed, then said, "Well, Angelo is in bed now anyway. I'll see him in the morning."

Now they were focused on Josie. "Well, sis, what about you? You're not off to meet with whatshisass, are you?"

Dickie added, "Bring him along. We need to ask him about his intentions with our little sister."

She rolled her eyes. "Not a chance."

Josie checked her phone again, remembering that she had placed it on silent, and was surprised to see a text had arrived. There was no message, only a series of photographs depicting a woman lying on a bed with an apparent gunshot wound to her chest, a rifle lying within arm's reach. Josie scrolled through the photos quickly and then went through them again.

Dickie moved over next to her, saying, "Is that Mina?"

She nodded while studying the details of the scene. The rifle lay next to her. The muzzle was near her head, and its butt was next to her right knee. Mina was propped up on a stack of pillows the way one might spend time reading or watching television before going to sleep—Josie doubted that Mina had done either before the Big Sleep came—and her ankles were crossed. She appeared relaxed and peaceful. A hairbrush lay on the bed not far from her right hand. There was no doubt in Josie's mind it was suicide.

Her partner quickly came to the same conclusion. "Suicide."

For the layperson, which could include cops who hadn't been trained in death investigation nor investigated hundreds of death scenes, like Jerry, and doctors whose experience with death was limited to unsuccessful emergency room life-saving efforts, like the cosmetic surgeon Dr. Fleming, most deaths raised some level of suspicion, especially deaths involving gunshot wounds. But for any experienced homicide cop, there were several illuminating signs present at a scene that told the story. People liked to be comfortable when they ended their lives. You often found them in their beds or favorite chairs, seated in their cars, or maybe leaning up against a tree on a mountaintop they had always enjoyed hiking or where they had spent their youth hunting birds. Seldom would you see someone shooting themselves while standing. For whatever reason, people were loath to fall even knowing they'd be dead when they hit the ground. So that was the first sign for the experienced investigator: Mina's relaxed pose. The second was the position of the rifle. If someone had killed her and tried to make it look like a suicide, they would have likely put the weapon in her hand or her hand on the weapon in some fashion. They likely would have used a pistol, not a rifle. And the truth was that rarely would a firearm that was used in a suicide remain in the victim's clutch. There could be the question of the gunshot wound location, but as she had previously told Jerry, it was a vanity thing with women; they almost never shot themselves in the head. But then the question was how did she do it? Some people shot themselves with a rifle by using a toe to depress the trigger. With Mina's ankles crossed, that wasn't likely. But Josie knew exactly how she had done it, and so did her partner.

"The hairbrush."

She nodded and then handed the phone to Lopes, who had not crowded in to see the images as Dickie had but instead waited with some anticipation. As he looked at the phone, he nodded in agreement. "Yep, she used the brush to reach the trigger and make it go boom. She was committed."

"But why?" Dickie wondered.

Josie pondered the question a moment. "I don't know, but that is certainly the half-a-million-dollar question."

Lopes handed her the phone, and she sent a message in reply to the photographs she had received: "Suicide."

Dickie said, "Now how about that drink?"

Josie was watching her phone, waiting to see if a reply would come. She said, "Yes, most definitely now." And then a new message arrived: "Jerry's gone, but I'll get him the message. Thank you."

Josie responded. "Who's this?"

"Dr. Fleming."

"Where is Jerry?"

There were bubbles showing he was typing his response, but then they stopped. Soon, they began again, and shortly after, a new message arrived. "I'm not sure."

What did that mean? She typed, "Is he okay?"

"He's upset, but I think he'll be okay."

"Okay, thank you. Please tell him to get in touch with me if you have contact with him."

The three detectives pulled out of the lot in tandem, each driving their own assigned county cars. Lopes led the way, Josie on his tail. Dickie brought up the rear. They were headed to Corina's for a proper debriefing.

38

Down the road from the *Caballo*, Jerry sat in Pablo's car with the gun from beneath the back seat now secured in his waistband. Pablo was at the wheel, but the motor and lights were off. They sat in silence while the festivities on *Avenida Revolución* boomed in the background—the street alive with colorful lights strung from poles and wrapped around trees and the neon glow of signs over businesses. Partygoers spilled onto the sidewalks from the various clubs, cocktails in their hands, the sounds of laughter and boozy jeers accentuating synthesized dance music blaring in the night.

Jerry hadn't arrived here lightly. In fact, his contemplations were those that one might have when he considered ending his own life: how will this affect my loved ones; what about my legacy; am I positively ready to end it all and say goodbye to this world that has grown ugly and troublesome; is there a life after death, and where will I end up? Because there was a better-than-fair chance he wasn't walking away from this if he went forward with his plan. But Jerry didn't have anyone to consider now, other than maybe Josie. He had burned his legacy long ago, and the ashes were cold and long forgotten. He believed he had a shot at heaven so long as he didn't take his own life. At least those were the teachings of the Roman Catholic church as far as he could remember—it had been a long time since he had attended Mass or lit a candle or confessed his sins or attempted any act of contrition. Regardless of his own sins, there were others who had committed worse and whose penitence mattered not to Jerry Townsend. It was time for retribution.

Pablo remained silent, patiently awaiting his next assignment. Jerry wondered if he had any idea what he had planned for Mr. Campo and any of his goons who might intercede on his behalf. He likely hadn't. His thoughts were probably on the *tetas grandes* that would no doubt be found on the other side of the heavy wooden door that was guarded by the two bouncers who stood out front, scrutinizing those coming in and, in some cases, patting them down for weapons or contraband. Jerry didn't think they'd pat him down. They knew him well enough, and they knew his handshake would include a note of gratitude—a U.S. Treasury note, that is, something always welcome in Mexico.

"Pablo, I think this is when we should part company, my friend."

Pablo looked at him, his youthful appearance more prominent without the big sunglasses he had worn during the day. He was, after all, just a kid. Whether he was seventeen or twenty-three, he was young and relatively innocent, and Jerry wasn't going to take a chance of him being killed or jailed because of whatever might happen next. His previous thoughts of having Pablo wait for him at the back of the club were ill-advised, he'd decided. He didn't want Pablo involved, and he didn't think the odds of him making it out alive were good, anyway.

"I don't mind waiting," he said.

"It's okay, Pablo, seriously. You've done more than enough, and I'm grateful. I wish I could pay you for your time, and I hope that someday I'll be able to."

Pablo waved him off. "Is no problem, my frien'."

Jerry had a thought. "Can I use your phone once more before you go?"

"Of course," Pablo said, handing it to him.

Jerry punched in Josie's number and sent a text:

Josie, it's me. This is Pablo's phone. He's been
helping me all day, driving me from place to
place. I owe him, but I have nothing after being
robbed. Would you please contact him later and
see how you can get some money to him? I have
substantial savings, and there is a debit card in
that safe deposit box. My pin is my badge
number. If you don't remember it, you can look it
up. He's a good kid. Send him half and keep the
rest for yourself. Love ya, kiddo. Jerry.

DICKIE SLAMMED ON HIS BRAKES AND SWERVED HARD TO THE LEFT WHEN
Josie suddenly stopped and pulled to the side of the road in front of him.
"Jesus, Josie!" He was alongside her now and saw she was looking at her
phone. He couldn't believe it. Anger flushed through him as the adrenaline
that had shot through his veins began to subside. He pulled up past her,
thrust his old Crown Vic into Park, and popped open his door. As he
exited, he saw that Lopes had come to a stop ahead of them—nearly a full
block beyond where Dickie had nearly creamed two county cars due to
Josie's idiotic maneuver—and now Lopes was in the middle of a three-
point turn, clearly intent on coming to check on them. Dickie was almost
to Josie's car when Lopes pulled alongside them and said, "What the hell
happened?"

Dickie had started to tell him that Josie was on her fucking phone
talking to God-only-knew-who! and she hit her brakes, nearly causing him
to plow into her… but he caught himself before saying anything at all
when he saw Josie wiping a tear from her eye. He stood frozen, fearing the
news that was forthcoming.

JOSIE JERKED HER CAR TO THE SIDE OF THE ROAD AND STOPPED AFTER
scanning Jerry's text that sounded like a last goodbye. She called the
phone that had sent the text.

"What the hell does this all mean, Jerry? Are you telling me you're
going to off yourself without having the balls to just say it?"

"No," he assured her, "I'm not going to off myself. I just might not be around much longer."

She brushed a tear away with the back of her hand. "Jerry, what on earth are you doing?"

Dickie was standing at her door now, Lopes in his car facing the opposite direction. Both stared at her, their expressions severe. She hit the button to lower her window and turned off her car while putting her phone on speaker so her partners could listen in.

"I'm going to have a chat with Mr. Campo, and it might not go over very well."

"Jerry, why would you do that?"

"Mina, Josie. That's why."

"Didn't you get my message, Jerry? Mina committed suicide. I'm sure of it. Dickie and Lopes think so too. We all looked at the photos, and there's no doubt about it. She killed herself, Jerry, for whatever reason, and there is no reason to throw your life away because of it."

The text she'd received had shocked her and she had found herself flooded with emotion due to the theme of it, the end-of-times tone of his instructions. His last request and final goodbye which had been sealed with an almost awkward term of endearment, his *Love ya, kiddo* bullshit. Yes, she knew he did, and she loved him too in the sense of their friendship and his mentorship in the early days of her career. It was a feeling they both felt and understood but rarely, if ever, were those emotions voiced. Now it was anger she felt as Jerry told her that either way, no matter if Mina had died at her own hand or had been killed by another, it was Campo that set it all in motion. He had to pay for his part in this, Jerry said.

"Jerry, listen to me. Nothing good can come from this. Have your friend there take you to the border, and I'll be there to pick you up in two hours, an hour and a half if the chippies don't interfere. Listen, Fur Face is working with the feds. He's an informant. We can put this all together if you keep a cool head and let us do our job."

Lopes had turned his car off too, even though he sat parked in the middle of the street. It was late, and there was no traffic in this part of Monterey Park where the bureau was tucked into an industrial area. He and Dickie were listening attentively, watching her carefully, weighing her words. The comment about the border had caused Dickie to raise his brows in question.

Jerry said, "What does it even matter anymore? Nothing's going to bring Laura back, and now I have Mina's blood on my hands as well."

Josie fought off the urge to remind him what and who Mina was—not someone to end your life over. Sure, she got it, Jerry had fallen for a whore and turned her into something other than that in his mind. It was his version of love and companionship, having lost his way in Mexico. Instead, she said, "Jerry, don't do this. If for no other reason, please think of me. I have always cared for you greatly, and I can't stand the idea of your wonderful, meaningful, and heroic life ending in the back streets or alleys of Tijuana like a stray dog shot and left for dead."

"I have to go," he said.

"NO! Jerry, please..."

But the line had gone dead, and Jerry was gone. Josie couldn't help but consider it an omen.

39

SHE SAT SILENTLY STARING AT THE PHONE FOR A MOMENT BEFORE MEETING the speculative gazes of her partners.

"I'm going," she said. It was simply stated and not negotiable.

Silence fell as the three partners and friends exchanged contemplative glances. There was nothing these three hadn't shared as brothers and sisters in law enforcement: deadly encounters, tragedy and triumph, the loss of partners and friends, the emotions of love and hate. They'd shared beers and tears and the bitter taste of fear, and they'd never wavered when push came to shove.

"I'm going with you," Lopes finally said.

Dickie glanced over his shoulder, looking in the direction of the office not far behind them, though gone from their view. He said, "Let's drop one car at the office. We may need two if something goes wrong or if a diversion is needed. And I've got a call to make."

Josie tilted her head like the RCA dog at the beginning of old movies, and a question formed in her eyes.

"My new sergeant friend in San Diego," Dickie said. He looked at Lopes. "America's Finest."

Pablo said, "You're going to kill him?"

Jerry handed his phone back without looking at him and ignored his question. "If you're ever asked, you picked me up hitchhiking from Rosarita. You don't know me, don't know anything about me, and never mention our mutual friend, Lucinda."

"*Mi prima*," he uttered in a sad and defeated tone.

Jerry reached over and mussed the tangle of dark hair on Pablo's head the way an old man might tease a young child or show a dog affection. Now it was Pablo who wasn't looking over. Jerry could see sadness in his eyes, and he didn't think it was because Campo would soon be dead. The kid had been on a mission. He had something exciting and worthwhile to do, something important with someone he likely presumed to have been a big deal at some point in his life. Lucinda had told him enough that he knew Jerry had been a cop in L.A., and Jerry knew how big that might seem to a kid trying to survive in Tijuana. Not only would he likely have viewed Jerry as someone important, but he likely would have thought him rich, too. Weren't all Americans? But Jerry also figured the kid had found a friend—Jerry certainly had.

"Why do you have to do it?"

Jerry drew in a long breath and held it a moment, wishing for a cigarette—one of his last, maybe. He said, "Pablo, Mina was my friend. She's dead because of Campo, I'm certain of it. He also knows things about the death of my wife, and I plan to find out what he knows. I'm not going in there to kill him, but I might have to. I hope not."

"Maybe he kills you," Pablo said, his watery brown eyes daring a glance.

He pulled his hand back. "I don't plan for that to happen, my friend. But I don't want you to be around here no matter how this goes, *comprende?*"

He nodded. "*Sí.* Yes, I understand."

Jerry offered his hand, and Pablo shook it, his hand feeling small and weak and wet with perspiration.

"*Adiós*, my friend. God bless you."

A tear rolled down the boy's cheek as he turned his head and Jerry walked away.

DICKIE HAD ASKED FOR THE WATCH SERGEANT AND WAS PLACED ON HOLD. The melodic instrumental hold music spilling through the Crown Vic's speakers was a sharp contrast to the hair-raising hundred-mile-an-hour two-car bullet train that was headed south through Los Angeles, Lopes tight on Dickie's tail as they raced through the night. Josie was with Dickie, waiting for the music to stop and the sergeant to pick up. The line was finally answered but not by Johnson; it was a woman who announced her name as Piotrowski, and Dickie was glad he wouldn't have to remember it or try spelling it. Johnson wasn't in, she said; he wasn't scheduled to be back until the day after tomorrow.

"Is there any way I can get a message to him? I need to speak with him, and it's rather urgent."

There was a subtle beep that was the universal warning that the line was recorded. Of course it was. Every police station's main lines are recorded, and it occurred to Dickie that it might be better that Johnson wasn't at work, at least if they were able to get that message to him and get a callback.

"And who are you, sir?"

He knew this was coming, and he had considered his response in the moment that had passed. "Richard Jones, L.A. Sheriff's Homicide."

"Oh," she said, a new tone in her voice, a bit more energy, and less apathy. "Okay, Detective. And a callback number?"

He gave it to her slowly to make sure she got it right, and then he repeated it with more pace. He could have said it with cadence two or three more times as they did on late-night commercials to make sure the jingle stayed in your head, but he opted not to and changed lanes to get around a slower-moving vehicle in front of him. She read it back and said she'd get Sergeant Johnson the message right away.

Dickie disconnected, and Josie raised her phone. "I'm going to call Pablo."

He glanced from the road with his brows furrowed in question. She said, "He's been driving Jerry around, and that's whose phone Jerry used to call a few minutes ago. Maybe Jerry's still with him, and I can talk some sense into him."

Dickie had no response. He knew from their previous meeting the man was unhinged, a lost soul in Tijuana with vengeance in his heart. And now, after the conversation Jerry and Josie just had, it was clear that he was either homicidal or suicidal at this point, maybe both. Campo was in his sights, and Dickie was trying to come up with a better plan than to cross over and head straight to the nightclub where he would likely be found, hunting down Campo. He didn't want to even think about the international crimes they would be committing by doing so.

Josie lowered the phone. "No answer."

"So do you have a plan?"

"No. Do you? I mean, nothing other than going straight to the *Caballo Loco* and trying to stop him before he does something stupid. Or at least be there to back him up and get him out alive."

"Yeah, not a great plan."

She shook her head. "No, it's not. So come up with something better, partner."

Dickie let out a heavy breath and glanced at his phone in its cradle on the dash, willing it to ring. "I'm hoping Johnson gets back to me soon. I think he has an ace or two up his sleeve in matters like this. We may have to donate to his pension fund or something if he does and we can pull this off without going to jail or losing our jobs."

Josie had no response. Dickie glanced over to see she was staring straight ahead but seeing something much farther away, something unpleasant that left her troubled. "It'll work out," he tried.

No answer.

His phone rang, but it was Lopes. Dickie glanced in his mirror as he answered the call, seeing Lopes still directly behind him. "What's up?"

"You tell me. Did you get ahold of that sergeant?"

"Not yet. They're trying to get a message to him."

"Okay, great. Any other bright ideas, Dickie, just in case your buddy doesn't come through for us?"

"Yeah, one."

Lopes said, "Let's hear it."

"Damn the torpedoes and storm the Bastille."

"Great fucking plan, Dickie. Maybe you can write songs after we're fired."

"Yeah, maybe. Now hang up on yourself, Lopes; you're starting to bore me."

Josie's phone rang next, and she answered it before it could ring a second time. "Hello?"

Dickie waited, listening and glancing over to try to pick up her emotion.

"Is this Pablo? I'm Jerry's friend, the one he called a few minutes ago."

She slipped into rapid Spanish, and Dickie wondered if she did so because it was Pablo's native tongue, or if she had something to say she didn't want Dickie to hear, or if it was just faster that way. He had always considered Spanish to be a fast, no-nonsense language—economical, one might say—but he really didn't know, not being able to speak or understand much of it himself.

When she disconnected, he waited to hear the details, filtered as they might have been.

"He said Jerry is at the *Caballo*. Pablo's still sitting down the street. Jerry told him to leave so that he wasn't part of anything that might happen, but Pablo didn't want to abandon him there. So he's waiting."

"What'd he say about a pistol?"

Josie looked at him, and he met her gaze. Dickie said, "I'm not a total idiot." There were some Spanish words that every cop understood.

She closed her eyes and opened them slowly. "Jerry's got a gun."

Dickie adjusted in his seat and kept his eyes on the road while considering the potential disaster they were walking into.

"Great. Where'd he get a gun? He say?"

"Apparently it came with the car."

Dickie looked over and frowned.

She shrugged. "It's what he said."

"Mexico," Dickie said as if that explained it. Buy a car and get a gun. Buy two cars, get a kilo and a gun. Sometimes he didn't get her people at all. "This just keeps getting better."

They were almost to Oceanside. The two-and-a-half-hour drive would be condensed to just a little over an hour and a half, thanks to the light traffic and the flashing *excuse me* lights on the rear deck, Dickie's blue and amber CHP repellent. Nobody could be more irritating than the

Highway Patrol when you were trying to get somewhere in a hurry and came across one of their traffic Nazis. He'd been lectured by them in the past. He had also been beefed by them when, on another occasion and during a similar mission, an officer with an attitude began his traffic lecture, and Dickie didn't have time for his bullshit. He explained as much in not-so-friendly terms, and the butthurt traffic cop made a complaint. *Chippies.*

Finally, the phone rang, and an unknown number showed on the display. Dickie pushed the button and lifted his chin slightly, sending his voice directly to the microphone attached to the A-pillar that framed the driver's side of the windshield. It was an aftermarket job, not a built-in fancy arrangement like the new cars came with.

"Sheriff's Homicide, Detective Jones," he said with some authority, and he knew Josie would give him shit because he never answered the phone like that. That was how she answered the phone, but it wasn't the way he did—ever. For some reason though, tonight he wanted to sound official and serious, suspecting that this was the San Diego sergeant returning his call.

"Good evening, Detective. Sergeant Johnson here. I got a message to call you."

Dickie thanked him for calling and told him he hated bothering him when he wasn't even on duty, but they had a very ugly situation developing across the border, and he really needed some help. There were questions, some answers, a little back-and-forth brainstorming, and when the call was finished, they had a plan. It wasn't a great plan, but it was a plan. Now they had to pray they could pull it off.

40

Jerry had slipped the doorman his usual twenty and asked how everything was going—cool as a cucumber—and made his way inside through the stagnant air that smelled of beer and cheap perfume. As he pushed through the crush of lustful patrons—most of whom were gazing at the various glittery naked ladies on any of the several stages surrounding them and barely noticed being brushed past and nudged out of the way—he spotted Campo and his boy, Carlos, across the crowded room. They worked their way through the crowd, and shortly after, they took a set of stairs to the second level. They moved along a corridor of VIP rooms and ducked into one of them at the end of the hallway.

Change of plans.

Jerry went to an open seat at the main bar and ordered a beer. He hadn't even considered what might have happened if he had stormed into Campo's office only to find he wasn't there. His timing had been lucky, and he thought maybe this was a good sign—off to a good start. He had all the time in the world and now a cold beer to quench the thirst that had suddenly overwhelmed him seemed to be just what he needed. He'd wait and watch, and when the boss man returned to his office, he'd make his move. In the meantime, he hoped to go relatively unnoticed.

But it didn't work out that way.

A hand touched his bicep and rested there. He turned his head to see it was the angel, the young entertainer looking up at him with a smile. She said something in Spanish, but it was more than he understood, so he smiled back and asked in English, "How are you?" Then he glanced back over his other shoulder at the VIP door upstairs where Campo and his righthand man had disappeared. The door was still closed, and Campo was not in sight.

The angel had apparently understood that much English. "*Bien*," she said, maintaining a lovely smile. Flashes of multicolored strobes reflected in her dark brown eyes.

Now she leaned into him, and he worried she might feel the Glock tucked into his waistband at the small of his back. He turned toward her in order to prevent that. In a mix of Spanish and some broken English, she asked about his lady friend. Josie, he presumed, since she had been with him the last time. But he wondered for a moment if she had meant Mina, and he knew she couldn't possibly know she was dead. Well, he wasn't going to talk about it—not here, and not now. He really didn't want to talk to her at all and wished she would go away, but he knew she was probably trying to hustle tips. After all, that's why they were there. That was the one and only reason these girls enhanced their boobs and took off their clothes and smiled and flirted and touched nasty men, and sometimes they did much more than that. It was all for money.

He raised his beer and asked if she wanted a drink. That was one of their gimmicks; the scantily clad waitresses—who were dancers on a break—would ask patrons to buy them a drink at the inflated cost, and they would never actually get themselves a drink; they'd just take the money. Of course, she agreed, and he gave her a five, and she said thanks and disappeared. He hoped she wouldn't be back. He turned back to his preferred vantage point and saw Campo and his boy, Carlos, coming out of the room upstairs. Amazingly—given the distance and the crowd—Campo locked his gaze upon him. So much for the element of surprise. Now he'd have to see Campo's next move and alter his own game plan.

Campo turned and said something to Carlos, and then they both looked directly at him. Carlos nodded with his eyes fixed on Jerry, then pulled his phone out of a pocket and worked his thumbs across the keyboard, probably sending a text. This wasn't going as planned. It wasn't going well at all, and Jerry decided it was time to leave.

As he pushed off his stool, a hand was on his bicep again. Only this hand wasn't dainty and soft like that of an angel; it was a large hand with a firm grip that betrayed the strength of the man it was attached to. It was Baby Face, one of Campo's goons. He said, "Come with me, *senõr*."

They went across the crowded main floor, past the center stage and through the crowd, and into the same hallway that he knew from his last visit led to Campo's office. Only this time, Jerry didn't think the meeting would have the same outcome as the last. This time, Campo would likely not be so gracious with him. But also, this time, Jerry had a Glock, and he was prepared to use it.

He wondered how it would go down. He had glimpsed Campo and Carlos on the staircase as he was being led into the hallway, so he knew they wouldn't be far behind. If Baby Face took him into the office and it was only the two of them for those few moments before others arrived, perhaps he'd take the first goon out and turn the odds of the final showdown a little more in his favor. Spin while drawing the Glock and put a 9mm right between the eyes of Baby Face. Move away from the fresh corpse and be ready to take out Campo and his boy the second they entered and paused for that deadly instant to take in the sight of their fallen comrade. But then he'd get no answers. Maybe take out Carlos first and then stick the barrel of his Glock in Campo's mouth and begin the interrogation. He'd have to work fast though, because even with the deafening music on the floor, someone might hear those first two shots. It was as good a plan as Jerry could come up with on the fly. He remembered in SWAT how they always trained to expect the worst, to anticipate that whatever could possibly go wrong probably would. *No operations plan ever survived the first contact.*

To emphasize this point, Baby Face nudged him from behind as Jerry slowed at Campo's door. "Keep going."

Where? The only thing beyond that door was an exit into the dark alley behind the club. Now he had to rethink his strategy again. He had no problem seeing his move to neutralize his escort—the man was too big and slow to get the drop on him once Jerry made his move for the gun. But then what? What would he have accomplished? Unless he went back inside and was somehow able to catch Campo unexpectedly, what good would any of it be? It made no sense to take out the muscle and leave without answers. Either way, he'd be scrambling to stay alive once this went down, and he no longer had wheels or an ally to help him put distance between him and his pursuers.

In SWAT they had a term for operations that went this far off track: FUBAR—fucked up beyond all recognition. And that was exactly how this was turning out.

He stopped at the door to the alley, and Baby Face nudged again. As Jerry reached to push the door open, a distant voice called out. "No, take him into my office."

It was time to drop Plan B and go back to Plan A but with a few minor on-the-fly adjustments. The goal was still the same: eliminate the threats and interrogate the boss.

Then what?

Jerry didn't know.

41

DICKIE PHONED LOPES AFTER HE HUNG UP WITH JOHNSON. "WE'RE meeting that sergeant at the trolley station in San Ysidro." Dickie pictured the place they would meet, the spot where he had waited for Josie to return the last time they were there, and where he and Johnson had shared a cup of coffee and a little bit about themselves as they bonded the way brothers in arms often did. He was willing to bet that if Johnson arrived before they did, he would be at that exact location even if there were plenty of other places to park and wait. Because Type A people were that way about things. When you went to a training class and picked a seat on the first day, you returned to that same seat—even though it hadn't been assigned to you—after each break and the following days and until the class was completed. And when you returned from lunch and found someone else had changed seats, taking yours, you felt violated, and you fought back your inner child that wanted to confront them and let them know that seat had been claimed. What was wrong with people?

"What's the plan?" Lopes wanted to know.

It was complicated, Dickie explained. Johnson had to make some calls and figure something out. There were a few options. There was a *federale* he trusted and had a rapport with, and if he were available to assist them, Johnson would have him meet them at the border. Johnson thought there was a good chance the *federale* would take them into Mexico, and Johnson believed he could get them back through customs easily enough. But if that didn't work, Johnson had another idea, one of which he had been reluctant to provide much detail about on the phone. "It has something to do with his four-wheel drive Bronco and an alternative route in and out of the country."

Lopes said, "Jesus, is he a part-time coyote?"

Whatever worked, Dickie told him. Then he hung up and handed his phone to Josie. "Do me a favor, would you? Send Emily a nice text and let her know I'm working late and not to wait up. But not too nice, or she'll think you sent it and not me."

Josie received the phone and started a text, but she didn't even smile at Dickie's attempt at humor. That was when he knew just how worried about her friend she really was. He said, "We'll get Jerry out of there."

She nodded but didn't seem confident.

They were a half hour out, and it was almost game time.

BABY FACE HAD BACKED UP TO PUT DISTANCE BETWEEN THEM AS HE TOLD Jerry to stop and turn around so they could go back to Campo's office. There were three of *them* in the narrow and dark corridor now, Baby Face right in front of him, and Campo and his boy not far behind, the two of them waiting near the door to Campo's office but watching Jerry closely. If Jerry drew on them now, he could take out Baby Face for sure, but he didn't like the odds of being able to take him down and then neutralize Carlos too. Campo likely wasn't armed, and Jerry didn't want to shoot him anyway. At least not yet. Not until he got some answers. He'd have to take his chances now and go into the office with them willingly and hope to be able to make his move there with better odds of surviving.

Carlos pushed the door to the office wide open, and the three of them stepped back, giving Jerry a wide berth. Their positioning and spacing would have made it impossible for Jerry to have any success with a physical assault had that been his plan. They apparently hadn't even considered that he was armed, and he hoped they wouldn't think of it now. If he got into the office without being searched, he believed he could pull this off, and as he saw it unfolding in his mind, he felt the rush of adrenaline pulsating through his veins, and he heard his heartbeat thumping in his ears. He stepped past them and into the office where he abruptly stopped inside the doorway, shocked by the sight before him.

The man sitting in the seat behind Campo's desk said, "Well hello, Jerry. What a surprise. I wish I could say it is a pleasant one, but both of us know that would be bullshit."

JOHNSON WAS WAITING AT THE TROLLEY STATION. HE WAS IN HIS WHITE Bronco that reminded Dickie of the OJ fiasco in L.A., but he wasn't a killer, and he wasn't being chased by a hundred cops and filmed by a dozen news helicopters. Instead, he was backed into the exact parking spot where he had parked to have a cup of coffee with Dickie on the occasion when they first met, leaving the space Dickie had used open for him. Dickie knew he liked this guy.

They wheeled in next to him, and Lopes whirled into the next spot over. Nobody turned their engines off—a sign that each of them had spent plenty of time working patrol in fast-paced districts where you left the motors running so you could leave in a hurry—and they gathered at the front of Johnson's Bronco for an impromptu briefing. Introductions were made, and Johnson got to it.

"My contact across the border might be able to assist, but he's probably still a half hour out," he said, glancing at the watch on his meaty wrist. "I don't know if you think we have time to wait or not, but there's always Plan B."

"The path of the coyote," Dickie said.

He nodded. "I can't tell you how I know about it or when I've used it, but when you've spent nearly thirty years working along the border, there are certain things that have to be handled discreetly on occasion."

Dickie understood that, and he knew Lopes and Josie were with him. There was the letter of the law and the spirit of the law, and the concept of it was applicable to both sides, the lawbreakers and the peacekeepers who pursued them. Not every law was enforced upon the citizen, and in fact, the more crime-ridden a community, the more relaxed the enforcement often would be. When Dickie worked patrol in South L.A., it was common to overlook the petty crimes. Many citizens would drive on suspended licenses, or none at all, and some would have a beer between their legs or a joint smoldering in the ashtray when they were pulled over by the cops. But if they were otherwise law-abiding citizens and on their way to or from a job—and if their attitudes were good—a warning was about the extent of any intervention in such matters. That was the spirit of the law rather than the letter of the law. There were also many laws in place regulating the manner in which police conducted their business, and the general public might have been astonished to know that the spirit and the letter of the law applied there, too.

One example would be when a crackhead was detained during a burglary investigation, and a small rock of cocaine was found on his person. If the person hadn't committed any other crime—such as the burglary the cop was there to investigate—then that rock might have been smashed on the hood of the patrol car with the cop's flashlight or dropped to the ground and crushed with the heel of a cop's boot. Possession of that rock was a felony. But with a dozen calls for service backed up and the cops stretched thinly across their district handling life-threatening calls and dangerous situations, and in the spirit of the law, sometimes a rock was just a rock. Technically, the destruction of that evidence was a crime in and of itself, and that being the case, Dickie and others had committed hundreds of crimes throughout their careers of enforcing the laws. But a reasonable person could see that the letter of the law, as it was written by sophisticated lawmakers in the comforts of their plush chambers, at times could hamper the efforts of the cops on the streets who were risking their lives to make the communities they policed a little bit safer.

The irony, considering the example of a felony crime ignored and another (technically) committed by the destruction of evidence, is that those same lawmakers, who would surely be at odds with the cops exercising their discretion in these matters, would later cast judgment on those who partook in the war on drugs by locking up the users, the drug addicts whom they now considered to be victims. The cops were ahead of their time, understanding the spirit of the law ahead of the scholarly anointed ones in their heavy robes.

And now this group of dedicated and committed law enforcement officers was going to apply that same spirit of the law—some international laws, in this case—to try to rescue one of their own. In the strictest sense of the letter of the law, it wouldn't be the first felony any of them committed, nor would it likely be the last.

Johnson said, "I'd suggest only one or two of you come with me, and someone else stay here to guard the horses and be ready for a rescue mission if one becomes necessary."

"I'm going with you," Josie said unequivocally.

Lopes said, "You're sure you can get us back across the border?"

Johnson nodded. "Pretty sure. There's always that chance, though."

Dickie looked at Lopes. "Well?"

"Go ahead," he said, the corner of his mouth turned up in a grin. "She's your sister. I'll stay back and man the fort."

Dickie nodded. "Thanks, partner. I appreciate it."

As they began loading up into the Bronco, Dickie turned back to Lopes. "If you have to come get us, take my ride. The trunk is full of adult toys made for just this kind of adventure. Have a look while you're waiting."

Johnson pulled out with Josie riding shotgun and Dickie in the back seat. They were headed south in the Bronco.

42

Now there was no need to interrogate Campo. The man behind the desk would have all the answers to Jerry's questions—Jerry instinctively knew it for certain the moment he laid eyes on him.

The door closed, and Campo walked past him and slid into one of the two chairs at the front of his desk, the chairs where Jerry and Josie had sat during their recent visit. He was glad she wasn't with him now. If he didn't make it out alive, he could live with that, so to speak, but he would never rest peacefully if his actions caused Josie to be killed. He already had enough blood on his hands.

Jerry glanced behind him and saw that only Carlos remained. Where had Baby Face gone? He didn't give it much consideration because he didn't much care. The main point was there was now one serious threat in the room that Jerry had to consider and plan to neutralize as a first action to his newly revised plan, and that was Carlos. The man at the desk could be a problem too, but Jerry was less concerned about him. Familiarity breeds contempt, but it can also bestow a false sense of security.

Campo was saying, "Come, sit with us, and let's have a talk. You and your old friend here probably have a lot to catch up on." The man enjoying his moment, completely relaxed in his kingdom.

But not for long.

Jerry took one step in the direction of the empty seat but stumbled and began to fall. He reached his left hand out to break his fall, saying, "Shit!" as he went down—playing it up all the way—and as he landed, he rolled to his left while pulling the Glock from his waistband with his right hand. He came up with the sights on Carlos and didn't hesitate. The two shots— a double-tap, in SWAT terms—hit center mass and Campos's bodyguard crumbled to the floor. But before the musclebound goon hit the ground, Jerry had rolled again, and his front sight came up on a new target. Another double-tap to center mass, and Campo was done running whores. Now it was just Jerry and an old friend who sat frozen behind the desk, and they watched each other like a pair of coiled vipers.

Campo sat in his chair with his gaze fixed far away, perhaps seeing his idea of Paradise: rolling fields of opium poppy tended by an infinite reserve of pre-pubescent girls with golden hair and bronze skin. The hell that awaited him would stand in stark contrast. A final breath escaped his body, wet and gurgled. It was the death rattle of those who believed it would never be them on that side of the muzzle.

"As you can see," Jerry said to his friend, "I am not disinclined to pull the trigger, not when it comes to killing bad guys. I never really was, to be honest with you." He lowered himself onto the chair across the desk from his old acquaintance and next to the cooling carcass of the former child pimp. Jerry glanced at Campo and smiled. "It was actually a pleasure to shoot this piece of shit, and I'm not uncertain that I won't take as much pleasure in killing you."

His adversary sat silent, unblinking.

"I now have no doubt that you know about Laura's murder. I've suspected at times that you might, but I always dismissed those thoughts as being ludicrous, the ravings of a madman. But now, with you sitting here in Mexico behind the desk of a cartel man—recently deceased, of course—I can see with a degree of clarity how it all happened. My only questions for you are who and why? And you'll want to be precise and forthcoming in your answers unless you care to join your gangster friends in the Great Hereafter."

"I have no—"

Jerry held up his left hand, the one that wasn't pointing a stolen Glock at the man's chest. "Don't you dare let one lie slip out of your disgusting cocksucker. One lie—one tiny little fucking lie from your nasty mouth—and you'll leak to death on this filthy floor."

"What do you want to know, Jerry?" he pleaded.

"Who killed Laura, and why?"

"It wasn't supposed to happen, Jerry, I swear to you. It was a fuckup. I'm sick about it—I've always been sick about it. You can't know how sorry I am." His eyes appeared glassy for an instant, but Jerry didn't buy it. The man could win an Oscar for his performances throughout his life. The thought of him screaming about a suspect grabbing his testicles came to mind.

"Who did it? Who was in my house that night while you and Wilkins and those other assholes were trying to keep us away from home?"

His gaze shifted away from Jerry and came back slowly.

"It doesn't matter anymore."

"It matters to me."

He nodded and looked down while shifting slightly in his seat behind the desk. Jerry could still see his hands wrapped around the armrests of his chair with the death grip of a man on a ledge, and Jerry knew he was stalling while contemplating action. His friend had never been opposed to violence and had always been quick to action. Jerry knew the man wasn't going to go out without a fight. But Jerry was ready for it—perhaps begging for it.

"Well, Benny Boy?"

Carmen took his time. He was thinking. Jerry couldn't afford to give him too much room to wiggle. It would be akin to letting your opponent land the first punch—it gave them a decisive advantage in the outcome of the fight.

He said, "Tell you what. Since I'm pressed for time suddenly—in a bit of a hurry to get back to my homeland—I'm going to give you a count to ten. That's all you get. Believe it.

"One…"

"Jerry, I—"

"Two…"

"It wasn't even my idea. Wilkins, he's the one that thought you were going to rat us out."

"Three…"

"We were always tight. You know that. I would have never—"

"Four…"

"It was Perry!"

"Who?" Jerry asked, his mind drawing a blank as the name rolled around in his head.

"Perry. Mike Perry."

He was a sergeant in Jerry's unit. But that made no sense. "Five…"

"Jerry, you have to believe me. He—it was him, but he was only supposed—"

"Six…"

"—to get the money back and look for any notes you might have been keeping."

"Talk faster. I'm at seven."

"It's why they gave him immunity. They knew they couldn't put him away without him rolling over on everyone."

"Eight…"

"It was that or kill him. He was just startled. You weren't supposed to be home."

Jerry shot him. You always wanted to catch them off guard, and Benny Carmen—of all people—would know that. He would have been moving on Nine, and then the outcome might not have been as clean.

But it was a gut shot, purposefully, no double-tap to the ten-ring on this one. Not yet. He still had some things to learn.

"Benny, why?"

He was crying now, writhing in pain, blood spilling over his hands that now clutched his abdomen. He said nothing.

"And how are you in with the cartel when it was them you were stealing from?" That was the part that puzzled him most.

Benny laughed through his pain. "You fucking dummy. You never see the big picture, do you?"

"One more question, and then I have to go."

The dying man waited.

"Who took out Mina?"

"Who?" he said, clearly puzzled by the name.

He'd never heard of her, so they had nothing left to discuss.

Jerry stood up from his chair and took a deep breath. His old buddy watched him closely, resignation in his eyes. Jerry turned and started to leave. You can't just kill your old partner in cold blood.

Unless letting him live would seal your fate.

43

"HEY KID, MOVE THE FUCKING CAR."

Johnson then repeated the order in Spanish, and Josie was surprised by how well he spoke the language. Even down to the pejorative, his translation was flawless. She said, "Looks like an old cop car."

The kid Johnson had yelled at had been leaning against the hood of a car parked in an alley to the rear of the *Caballo Loco*. He seemed frightened and confused as he began to move to the driver's door. Suddenly he stopped, looked back at the trio in the Bronco, and started for them.

Johnson drew and readied his gun beneath the frame of the door as the young man approached. In nearly perfect English, he said, "Are you friends of Jerry?"

Josie leaned forward to look around Johnson and make eye contact with the kid. She recognized his voice. "Pablo, it's me, Josie. Where's Jerry?"

Johnson shifted the Bronco into Park and shut off the engine. Josie popped out and started around the hood to meet him. Pablo said, "He's still inside, as far as I know."

But there was something else; she could see it in his eyes. "What's wrong? What has happened?"

He shrugged. "There were gunshots."

She went to the door. It was locked.

Dickie was beside her now. She looked around for something to use to pry the door open. Since it opened outward, there was no way to kick it open or bust through it from this side.

Dickie turned to Johnson. "Tire iron."

Johnson started for the back of his vehicle just as the door to the nightclub flew open. It was Jerry, and he almost knocked Josie down as he hurried through the door. She grabbed him, and they hugged. They pulled apart, and Jerry looked at Pablo. "You are one loyal companion, my friend."

"We need to get out of here," Johnson said. "I have a feeling it's going to get hot in a minute."

Dickie followed Johnson to the Bronco, but Josie hung back with Jerry. "Come with us."

He hesitated, and she could see his mind racing with the possibilities.

"Come on, Jerry. We're getting across, and you won't need ID." She indicated the Bronco with a nod. "Sergeant Johnson's going to take us across the desert."

Jerry was nodding when his eyes brightened with a thought. "Yeah, okay. But give me one second." He turned and started for the door back to the club.

"Jerry!"

He was through the door as he called out, "I'll be back. One second!"

Dickie yelled, "Let's go! Come on, Josie. He's lost his fucking mind!"

"Hang on," she shouted back. "Just one second."

Josie stayed at the door, waiting, watching.

The narrow and dark hallway was ominous. The bright flashing lights of the club bounced off the walls beyond the corridor, and the music spilled out in waves of thumping bass tones and shards of piercing synthesized distortion.

Jerry appeared at the far end and met her gaze, turned back, and was encouraging someone to come. The angel appeared next to him, and he ushered her forward. She came down the hallway ahead of him, moving quickly in her white bikini bottoms and paper wings, tassels swinging from her otherwise bare breasts.

As they neared the exit, Jerry shouted over the music. "Take her with you."

"Come on, Jerry, let's go!" Josie said again.

"Take her."

"We will. But you're going too."

He shook his head, started to say, "No, I can't..." and his legs folded beneath him. In the hallway now she saw Baby Face coming from behind him, a gun extended in his hand. There was a flash and then another, and Jerry was down. Josie pushed the angel out the door while drawing her weapon. She fired two shots at the cartel goon, and it stopped him. He cringed and fell against the wall. She fired again, and then she was grabbed from behind. It was Dickie. He pulled her from the doorway and pushed her toward the Bronco.

The naked angel was climbing in, and Josie followed, the two of them climbing into the back seat. She had lost sight of Dickie, and realized he must've gone into the club. She turned to go back for him, but the door flew open again, and Dickie came out with Jerry over his shoulder.

Dickie pushed him into the Bronco, behind the front passenger's seat into the back with Josie and the angel. Dickie jumped into the front. He slammed his door shut, and Johnson gassed it. But he had only gone a few feet when he suddenly stopped.

Pablo stood next to the old Crown Vic, his face a mask of confusion. Johnson backed up a few feet to come alongside him. "You want to go with us?"

He smiled.

"Come on," the old sergeant insisted. He opened his door and pulled the kid in, across his lap, and into the backseat. "What's one more felony?" he mused and then drove off.

44

When they hit the outskirts of the city, Johnson pulled off the main road and started across the barren landscape over shrubs and around cacti and across dunes of powdery sand that glittered beneath a harvest moon, a cloud of dust marking their trail. Angel removed her felt-covered poster-board wings and the halo and tossed both out the back window. They whirled in the blowing sand and crashed down against the harsh desert terrain, and the angel who had been no saint was now delivered from her living hell. She pulled her knees to her chest and wrapped her tiny arms around her bare legs with a newfound gesture of modesty.

As lights from the city faded behind them, Johnson slowed and eventually stopped to evaluate the damage to his gunshot passenger before they began the roughest stretch of their escape. Jerry leaned against Josie who compressed a wadded shirt against his side where the bullet had torn through his flesh. It appeared to be a minor wound, relatively speaking, having entered his lower back at an angle and exited just above his hip. Of course, the term "minor" when describing a gunshot wound is only used when referring to the trauma of another, not oneself. Sweat beaded on his forehead and trickled down his cheeks, but he was alert, and his eyes were clear and complacent.

"How bad is it?" Johnson asked.

Josie lifted the bloody rag she held against the wound and was comforted to see the bleeding had mostly stopped. "He needs a doctor, but he'll survive."

Johnson went to the back of the Bronco and dropped the tailgate. He moved a few things around as if searching for something, and a moment later he tossed a Padres hoodie over the seat to Angel. It was large enough to blanket three of her, but she was elated to lose herself within it. Next, he handed a first aid kit over the seat to Josie.

"You know basic first aid, I assume."

"Of course."

"Let's clean up that wound and put some fresh bandages on it for the ride north. I've got painkillers in there, too, if he needs anything."

Jerry shook his head.

She said, "We'll see how he does."

Johnson nodded, closed the tailgate, and they were off again, headed north with the stars shining bright above them and the bawl of a coyote's song fading in their wake.

AN HOUR LATER, THEY WERE ON AMERICAN SOIL SOMEWHERE WEST OF THE Otay Mountain Wilderness, and half an hour after that, they arrived at UC San Diego Medical Center where a team of surgeons waited to patch Jerry up. Johnson had called ahead and told them a cop had been shot, and emergency staff were ready and waiting. Dickie was grateful for the sergeant's assistance and amazed at how much risk he had taken to help his fellow law enforcement brethren, even though he had barely known them. He was a dinosaur and a dying breed of cop, and Dickie didn't think he could ever repay him.

They left Jerry at the ER, and Josie told him she'd be back to get him in a day or two when he was ready to go home. Jerry argued he didn't have a home, and Josie quipped back, "You and half the people in that Bronco, pal... We'll work something out."

THE NEXT EVENING, THE TEAM RETURNED TO LONG BEACH AND KNOCKED on Mike Perry's door again, this time with a new agenda but the same Columbo-like demeanors, showing no hint of what they now suspected to be true, that Perry had killed Laura Townsend. Benny Carmen had said so while under a great deal of duress in Campo's office, dead cartel members scattered about and rapidly cooling, but that didn't make it so. It was certainly worth consideration and exploration, but they had no evidence that it was true. Not yet anyway. His physical description matched what Jerry had reported back then, but so did every other male in Los Angeles of average height and weight and of white or Hispanic descent. The black clothing and ski mask the killer had worn eliminated the possibility of a positive ID. The odds were against solving the case absent the discovery of some type of evidence, such as the gun that was used or a suspect's confession. The odds of obtaining either were heavily against them.

Inside they each returned to the places they had sat on the previous visit. Perry seemed more nervous than he had before, and Dickie couldn't help but wonder if they were unknowingly giving off a different vibe due to Benny Carmen's allegation that Perry was the killer. Or maybe it was as simple as that their previous visit had rattled Perry, and he was worried about something else coming down on him. It made Dickie think there could be something to Perry being the burglar-turned-gunman that night if their previous visit had stirred some emotions in him that he had been suppressing for a decade now. No matter how much time passed, when homicide detectives knocked on a killer's door, that door was never opened lightly.

Lopes began by showing Perry a picture of FBI Agent Williams. "Is this the dude that was in Carmen's office that day you agreed to a deal?"

Perry studied it longer than Dickie thought necessary, almost making a show of it.

Eventually, he said, "I don't think so. I really can't be certain though."

"Try," Lopes encouraged. "It's important."

Perry pushed back in his seat, getting comfortable now that they had started with their focus on someone other than him, or at least that's how Dickie saw it. "Okay," he said, "the more I look at it… I don't think this was the same guy."

Lopes had said on the way over, "That meeting with Carmen and the black dude would have taken place after the Townsend murder." Dickie hadn't thought of that. It was all at about the same time, and he hadn't considered the time frame of it until Lopes mentioned it. Josie had commented, "Right, so Perry stood in that office knowing he killed Laura Townsend, and the chief would have also known that Perry killed Townsend, and yet there's this federal agent there dictating the terms of a plea agreement." Which they can't do, Dickie had retorted, saying that it made more sense that the black guy was a prosecutor. Now Dickie was convinced he was right. It hadn't made sense to think Williams would have been part of that meeting, and Dickie was relieved that Perry had failed to identify him.

Now it was time for the confrontation, and that was Dickie's lead role.

"Where were you the night Laura Townsend was murdered?"

Elvis could have parachuted into the living room and not surprised Perry more than Dickie's question—and its implication—had. He looked from one investigator to another but never settled long on any of their watchful eyes until he could finally manage, "*What?*"

It was like every other crook buying time, a natural reaction. Hey man, where'd you get that watch? Huh? Who, me? And then the lies began. *I found it. Some dude gave it to me.* Anything to avoid admitting that they jacked a dude to get it. In Perry's case, he began, "How would I know? That was a long time ago, man." He licked his lips and waited, but when the detectives only maintained their poker-faced stares, he said, "I didn't even really know Townsend, and I never met his wife."

A non sequitur response to a rather clear and pointed question.

Dickie said, "Let's try this. When did you hear about the murder?"

He shook his head, his eyes still darting about the room nervously. "I —I don't remember. Why would I remember…"

"Jerry Townsend was your captain at the time. His wife gets murdered when the two of them return from an evening out with colleagues and surprise a burglar. You don't remember where you were or what you were doing when you heard about it?"

He sat shaking his head slowly, still feigning confusion and shock at the line of questioning.

"You remember where you were and what you were doing on nine-eleven?"

Now he nodded.

"Do you remember where you were when the Northridge quake rocked Southern California?"

He nodded again.

"My point, we remember the significant emotional events in our lives. When your captain's wife is murdered, you remember where you were and what you were doing when you got that news. Unless, of course, it wasn't news."

Perry frowned. "I don't know what you mean."

Dickie looked at Josie as a cue. They had planned to ruffle Perry's feathers and then allow him to feel the comfort of Josie's embrace, so to speak. It was the good cop/bad cop routine but with somewhat of a beauty and the beast twist.

Josie led off with a personal touch to further weaken his defenses. "Mike," she said as she reached over and lightly touched his knee with her hand, "we're not here talking to you again by accident or because of whatever deal you made with Arco Narco. We're here to talk to you about Laura Townsend's murder, and we are acting on some compelling information that has come across our desks."

"Oh?"

"Let's step back a minute, though, and talk about what happened. Someone broke into their home. That someone was surprised by the Townsends coming home early. Someone panicked, and in the heat of the moment, a shot was fired. That's not premeditated murder, at least not on the surface. I don't think it was a premeditated murder," Josie said and paused to look to her partners for affirmation. Both shook their heads, *No, no, definitely not a premeditated murder.* With that part of it played down, she went on: "So you have a burglary and an accident—that's how someone might see it." Not her and not her partners, but someone, somewhere might see it in that light.

Perry was all hers, leaning into her now for more of the comfort she was offering before his execution.

"See, but the reason we know even that much," she said, "is the same reason we know who that someone was. Because others were involved. No, no, they weren't there that night—only one person was there—but there were accomplices who, let's just say, didn't sign on to be caught up in a murder investigation. So you know how that works, Mike… they want to talk. They want to cut deals. Now that we've turned the heat up on this unsolved case, people are dying to talk to us." Perry would have no idea just how reflective that last statement was.

He began shaking his head again. "They're not saying it was me…"

"You're that someone I spoke of, Michael. The someone who broke into the home. The someone who was surprised by the Townsends' early arrival. The someone who panicked."

He leaned back, trying again to distance himself from Josie on the sofa. She scooted toward him and again touched his knee with her hand. "But you're not really a killer, Mike. You didn't go there for that reason. In fact, it wasn't your idea to go there at all. You were told to go there, told by one of your superiors, and you probably didn't think you had a choice. We already know all that."

The gazes of Dickie and Lopes never left Perry's face. They studied his every mannerism, his physical responses, and his emotions. Dickie was impressed with Josie's skills in the interview room. She had always been better at getting people to talk than anyone he'd ever worked with before. People wanted to talk to her. They wanted her to like them, to accept them for whatever they might have been. They wanted her to understand their part in whatever heinous crime she was investigating, and they hoped she'd forgive them for it. Later, in court, they'd hate her—each and every one of them. Because they'd been had, and by the time they figured it out, it was too late. She was on the other side after that, sitting at the table with the prosecutor who meant to put them in prison for as long as the laws would allow.

Perry cast his gaze to the floor, and the room went silent. They would wait for however long it took because these were the moments that preceded confessions. It was a time when the suspect reflected on the surreal events he had tried to forget but that still haunted him, and he would try to reconcile what was happening at that moment when their worlds were seemingly coming apart. A sociopath would give no thought to it at all, but civilized people would oftentimes be grasping for relief after having spent years living with such dark, burdensome secrets. People inherently wanted to confess their sins and receive absolution, and it took time and patience to allow them to resolve their internal conflicts. On the one hand, they'd be confessing to murder. On the other, it was a relief to stop living with the guilt and hiding from the world. It was liberating to confess one's sins.

As their primary suspect continued to writhe before them, Dickie thought about Benny Carmen, the mastermind of all of it—the dope rips, the attempted burglary that cost an innocent woman her life and ruined the lives of many others—and how he met his demise in a Tijuana whorehouse. Good for him, the piece of shit, he thought. Let him rot in hell. But they had others who mattered, not the least of which was the commander, Don Wilkins, and County Supervisor Charlene Anderson. And Dickie wondered what Perry might be able to give them to implicate each of them. As Perry considered his fate, Dickie knew there was a better-than-fair chance he'd shut off and tell them he had no idea what they were talking about. He was likely weighing those odds now: Do they have enough to hang me, or do they need my confession? And before he dropped that bomb on them, that he had nothing more to say, Dickie wanted to give him one more glimmer of hope, one more chit to hold onto.

He said, "Perry," just to get his attention. Perry looked up slowly and met Dickie's gaze.

"They hung you out to dry, my friend. Now you have the chance to put it all back on them. All of them, Carmen, Wilkins, and even Charlene Anderson."

His eyes widened at the revelation of Anderson, and Dickie thought he'd landed a fight-ending blow when he let this cop-turned-killer know that they were looking at the others, that they knew about the whole deal. But a grin crept onto Perry's face, and Dickie knew at that moment they had lost him.

"I don't have anything else to say," he said, "and I'll see you out now."

45

———————

"WE KNOW CARMEN AND WILKINS WERE INVOLVED, SO WHAT DID I SAY that flipped his switch?"

They were back at the office having a roundtable discussion. None of them were happy with the outcome of the Mike Perry interview. Dickie felt he had undone everything, that his final comments had turned Perry in another direction.

Lopes huffed out a heavy breath and said, "I think it was when you mentioned Supervisor Anderson. That's when the lights went on in his tiny little head."

Dickie thought so too. "Does that mean she wasn't involved?"

"We have nothing on her. She was a champion of the Narco guys and their war on drugs, and she showed up for their post-bust press conferences praising them. She campaigned on her record of being tough on crime. So maybe her relationship with Carmen and company was strictly political. We have nothing to connect her to any of the criminal activity."

"But they were all together the night of the murder," Dickie reminded. "It was Carmen, Wilkins and his wife, Anderson and her husband..."

Lopes shrugged. "She was an ally to Benny Carmen and his war on drugs. They were friends, or at least they had a working relationship. Maybe she was invited that night so that Carmen and Wilkins would have the solid alibis of being out with a county supervisor in the event anything ever came back on them."

"Yeah, maybe."

Josie weighed in. "Don't beat yourself up, partner. He wasn't going to confess."

Dickie was surprised by her statement. "You don't think?"

She shook her head. "I thought I had him for a while. I was close, and he was on the ropes toward the end. But when the silence continued for as long as it did, I knew in my heart the interview was over. I knew we'd lost him somehow. When you offered up the others to bait him into cutting a deal, I was glad that you did. I thought, there you go, that might bring him back. I thought it was the only chance we had then because I somehow knew he wasn't going to confess."

It was something, but Dickie still felt that he had blown it. He started thinking of how to resurrect the investigation without Perry, without a gun, and without any other evidence. They didn't have enough probable cause to get a search warrant on Perry's house, much less a wiretap on anyone's phones. With Benny Carmen dead in Mexico, the only other option was Wilkins. They could try to turn him, but Dickie knew their case was too thin without Perry's confession. Wilkins would likely know the same.

But what else did they have? Dickie had lost his appetite for a trip to Idaho. He didn't think Brett Walker, who, along with Victor Robles, had originally investigated the case could shed any light on anything they didn't already know. In fact, he likely knew far less than what they now knew about Laura Townsend's murder. They had Williams's informant, Fur Face, who claimed that Jerry had had her killed because of an affair, but there was absolutely no evidence to support that claim, and Dickie didn't buy it. Maybe with the aftermath of the Tijuana fiasco, Fur Face might be more forthcoming. After all, his boss was dead. His buddy Baby Face was likely dead or dying, given what Josie had said about her shots hitting him and taking him down. But whatever impact any of it might have had on the case was yet to be seen. In fact, there hadn't been a word from anyone about what happened in Tijuana—at least not yet—and Dickie wondered when that storm was going to hit.

He said, "What about Wilkins? Should we pay him a visit?"

Lopes said, "Sure, why not? I always like slamming my meat in the door after stepping on it first."

Apparently, Lopes also expected the storm to come ashore soon enough.

"What about you?" he asked Josie.

"You boys go on. I have to check on Pablo and Angelica."

It turned out that the young woman they had been calling Angel was Angelica Alvarado. Angel, as it turned out, is what everyone called her, and that was the reason for the wings and halo outfit she wore at the club.

"And the good news is," Josie continued, "she's an adult—barely, but still—and she and Pablo are hitting it off. So they can hang out together in the motel for a few more days until Jerry gets out of the hospital and we figure everything out."

"An adult, huh? I thought she was fifteen or sixteen."

Josie shook her head. "The sad part is, she's been working there since she was fifteen."

"Shame," Dickie said.

"Uh-huh."

"Okay," Lopes said, rising from his chair and looking at the clock on the wall, "Let's get to it if we're going to see Wilkins. I am going to need some cocktails tonight, and you guys are running into my social hour."

They turned out the lights and walked out together into a warm summer night in Los Angeles. You could hear the distant hum of steady traffic on the nearby freeway and smell the sweet perfume of the night-blooming jasmine that adorned the landscape around the buildings and along the walkways of the office. If it weren't for the bloody trail that had been left in Mexico and the weight of having smuggled two Mexican nationals and a gunshot *gringo* across the border, it would have been a lovely, carefree night in L.A., the type on which you would sit on a patio and think about your day with an adult beverage or two. But as it was, the investigators had work yet to do and trouble on the horizon. There would be time for cocktails when the smoke cleared.

JERRY AWOKE IN THE HOSPITAL WITH A CLEAR HEAD. HE REMEMBERED everything that had happened in Mexico, first with Mina, then at the club with Benny Carmen, the boss, Campo, and his boy, Carlos. He remembered every detail of shooting Carlos and Campo, and he had no regrets about doing it. He figured he was a dead man if he didn't, so it was no different than pulling the trigger on a man who aimed his gun at you. Some people just needed to be ventilated. Jerry remembered his conversation with Carmen before shooting him too, and the revelation he'd made sat on Jerry like a boulder.

He reflected on the moment he was shot. Josie was at the door, and he was going toward her while prodding the angel ahead of him. He didn't hear the gunshot, but he knew he'd been shot when the bullet tore through his flesh. As he fell, he looked behind him and saw Baby Face with a gun. Josie guided the angel through the door and stepped between her and the gunman as she drew her gun and fired. And he remembered Dickie grabbing him and carrying him out over his shoulder. It all seemed to happen over a long period of time, but Jerry knew that wasn't so. He had experienced this phenomenon before where time seemed to slow or stop during life-threatening situations, and the brain processed every action in extraordinary detail. The time warp seemed to wane as Dickie carried him out, and Jerry still didn't know how he had done it. He didn't know if it was one of those things you heard about where superhuman strength is witnessed during life-saving efforts or if Dickie was far stronger than he appeared—stronger than what you would expect of a man of his age with a desk job.

Jerry was unclear about when this all happened. He had no idea how long he'd been at the hospital, though he did recall being brought in by Dickie and Josie and some dude in a Bronco. Who was that guy, anyway? He seemed to recall someone calling him a sergeant. Whoever he was, he had likely saved them all with his detailed knowledge of the backcountry that allowed him to sneak back over the border. Jerry recalled the rough ride across what must have been a goat trail at times, the Bronco twisting and crawling as it climbed steep hills and eased down others, Jerry being jostled left and right and bumping along as pain shot through his abdomen like a flame.

The room was no different than any other hospital configuration with its strong odors of antiseptic cleaners and bleach. A machine behind him beeped steadily, and the sounds of voices and phones and doors opening and closing were constant. Occasionally the sound of a gurney or wheelchair rolling along in the hallway outside his room would be accompanied by groans and moans and sometimes the cries of other patients. As for his level of comfort, Jerry felt damn good for having been shot. Good enough that he wanted to get out of there. He had the room to himself, though he knew the empty bed next to him could be filled at any time.

He felt around for the remote that could be found attached to every hospital bed he'd ever been in or seen. He wanted to raise the back of his bed so he could sit more upright, and he thought he'd summon a nurse while he was still awake. He was dying of thirst, and he also wanted to ask a few questions: What day was it? How long had he been there? What was his prognosis and when could he get out? He found the remote and raised the bed to his liking, and then he pushed the button to call for a nurse.

The view outside his window was of a sprawling city, and he remembered that he was in San Diego, back in the relative safety of the United States. He wondered what might happen to him following the ordeal at the *Caballo*. Would he be named as a suspect in the deaths of the men he had shot? Would the authorities ask for him to be returned to stand trial? What would the authorities here do about it? He didn't know. He knew if the roles were reversed and he was a Mexican national who had killed someone in America and fled across the border, there would be no guarantee that his government would send him back to face trial. In fact, oftentimes, they did not, usually citing their opposition to the death penalty as their primary reason. But Jerry suspected that in many of those cases, there was more to it. Status and wealth, political connections, cartel influence… Maybe his government would protect him in a similar fashion and refuse to send him back. They might not believe in the death penalty in Mexico, but everyone knew if a *gringo* was locked up down there for any serious crime, a death sentence was handed down at the prison level. Jerry couldn't imagine what they'd do to someone who killed cartel members.

He thought about what his old friend Benny Carmen had told him about his wife's murder. Mike Perry, of all people, was the masked man that night. Could he believe it? It seemed a stretch, but why would Carmen lie about it when he likely knew he was about to die?

Had Benny Carmen died?

Jerry had considered finishing him off before he left, but he couldn't do it. He'd shot him in the gut, and that might very well have killed him—especially being in Mexico where trauma care was a century behind that of the States—but he hadn't had the ability to finish the job before walking out. It wasn't easy shooting your friend.

Benny had called him a fucking dummy and said he never saw the big picture. It was in response to Jerry asking how Benny could be involved with the cartel when it was the cartel he had been stealing from. What was he missing? How did that make sense? What was the big picture?

The nurse arrived. Jerry had pictured a cute blonde with a great smile to be the one who would care for him during his stay and perhaps expedite his release with just the right amount of flattery and flirtation. But no, they sent in a gorilla. Jerry's nurse was well over six feet, nearly in each direction. His name tag read Hemi S., the S the first initial of his last name. They likely did that to protect the nurses from creepy weirdos and stalkers. But they could have listed Hemi's full name, social security number, home address, and a picture of his beautiful daughter—if he had one—and Hemi would have no worries. He was Samoan—Jerry asked—twenty-six, and single. He graduated from the University of San Diego with a bachelor's degree in nursing, his education paid for by a full-ride football scholarship. And yes, he'd heard the Hemi jokes before, a Hemi being Dodge's powerhouse gas motor, and no, he hadn't been the offensive line for the Toreros, just a big part of it.

Jerry said, "Look, Hemi, I need to get out of here. What do you think, can we get some pain meds to go and my discharge papers?"

"What I think," he said, his voice a dull rumble like distant thunder, "is you'll be here till the doc says otherwise, *capiche*?"

Yes, Jerry clearly understood. And with that, he lowered his bed and shut his eyes.

46

Dickie turned from Don Wilkins's front door and shook his head.
Lopes nudged past him to see for himself the note that had caused Dickie's
annoyance. Though the message wasn't addressed to anyone in particular,
it had clearly been left there for them. The former sheriff's commander
had no intention of speaking to any lowly cop. The note was concise:
Contact my lawyer.

"Perry beat us to the punch," Lopes said, turning to join Dickie, who
had started back for the car.

Dickie didn't bother with a reply. Of course Perry beat them to the
punch. It proved what they now believed: that Perry was the killer and
Benny Carmen and Don Wilkins were collaborators. Dickie didn't think
they planned to kill anyone that night, but that didn't matter. Laura
Townsend had been killed during the commission of a felony—residential
burglary—and that made it a first-degree murder case. Though Carmen
and Wilkins weren't there when it happened, it was clear that they had at
least known about it and authorized it if they hadn't planned it and ordered
it done. But with Carmen dead and Perry and Wilkins hiding behind
lawyers, the path to retribution was anything but clear.

They rode back in silence and parted ways at the office. Dickie
called Josie on his way home. She said "the kids" were settled in and

enjoying their time together with pizza and sodas and 180 channels on cable TV.

"What happened with Wilkins?"

Dickie told her about the note and said he thought they were dead in the water. "There's just nothing to tie any of them directly to the murder."

She didn't disagree.

Dickie knew it was the type of case that could be impossible to prove, and that was when it didn't involve former department executives. Without compelling evidence, they would likely be told to shut it down, that they weren't going to embarrass the department with these wild accusations and nothing to substantiate any of it.

He told her he'd see her tomorrow at the office, that they'd try to figure it out then after they rested and had time to think.

Josie agreed and said, "Hey, partner, thanks for everything."

THE FOLLOWING DAY, DICKIE ARRIVED AT THE OFFICE WITH THE FEELING he would have as a child when coming home from school knowing that his parents had been notified of his bad behavior. It was the butterflies in your stomach that made you feel nauseated and ruined your appetite for fear of being sick. What they had done by going into Mexico and leaving in their wake a smattering of dead bodies could add up to multiple felonies, and who knew how many international law violations. The killings in Mexico could be prosecuted in the U.S. under extraterritorial jurisdiction, a concept that had been increasingly utilized by the United States to prosecute both U.S. citizens living and working abroad, as well as foreign nationals who have no connection to the United States. Or Mexico could prosecute them and demand extradition. The problem they would have, in Dickie's opinion, was proving their case. Unless there was a video of the *Caballo* fiasco, what evidence would they have? The witnesses were dead, and there was no way anyone in the club remained to provide their information to authorities once the shooting had started. Most likely, the other patrons there hadn't even known it happened. Also, it was only Jerry whose actions south of the border were questionable. When Josie put Baby Face down in the corridor, she did so in defense of others and in self-defense as well. Moreover, according to Jerry's account of the other killings, one could make a solid argument for self-defense in his case too.

But Dickie knew it was all a moot point when he walked in and crossed paths with the captain.

Stover was out on the floor, mingling with the troops, and their gazes met as the door closed behind Dickie and the cone of daylight that shrouded him disappeared. Dickie expected the captain to end his other conversation with another detective and confront him, maybe a simple *In my office, Jones* from the boss man and a long walk down the hall. Or maybe a stern look to let him know he wasn't happy, and they'd be speaking about it later. But Stover nodded a nonchalant greeting and otherwise paid Dickie no attention at all. Dickie beelined to his office thinking it was too good to be true, that surely shit would hit the fan, now or later.

In Unsolveds, Josie sat at her desk filing her nails. Lopes had rolled his chair over by her and was sipping coffee while they visited. Everything was as normal as if Rockwell had painted the scene himself.

"What's up, asshole?"

Lopes's friendly greeting caused Josie to look up from her manicure and catch Dickie's eye. She said, "Hey, partner."

Normal. Everything was so normal it was weird. It was like a surprise birthday party going south, and everyone was feigning business as usual until the girl jumped out of the cake. Dickie looked around the office for evidence of any such deception taking place, but none was detected.

"What's going on?" he asked, his tone low and guarded. "Nothing happening?"

Lopes smirked and shook his head.

Josie shrugged and raised her brows in question. "Not a peep from anyone. The captain seems to be in a good mood."

"Well, that can't be good," Dickie said. "Maybe he's happy because the feds are on the way here to take us into custody."

Lopes finished his coffee and tossed the Styrofoam cup into a yellow metal trash can with a clear plastic liner that was half-full of other cups and wadded papers. "I think we're okay."

But how could they be? Dickie voiced his skepticism and asked his partners rhetorically how they thought a former chief could be whacked in Mexico, and no one seemed to care. How had Perry or Wilkins not called in a beef against them or had their attorneys fire off cease and desist letters with elegant letterhead printed on linen paper? How was the Attorney General not drawing up papers for extraterritorial prosecution as they spoke?

"Relax," Lopes said, "we're fine."

"*We're fine*," Dickie mocked.

"Look, Carmen will never be heard from again. He's probably been fed to hogs by now because nothing good can come from his being killed in a Tijuana nightclub."

"Whorehouse," Josie corrected.

"Worse yet," Lopes said. "As far as Perry and Wilkins, they're shitting themselves wondering if we have enough to file on them. They'll go to bed every night now hoping SWAT doesn't hit their doors with warrants. They don't know what we have, but they know they're culpable and they'll live out their days looking over their shoulders. You think they're going to poke the bear?"

"I don't know."

"They're not—trust me."

"But how do we ever get enough on them to take 'em down? Our whole goal here was to solve the Townsend murder."

Josie weighed in. "It's solved; we just don't have enough evidence to prove it. And chances are, we're not going to get it. Perry wouldn't roll so we have nothing."

"I was hoping Wilkins would roll," Dickie said. "I mean, the guy didn't sign on for murder—you know that much. They were all dirty, but I believe what Carmen said about them only wanting to get the money and search for any evidence that Jerry was building a case against them. If we could convey that to Wilkins, maybe he'd be inclined to take a deal."

"Yeah, well, Wilkins has lawyered up," Lopes reminded, "so we're out of luck there. Too bad Jerry smoked his buddy."

Dickie agreed. Killing Benny Carmen was bad mojo on several fronts, not the least of which was eliminating a potential witness against the shooter. "He should've just wounded him, then pulled a Dirty Harry and stood over the dude mashing his heel into the gaping hole until he answered some questions."

Josie put away her nail file and turned to her computer where she began going through her email. Lopes rolled back to his desk and busied himself with a thick folder that was opened in front of him, apparently moving on to a new old case. Dickie lumbered to his own desk and lowered himself into his chair carefully. His back was out. He figured it was from the off-road excursion or from his fireman carry of Townsend out of the *Caballo*. He'd surprised himself that he was able to hoist the man onto his shoulder the way they had been trained in some type of riot training or something else he couldn't remember now, but it had worked. Fortunately, over the years and through the self-inflicted abuse to his own body, Townsend had withered into a scrawny shadow of what he had once been. But still, Dickie had hoisted a grown man onto his back and carried him. Now he was paying the price.

Dickie began going through his emails as if it were just another day at the office despite the pit he still felt in his stomach. Just because the hammer hadn't yet fallen didn't mean someone didn't have their arm cocked back, ready to let it fly. There were the usual administrative emails of which Dickie generally browsed the subject lines and deleted without opening. There were forwarded emails from friends who apparently had less of a workload than he did, and he deleted those without prejudice as well. After cleaning up the garbage, there were twenty or so work-related emails he needed to read and, in some cases, respond to. These were from other detectives, from prosecutors, and in some cases, from defense attorneys. And it was in that order that Dickie handled them.

But his reading was distracted when Josie took a call and turned in her chair to face him as she said into her phone, "Good morning, Agent Williams... How may I help you?" and her eyes revealed her apprehension.

47

Dickie paced while waiting for Johnson to answer his call. He was standing outside the office in the shade of a sycamore, avoiding the heat of the mid-morning sun. His shirtsleeves were turned up, his collar loosened, and his straw fedora sat high on his head. He wished he'd brought his sunglasses outside with him. He stopped pacing when the voicemail picked up and a recording began that he'd reached the voicemail of Sergeant Johnson of the San Diego Police Department…

Dickie turned and started back inside when his phone rang. It was Johnson.

"Sarge, we've got a situation."

"Another one, or did the last come back to bite us?"

Dickie thought about how to say what he needed to ask of the sergeant. He already felt he was eternally indebted to the man, yet here he was, ready to beg for another big save.

"Nothing has come back to bite us yet, my friend, but we've got another situation at the border, and we may need your help. And if this goes the way I'm hoping it will, we shouldn't have anything to worry about as far as the other night."

"You're going to owe me a fat, juicy steak and several beers, Detective."

"At the very least. Thanks, Sarge."

———

THEY STOPPED AT THE HOSPITAL TO CHECK ON JERRY SINCE THEY WERE AT least an hour ahead of schedule. Josie had driven, and Dickie rode shotgun. Lopes had court and had to sit this one out. But if all went well—if this worked out the way Agent Williams had said it should—there would be no need for Lopes to be along. They mostly needed Johnson and his *federale* friend and a helping of luck.

Dickie pointed out an open parking space. Josie glared at him and turned into a different one. She locked the car, and they went in through the emergency room doors, past the crowded waiting area, and with a flash of their badges, past the security checkpoint and to the elevators. In his room, Jerry was sitting upright in bed with a smile on his face while visiting with a male nurse the size of a small box truck. A grin was stretched across *his* face, too, his white teeth shining against his cocoa-colored skin. Jerry greeted them and introduced his nurse as Hemi.

Dickie said, "That's a great name for a guy your size. Nickname I assume?"

"No sir," Hemi said, "it's my given name. I had to grow into it."

"You remember the defensive tackle back in the eighties they called The Refrigerator?" Jerry said. "Played for the Bears?"

Dickie nodded. "Yeah, I remember."

Jerry grinned again. "That's him."

Dickie frowned as if he wasn't too sure.

Josie knew Jerry was pulling his leg because this Hemi guy couldn't have been thirty. She said, "Yeah, right. Whatever."

Jerry laughed a little. "I'm messin' with you. But he was a star lineman over here at the university," he said, tilting his head toward the window as if you could see the campus from there. You couldn't.

They stayed back to allow the man to finish his work—he needed the space to move about. When he finished, he told them it was nice meeting them and promised he was taking good care of their friend. Then he left, whistling a tune.

Josie went to his bedside, and Dickie remained at the foot of the bed, allowing some space. She said, "Quite the nurse you have."

"I was trying to get outta here, but Hemi said nuh-uh, and I decided not to push my luck. Any news with that..."—he glanced at Dickie and came back to Josie—"that fiasco down there?"

"Well," Josie started, and now she glanced at Dickie before continuing, "as a matter of fact, there is some news."

She let that hang a moment in the sudden tension of the room.

"Don't keep me in suspense," he said.

"Benny Carmen is alive."

They stared at each other with solemn faces as Josie waited for his reaction.

Jerry smiled. "That's outstanding," he finally said. "That tough old *dago*. You know, I almost put two more in him before I left, but I couldn't do it. That would have been murder. I shot his cartel buddies in self-defense—the one was armed, and Campo was going to have me killed—he wouldn't have let me leave there alive. Anyway, the only reason I shot old Benny Boy in the gut was to get him talking, and it worked. Where's he now?"

"He's at a cartel safe house in Tijuana currently. But if all goes well, he'll be back across the border and in our custody in an hour or two. We're hoping he's still in the mood to talk."

Jerry took a moment to consider this information before asking, "How are you pulling that off? Your boy, Mickey Thompson, helping you out again?"

"Who?"

Dickie explained it to her. "Mickey Thompson was a famous race car driver and an off-road racer and promoter. He's referring to Sergeant Johnson."

"Yeah, Johnson," Jerry said, as if suddenly remembering his name. "Anyway, how are you getting Benny back? And how the hell did you know where to find him?"

"I told you about that one goon being an informant," Josie said, "the one I call Fur Face?"

He nodded.

"He's working with the feds. This fed, Williams, got ahold of me this morning, and this Hector Romero—Fur Face—said Carmen was alive, and he knew where they could find him."

"So this isn't verified."

Josie shook her head. "The fed says this guy is rock solid. If he says Carmen is alive and well, we could count on it. Let's hope that's true."

Jerry turned his head away from Josie, where his gaze seemed to settle on the window overlooking part of San Diego. It was hazy and cool there, a contrast to Los Angeles. Josie gave him the time he needed.

"Okay, so what does this mean if you can bring him back? Can you make a case against him?"

Dickie stepped closer and interjected. "The feds are moving forward with additional charges related to the dope rips by going with conspiracy charges against all three of them, Carmen, Perry, and Wilkins. They'll let Carmen plead out if he'll testify against Perry on Laura's murder. Perry and Wilkins have both lawyered up, so it's our last hope. We were relieved to know he was still alive."

"We're going to seize that money, Jerry," Josie said. "You'll have to stay around to appear in front of the grand jury and tell them your story."

He nodded slowly.

Dickie said, "And if Carmen won't testify against the others, he'll be prosecuted on the dope rip cases. Unfortunately, I'm not sure we'd ever be able to charge Perry with Laura's murder unless one of them flips."

"And then what?" Jerry eventually said.

"And then you're a free man, Jerry," Josie said. "You'll be vindicated, and you won't have to run anymore."

He took a deep breath and let it out slowly while holding her gaze. Finally, he nodded, but Josie could tell he wasn't convinced about any of it —that he could be vindicated, that he might be free, that he could somehow be able to go on with his life unaffected by all of the killing and betrayal.

She said, "Well?"

After a moment, he said, "Where's Pablo and the girl?"

"Angel?"

"Yes, the angel."

"We have them stashed away. I figured when we can get you out of here, you can join them. Eventually, we'll have to try to get them visas and maybe help find them jobs and places to live. Right now, we're calling them witnesses so we can spend some county money to put them up, but that's a very temporary fix. We'll have to figure something else out."

"I get out of here," Jerry said, "I'll take care of getting them set up. I owe Pablo at least that much. And the girl, she's just a kid. What are you going to do with her?"

"Turns out she's eighteen," Josie said. "And that makes things a lot easier on all of us. Besides, she and Pablo have become good friends—maybe more."

Dickie checked his watch. "We better get going, partner."

Josie nodded and reached over to touch Jerry's arm. "We'll keep you posted. Let me know when that moose is planning to let you out, and I'll come get you."

Jerry smiled. "I'll be sure to tell Hemi you called him a moose."

She shrugged, proffered a smile, and they left.

AN HOUR LATER THEY HAD LEFT THE CHARGER AT THE SAN YSIDRO station and were riding with Johnson in his black and white Ford Explorer with America's Finest across the door. He was taking them south to the border. They arrived at the United States Customs House and parked in front, then walked along a winding sidewalk that took them to the west side of the building. They were now within throwing distance of the border and near the dozens of traffic lanes filtering those traveling north into the customs portal where they were scrutinized, searched, and recorded as they sought entry into the United States. The air was stagnant and reeked of exhaust fumes, and the sounds of idling cars and trucks droned in the heat of the day.

The first question Dickie asked was, "How the hell are they going to get through all that traffic?"

Johnson smiled. "The same way we do."

They waited nearly a half hour before the sergeant nodded to the south and said, "Like that."

A dark blue Dodge Charger with a white racing stripe across the hood, over the top, and down the trunk was headed toward them. The light bar on top flashed red and blue as the vehicle continued along some type of private access road skirting the congested lanes of northbound traffic. Dickie assumed the narrow strip of otherwise vacant pavement was designed for just this type of travel by emergency vehicles. The car came to a stop just shy of the border, and Dickie took notice of the decals across its side: a state trooper-type seven-point star and the words *POLICÍA FEDERAL.*

There were two men up front: the driver in his dark blue uniform and a Keystone cops police hat with its shiny brim and silver badge, and his bearded passenger in civilian clothing. It was Fur Face. The cop got out and opened the back door. Benny Carmen, his hands cuffed in front of him, slid out and came to his feet unsteadily. He was a shadow of the man Dickie remembered, who had strutted like a banty rooster and flaunted his power like a mafia boss. Now he appeared beaten and weak like a man who was ready to lie down and beg for mercy.

The two men walked slowly to a gate where two U.S. Customs officials waited. Carmen was hunched over in apparent pain. Fur Face stayed by the car, his eyes fixed on the action before him. After a short discussion at the fence, the gate was unlocked, and Benny Carmen stepped through. He was back on U.S. soil.

Josie went forward with Johnson at her side. She placed her handcuffs on Carmen and then removed the pair he wore, handing them back to the *federale* who delivered him. There was something about watching Josie put handcuffs on a former chief that Dickie found particularly enjoyable. She thanked the Mexican cop in Spanish, then locked gazes with Fur Face, who stood watching. Johnson shook hands with the *federale* and bid him farewell, and the gate slammed shut.

Josie placed Carmen in the back seat of Johnson's vehicle and fastened his seatbelt. Dickie and Johnson stood behind her, watching. Dickie said, "No paperwork?"

Johnson shook his head. "He's a U.S. citizen who wanted to come back." He smiled. "What a coincidence we were here at just the right time to receive him."

"Imagine the odds," Dickie mused.

"The *federales* can be very accommodating at times. Especially when they owe you a favor."

Dickie thought about what Johnson might have done to cultivate such a reliable contact on the other side of the border. Whatever it had been, Dickie knew it came down to old-style police work at its finest. You worked the streets and its players, and you made allies and enemies alike. If you were good at what you did, both knew to take you at your word.

However Johnson's Mexican ally managed to get Carmen out of a cartel safe house and deliver him to the border, Dickie didn't care. Mexico was like Vegas: what happened there, stayed there. And Dickie wasn't about to ask. There may have been payoffs, or there might have been some deal made between the cartel and this Mexican *federale*, but none of it was Dickie's concern. What mattered was that Benny Carmen was on American soil and in their custody. Soon he would hear his choices: cooperate and testify against Perry or try doing time as a former cop who had ripped off drug dealers.

48

DICKIE WASN'T THERE WHEN THE FEDERAL PROSECUTOR LAID HER CASE out before Benny Carmen and the attorney who represented him, but he heard about it firsthand when Emily arrived home from work that night. Dickie had taken some time off so that he could stay home with Angelo while Rosalva went away to Vegas for a few days. She and a girlfriend were excited to play the nickel slots and feast at the buffets. Maybe they would even catch a show. As for Dickie in his temporary stay-at-home dad role, he couldn't have been happier. It was all about balance, he had learned over the years.

They sat out on the patio eating hotdogs that Dickie and his son had barbecued on the Traeger. Angelo loved hotdogs, and he loved to help cook. He especially enjoyed it when Dickie used the pellet stove because the clouds that rose from its smokestack were not unlike the puffs of black clouds that issued from the tractors he watched across the street as an old home had been torn down and new construction began. He also liked to open the lid to the hopper and smooth the pellets with his hand while reporting to his dad whether more pellets were needed—he always said they needed more.

Emily gave him the highlights while squirting mustard and then scooping relish and onions onto her dog. "His attorney started in with statute of limitations and lack of credible witnesses and coerced admissions—"

"What admissions?"

"Exactly. He thinks we're trying to use the Tijuana debacle as evidence against his client. I explained that we didn't need admissions because Jerry Townsend turned over the cash he'd accumulated, and Carmen's prints were on the envelopes."

"His prints are on the envelopes?" That was the first Dickie had heard of that.

She shrugged. "I doubt it, but maybe."

Dickie smiled.

"And I mentioned that those deputies who took their falls behind the original Narco scandal were all out of prison now and that several had already come forward, anxious to testify against him."

Now Dickie chuckled. "You're worse than me."

"Hey, some of them might be. He doesn't know."

"But ultimately, he saw the writing on the wall."

She nodded and finished chewing a bite of hotdog. "I told him he was looking at a hard twenty with the federal charges and the state could still come after him once we finished with him."

"So he agreed to a deal."

She shrugged. "The attorney said he'd talk it over with his client. I gave him two days. I said, 'Friday afternoon I'm leaving early, and I'm off the next two weeks. I want this off my desk before I go.' Eat your hotdog, Angelo. No more chips until you've eaten this much," she said, placing a polished fingernail at about the halfway mark of his dog that was garnished only with ketchup.

"About that trip," Dickie started.

Emily froze just before taking a bite, then lowered her hotdog. "You better not—"

He smiled. "I was just going to tell you that I've upgraded us to first class."

Her eyes sparkled as she took an enthusiastic bite and held his gaze.

"Both ways," he said.

"Okay, what did you do?" she asked around a bite.

Dickie chuckled. "Grown up a little, maybe. I'm beginning to see the bigger picture."

"I'm growing up too, Daddy. And I can make you a picture."

Angelo bolted from the table before either of them could object. Emily rolled her eyes and shook her head. "He probably won't starve to death."

Dickie reached across the patio table and pulled his son's plate over. "No, he won't. And neither will I," he said, cramming the rest of Angelo's hotdog into his mouth.

***

Justin McKnight rode with Josie to San Diego to fetch Jerry Townsend and bring him back to L.A. She had been able to secure a rental in Norwalk, and that was where he'd be until he figured something else out. On the phone, Jerry had told her, "I don't even have a driver's license." She said she remembered that he was robbed, and Jerry said, "No, I mean I don't have a driver's license, period. It expired two years ago, and I didn't need it living in Mexico." She suggested he go in and apply and tell the lady at the DMV he'd been in prison—that was more believable than the truth and easier to explain. In fact, she had told him, they'd probably treat him better thinking he was an ex-con than a rogue cop. "Rogue cop?" he had said incredulously.

They were halfway to San Diego, moving slowly in the evening traffic. Josie knew she should have left earlier, but when McKnight said he wouldn't mind going for the ride if she could give him an hour or so to finish up at work, she had decided the company would be good. Besides, better that McKnight meet this friend of hers he'd been hearing so much about than to leave him wondering.

"So, the kids are at the rental?"

"Yeah. They each have their own rooms, and Jerry will have the master. I don't know what any of them are going to do long-term, but it's a start. Pablo said he could easily get work. He's lived here before. Angel is a bit lost. She might need to get a GED or something, and I can probably help her with that. I don't want her heading over to the Spearmint Rhino for another stripping job."

"Hey, a girl's got to do what a girl's got to do."

Josie shot him a look through her Pradas. He shrugged it off. She said, "And Jerry's set. His pension has been going into the credit union while he lived in Mexico like a pauper. He can live happily ever after, so to speak."

"Plus he's got his secret stash."

She shook her head. "Not anymore—it's been seized and booked as evidence. Jerry was happy to have it gone. It's been this thing hanging over his head all these years."

"The feds aren't going after him?"

That had been her and Jerry's concern, but Benny Carmen gave the *federale* a full statement before he was delivered to them, which included an admission that Jerry had never come aboard with the dope rips. The confession was part of Carmen's deal. He was given a choice to tell them everything and cooperate with the U.S. authorities, or the *federale* would turn him over to the cartel rather than take him to the border.

When Josie finished explaining that, McKnight said, "I thought he was working with the cartel? Didn't you tell me he was in with the guy who runs that nightclub?"

"Whorehouse," Josie corrected. "Yes, he was. They were tied in with the Tijuana cartel. The dope rips always targeted their rival, the Jalisco cartel. When this story hits the press, the ongoing rivalry between them will likely turn into a full-blown war."

Hemi brought Jerry out in a wheelchair. He appeared to have put on weight since Josie last saw him, and she mentioned it to him.

"Yeah, we eat good here," Hemi interjected, a smile stretched across his big face. "I told him if he wants out, he'd better get healthy. You don't get healthy if you ain't eatin'."

Jerry got out of his wheelchair and gave Hemi a hug. "See ya later, big man."

Hemi smiled, a gold tooth sparkling in the sunlight. "Take care of yourself, my man. And keep your ass on this side of the border from now on."

Jerry shrugged, unwilling to commit to that just yet. He thanked Hemi for taking good care of him, and they loaded up and headed north.

49

"A good man deserves a drink. When he has a drink, he becomes a new man. That new man deserves a drink, and when he has it, he too, becomes a new man. And so on," Lopes waxed poetic, hoisting a beer to emphasize his point. He was standing on his patio in board shorts and a tank top, dark sunglasses concealing his stoic gaze. His audience: a sinewy, ponytail-wearing man with steely eyes, and a second man, more subdued, clean-cut, and dressed for the country club. Lopes called him "Doc." The three men clinked their longneck bottles of beer and toasted their newer, better selves.

Pablo dove into the deep end of the pool and spiraled to the bottom like a porpoise, resurfacing moments later with rubber-coated rings grasped in each hand. He spat a mouthful of pool water and gasped for air, a smile stretched across his narrow face. Lopes called his name to get his attention, then said, "Don't pee in my pool." Pablo laughed and went back under.

Angel bobbed around in the shallow end, clasping the small hands of Angelo, who kicked his legs and motored about with floaties on his arms. Dickie watched all of it from a nearby table where he sat on a soft-cushioned patio chair beneath an umbrella that shaded his fair skin from the summer sun. He was very content with a cold beer in his hand, and he had no intention of leaving this spot while his son was in the pool. But he couldn't think of anywhere he would rather be at the moment either.

Hemi was behind Dickie at the barbecue in his 4-X fat bastard (his words) Hawaiian shirt that he wore half unbuttoned to reveal a dark, hairless chest. His big brown head beaded with sweat as he worked beneath the afternoon sun, grilling a meal he claimed to be an islander favorite: barbecued chicken and coconut rice with pineapple. He alternately waved the smoke from his eyes and sipped an icy ginger mojito while swaying to a Samoan reggae tune called *Baby Why*. Hemi was no Richard Parker, whose soothing warm voice oozed through a pair of suspended patio speakers, but he enthusiastically joined in the chorus nonetheless, crooning: *Tell me why, oh why, oh baby baby why you left me behind...* and Josie hula-ed through the rear slider with bowls of chips and dip and a platter of appetizers, comfortable in her loose-fitting drawstring shorts and a floral-print bikini top.

McKnight stood at the kitchen counter cutting up a couple of melons he and Josie had brought with them. Emily stood next to him, preparing a pitcher of margaritas while watching Angelo through the kitchen window. The talk turned lawyerly, and Emily told McKnight about Benny Carmen's plea bargain and her creative filing of federal murder charges against Mike Perry by classifying Laura Townsend's death as a drug-related killing. She shrugged and said over the whir of the blender, "When we're done with him, you guys can have him." Then she poured two margaritas and leaned against the countertop, locking her gaze on McKnight. "So, refresh my memory," she said as if she hadn't remembered everything Dickie had told her about the man, "How long have you been with the DA's office?" She went on to ask where he had attended law school, what he saw in his future with the district attorney's office, and whether he had ever considered going into private practice. There was a little back and forth, him providing the details, Emily allowing the appropriate *Uh-huhs* and *Oh reallys*, and then she hit him with the question she'd been holding back until just the right moment: "What are your intentions with Josie, Counselor?"

McKnight was ready to raise his objections to the last question: *It's leading, your honor. Vague and ambiguous. Argumentative. Outside the scope of examination. Lacks foundation. Speculative. Unfair extrapola-*

tion. Your honor, this is all hearsay!... But there was no arbiter to whom he could make his protests, so he tried to untwist his tongue and give her something fairly noncommittal.

Josie saved the day by dancing her way back into the kitchen before McKnight had a chance to answer the awkward inquiry. She set down an empty bowl she'd brought in and accepted a margarita Emily offered, saying, "Thank you—this is just what I needed!" and continued grooving to the music. She came up behind McKnight and wrapped her free arm around him, and they moved their hips together to the pervasive island beat.

After dinner, the kids—which included two young adults with questionable legal statuses—were back in the water. But they had moved their party from the pool to the hot tub, where they splashed and kicked as the waning sun cast a long shadow across the pool and fleeting rays of sunlight streaked through the foliage of a towering eucalyptus.

The others were gathered around the open flames of a gas fire pit where they sat nibbling cookies or forking bites of cheesecake and sipping coffee or another cocktail. A stillness settled in, and Josie knew that the weight of all that had happened hadn't yet been realized. Laws had been broken. Feathers had certainly been ruffled. New friendships were made, and others were lost. And people had died. The right people, in Josie's opinion, but still...

The next morning, Josie returned to her neighborhood coffee spot to be anonymous and alone in her reflections. It was later in the morning, so the patio was largely empty. Josie sat with her chair pulled out and turned perpendicular to a table to allow the sun to kiss her legs. An older couple sat a few tables over. The woman stared at her phone, and the man quietly read a paperback novel. Josie wondered how long they'd been married, how many children they had raised, and if they were happy in their marriage—they were clearly empty nesters by now. These were things she sometimes pondered when she thought about her own future and contemplated the idea of growing old alone. Her mother wouldn't be there forever to fill the void.

She thought about Pablo and Angel being alone in a strange country, the two bonding as a family or maybe just casual lovers as they cohabitated and filled one another's voids. Now Jerry was there too, and the three seemed happy together, a trio of misfits in a ruthless world. Pablo's parents were both deceased, and only aunts, uncles, and a few cousins remained in Mexico. His brother had died somewhere in the desert during his quest to migrate to America, and his remains were never found. Angel was a whole other story—a Dateline special. She had been born in Guatemala, but her family migrated to Mexico with the intent of coming to America. Somewhere along the way, Angel was separated from her family—a mother, father, uncle, and two brothers—and she hadn't seen them since. At fourteen she found herself homeless and alone in a foreign land. Her striking looks both saved and destroyed her—she seldom went hungry and often found refuge in various homes and shelters, but the price she paid was astronomical. It was no surprise she ended up at the *Caballo Loco* in Tijuana; she knew of no other way to survive.

The first thing Jerry did after settling in with the kids at the rental was to get Pablo signed up for night classes at the community college and to help him apply for a work visa. Jerry also enrolled Angel in English classes—Pablo was helping her learn the language—and they met with a counselor to map out the course for her to get a GED. More importantly, Jerry was able to get her into a counseling program for victims of human trafficking and sexual assault. Josie was pleased with this more than anything else. She felt that with a solid support system in place, Angel could thrive in her new environment. She was smart and full of life and pleasant to be with—in fact, it turned out, she had quite a sense of humor. But she needed the knowledge and tools to heal her wounds. The process of helping the kids was also therapeutic for Jerry; he was back to contributing to society rather than being another blemish on it.

The elephant in Josie's house though, was her status as a single woman with a biological clock ticking away and a nurturing woman in her home who wanted nothing other than to be an *abuela*. Esmeralda was persistent with the reminders that Josie wasn't getting any younger, that she was running out of time, and that she needed to start a family of her own.

Josie glanced at the old couple across the patio and thought that whatever they had and no matter what they were lacking, they had each other, and they seemed content in knowing it. As for her own looming void— that elephant in the room—there were options now for her to consider, and that was what she contemplated today as she sat in the sunshine with her iced caramel macchiato enjoying a day away from the business of death.

Behind the oversized Pradas, her gaze settled on a pair of mothers across the street unloading children, strollers, and diaper bags from a minivan with a stick-family decal on the window. Josie certainly wasn't ready for *that*, but she couldn't stop thinking about the final moments of last night's party at Lopes's house. McKnight had taken her by the hand and led her away from the others and into an open room down the hall. The room, it turned out, was a combination man cave and *I love me* room, crammed with weightlifting equipment and a treadmill, a giant television in front of dual recliners, and photographs, certificates, and awards framed and mounted on the walls. McKnight had pulled her close beneath a shadowbox that displayed Marine Corps insignia and medals which hung next to a gaudily-framed painting of a nearly naked angel. He kissed her passionately, then dropped to one knee and took her hand. He popped the question, and Josie said maybe.

She had to think about it, she told him. Plus, he didn't even have a ring, he was somewhat intoxicated, and it felt rather spur of the moment, so she wasn't even sure he was committed to the idea of it. He told her to consider the proposal a trial run and asked her just to think about it so that when he popped the question in the proper fashion, he could expect a definitive answer. She assured him she'd be thinking about it—there was no maybe about *that*.

Josie knew instinctively that there had to be more to life than just the job. She thought of the barista she had met the last time she was here who said that her husband, who had been a cop, was deceased. Did she work at the coffee house to fill that void? How lonely was it in her living room each evening or at the dinner table without a companion? Josie couldn't imagine her own home being empty, but she knew that someday it might be so.

But McKnight? The preppy prosecutor with his exquisite home with its modern chic décor, all the amenities for overnight guests, and a hairless Chinese crested toy dog that was probably higher maintenance than any woman he'd ever allowed to stay overnight—certainly more demanding than Josie would ever be. Could *he* be The One?

Well, maybe…

A burgeoning smile parted her lips as she saw herself walking down the aisle in a flowing gown of satin and lace, McKnight in his impeccably tailored black tux awaiting her. Dickie at her side because someone would have to give her away, and she could think of no one other than Dickie for that duty. He would be dressed in his sharpest suit and wearing his best fedora, one with a feather in the band. She wondered if he'd cry. After all, for all the armor he wore, she knew he was truly just a big marshmallow. Or they could do a destination wedding and forgo all the hullabaloo. Hawaii, maybe. Or the Bahamas. Cozumel? Or maybe just do Vegas and keep it simple, get it over with before she got cold feet. See what McKnight thought about that.

So yes, she thought, her face turned up to the warm morning sun, a union with the counselor was a definite maybe.

PREVIEW OF NOTHING LEFT TO PROVE

"The sharp, hardboiled prose you would expect from a detective novelist... Smith shares vivid details, hard-earned insights, and stories of courage and terror, told with crisp, raw dialogue, a feeling for the drama of potentially violent confrontations, and an undercurrent of despair, despite many heartfelt tributes to cops he trusted and the mentor whose murder he had to look into."

- BookLife Review

NOTHING LEFT TO PROVE

A LAW ENFORCEMENT MEMOIR

Get your copy today!

ALSO BY DANNY R. SMITH

THE DICKIE FLOYD DETECTIVE SERIES

- A Good Bunch of Men
- Door to a Dark Room
- Echo Killers
- The Color Dead
- Death after dishonor
- Unwritten Rules
- The Program
- The First Felony
- Hard-boiled: A Dickie Floyd Boxset

THE RICH FARRIS DETECTIVE SERIES

- The Outlaw

DICKIE FLOYD SHORT STORIES

- In the City of Crosses
- Exhuming Her Honor

AVAILABLE AUDIOBOOKS

- A Good Bunch of Men
- Door to a Dark Room
- Nothing Left to Prove

NON-FICTION — MEMOIR

- Nothing Left to Prove: A Law Enforcement Memoir

SUBSCRIBE TO MY NEWSLETTER

I love staying connected with my readers through social media and email. You can also sign up for my newsletter at murdermemo.com and receive bonus material, such as the Dickie Floyd short story, EXHUMING HER HONOR.

As a newsletter subscriber, you will receive special offers, updates, book releases, and blog posts. I promise to never sell or spam your email.

Danny R. Smith

Dickie Floyd Novels

BOOK REVIEWS

Independent authors count on word-of-mouth and paid advertising to find new readers and sell more books.

Reviews can help shoppers decide about taking a chance on authors who are new to them.

I would be grateful if you took a moment to write a review wherever you purchased the book.

Thank you!

Danny R. Smith

ACKNOWLEDGMENTS

I'd like to thank my editor, Patricia Barrick Brennan, for her ongoing support, her relentless pursuit of editing perfection, and most of all, her friendship.

My beta team provides me with terrific insight and feedback before my stories are published, and they are terrific at catching typos or grammatical errors, the manuscript gremlins that plague all writers. I would like to recognize and thank each of them for their continued commitment and dedication:

Phil Jonas, Deac Slocumb, Moon Mullen, Bud Johnson, Michele Carey, Scott Anderson, Andrea Self, Teresa Collins, Heather Wamboldt, Kay Reeves, Michele Kapugi, Jacqueline Beard, Ann Litts, Sherry Shelgren, Jake Needham, Schauer, Lesli, and "the girls."

I would also like to thank Detective Sergeant Eric Drilling of the San Diego Police Department for his time and technical advice on law enforcement matters concerning the border of Mexico. The exaggerations and creative licenses on the border topics are mine and not those of *America's Finest*.

ABOUT THE AUTHOR

Danny R. Smith spent 21 years with the Los Angeles County Sheriff's Department, the last seven as a homicide detective. He now lives in Idaho where he worked as a private investigator and consultant until retiring from his second career in 2022. He is blessed with a beautiful family and surrounded by an assortment of furry critters whom he counts among his friends. When he's not writing, he's golfing. When you're waiting for his next book, you should pray for bad weather.

Danny is the author of the *Dickie Floyd Detective* series and the *Rich Farris Detective* series. He writes about true crime and other topics in his blog, The Murder Memo.

He has appeared as an expert on numerous podcasts and shows, including True Crime Daily and the STARZ channel's WRONG MAN series.

Danny is a member of the Idaho Writers Guild and the Public Safety Writers Association.